PIXIELAND DIARIES
ENHANCED EDITION

BOOK ONE OF THE PIXIELAND DIARIES

CHRISTINA BAUER

COPYRIGHT

Monster House Books
Newton, MA 02434
ISBN 9781946677785
First Edition

DEDICATION

For All Those Who Kick Ass, Take Names
And Read Books

COLLECTED WORKS - CHRISTINA BAUER

Pixieland Diaries
   About sassy pixie Calla and her love-crush-nemesis, the elf prince Dare
   1. Pixieland Diaries
   2. Calla
   3. Dare
   4. Winter Prince
   5. Ley Queen

Angelbound Origins
   About a quasi (part demon and part human) girl who loves kicking butt in Purgatory's Arena
   1. Angelbound
   2. Scala
   3. Acca
   4. Thrax
   5. The Dark Lands
   6. The Brutal Time
   7. Armageddon
   8. Quasi Redux *(coming 2020)*

Angelbound Lincoln
   The Angelbound experience as told by Prince Lincoln
   1. Duty Bound
   2. Lincoln
   3. Trickster *(coming 2020)*

4. Baculum

Angelbound Offspring
The next generation takes on Heaven, Hell, and everything in between
1. Maxon
2. Portia
3. Zinnia
4. Rhodes
5. Kaps
6. Mack
7. Huntress

Fairy Tales of the Magicorum
Modern fairy tales with sass, action, and romance
1. Wolves and Roses
2. Moonlight and Midtown
3. Shifters and Glyphs
4. Slippers and Thieves
5. Bandits and Ball Gowns
6. Evil Queens and Goblin Kings (*future*)

Dimension Drift
Dystopian adventures with science, snark, and hot aliens
1. Scythe
2. Umbra
3. Alien Minds
4. ECHO Academy

Beholder
Where a medieval farm girl discovers necromancy and true love
1. Cursed
2. Concealed
3. Cherished
4. Crowned
5. Cradled
This is a completed series.

CONTENTS

THE PIXIELAND DIARIES

ALSO BY CHRISTINA BAUER

CALLA - EXCERPT

APPENDIX

THE PIXIELAND DIARIES

DAY ONE OF THE NEW ME

*D*ear Diary,

Goodbye, old me! This journal will track my transformation into an all-new Calla. Not on the physical side, mind you. I'll still be a fifteen-year-old pixie, five feet tall with pink hair and violet eyes. Instead, what will change is this: as of today, I shall never play another prank for as long as I live.

Definitely.

Maybe.

Hopefully.

Okay, having a diary means being totally honest. It's true that I've made this no-prank promise before. But today, the Elven High Council gave me another super-long lecture on my so-called *silly attitude*. What a bunch of grumps. All their panties were in a twist, too. Why? I just cast one little enchantment that transformed the council's shampoo into hair remover.

Which was awesome, by the way. The council are way too snooty and into their looks. Plus without their hair, the council rocks an alien vibe. And their silken tresses will all be back to normal after a spell or two. I think. Prince Darius says my magic is too powerful for my own good. He's too cute for his, so we're even.

Anyway, back to the council's lecture. They reviewed this crazy-long list of how I should act going forward. I wrote it all down super carefully:

Act mysterious – always

Be frivolous – never

There was more on their list but what can I say? I got bored. The council also *waah waah waah-ed* that if I didn't change my personality and soon, then this was my last warning. One more infraction and I would be kicked out of Pixieland, my home within Faerie. Or even worse, they might put me in a supernatural prison.

Either of those options sound pretty nasty, so I'm putting together a New Me plan.

Next steps to the New Me: swap out my gossamer wings for a bat look… Only answer questions with a long and mysterious 'maaaaaaybe'… And no pranks.

For real, this time.

-The New Calla

DAY TWO OF THE NEW ME

*D*ear Diary,

These bat wings itch like you wouldn't believe. Even worse, the Elven High Council will hold another revel next week. I'm ordered to join. *Ugh.* Which means I must pick a human to kidnap and force into dancing themselves to death.

And this is supposed to be fun?

New Me. New Me. New Me.

-Calla

DAY THREE OF THE NEW ME

Dear Diary,
   I found a human I'd like to kidnap. Name's Griffin. He might be cute. And funny. And enjoy pranks.
   I am in deep trouble.
   -Calla

DAY FOUR OF THE NEW ME? MAYBE NOT SO MUCH.

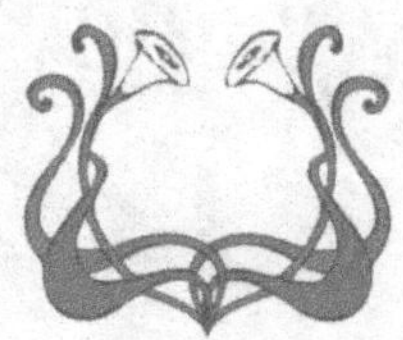

*D*ear Diary,
    I tried, really I did. But I couldn't make my human dance himself to death at the revels. Instead, I cast a spell that forced the High Council into doing the Macarena for three days straight. Prince Darius says I'm in deep doo doo.

Exile is imminent. Or worse.

Yipes.

-Calla

DAY FIVE OF THE NEW ME

*D*ear Diary,

Today I chatted up the naiads for advice. Most of Faerie won't talk to me—they think I'm trouble or something—but naiads are magically attached to their trees, so it's not like they can avoid conversation. Anyway, Nicola the naiad was the most helpful. She said to be *super specific* in my diary. As in, I should slow down and write details about every little thing.

Good thinking, Nicola.

With that in mind, I now take this solemn vow:

I, Calla, do hereby seriously promise to fully describe each eentsy beentsy thing that happens to me. No excuses. No exceptions.

Whew. Just writing those words makes me feel better. Next I'll describe something that happened to me in crazy detail. And to make it super-official, I shall add a cool title.

Calla's Amazingly Detailed Story Of Chatting Up Nicola

Verdict: adding a title is clutch.

Here's what happened. Nicola lives with her sisters in a massive yellow tree within Pixieland's Golden Vale. The naiad's realm is sandwiched between the Pink Forest (where I live) and a Troll Swamp (ick). In terms of looks, Nicola and her sisters remind me of human ballet dancers, only with bark for skin.

Hmm.

Okay, I know I just promised that I would describe stuff in super detail. But I already explained my chat with Nicola. Not much new territory to cover. Therefore, I shall make a slight change to my mega-serious vow.

I shall record every detail, unless I pretty much told it already.
And/or it's boring.

Thus endeth the story of Nicola.

Moving on.

After chatting up Nicola, I head home. This brings up a critical question. How do I get around? Answer: with cute pink wings that sprout on my command. When I'm flying, I leave behind sweet arches of pink fairy dust. There are two reasons for this.

One. Pink lines are really cute, and we all need more cuteness.

Two. Fairy dust is hard to make. Not for me, though. The fact that I toss it around always turns heads. Even the dwarves look up from under whatever rock they're hyper-focused on smashing.

Needless to say, I could stop leaving dust trails, but why? I work super hard at the Pixieland Citadel of Magical Knowledge. I spend hours practicing how to summon orbs of power, which are the magical spheres behind higher-level spells. Plus I help out Bilge, the ancient hobgoblin who runs the place, along with his piggy familiar, Oinky. In my opinion, I've earned the right to have fairy dust fly off my butt.

Back to my day.

I flit along, looking awesome, and leave a totally cool trail behind me. Then I reach the massive red oak that's my home. Specifically, I live with my parents in an oversized acorn on that tree. Anyway, my arrival requires that I pause and shake my hips extra fast. That way, I release enough fairy dust to shrink down to the size of a honeybee.

On second thought, make that a wasp. They're way more badass.

Once I'm tiny, I zoom in through a gap in our acorn's cap. Inside, our home acorn is carved up into three stories, complete with furniture. This late in the day, my parents—Poppa and Muti—hang out at the bottom level, which is where we chow down. I swoop to that spot.

Like the rest of our place, the dining room is pretty basic. There's a wooden table. Matching chairs. Mandatory pictures of me on the walls. And, of course, Poppa and Muti. They're silver tree sprites with crinkly faces, long gray hair and short white robes. Wooden bowls sit on the table before them. Clearly, they've been using these containers as pillows.

How do I know? Spit puddles.

As I approach, the pair sit ramrod straight, like they've been waiting for dinner instead of snoozing. Not that I blame them for napping. They're both at least forty thousand years old, and that's in fae time. If I were them, I'd snore inside an acorn, too.

"How was your day, Calla?" asks Poppa in his warbly old-guy voice.

"Fine," I say. "You know, the usual. Flying around. Trying not to get exiled or locked up. That kind of stuff."

Muti has overlarge eyes surrounded by layers of wrinkles. She widens them now. I call this her *hopeful look.* "What have you done today that's selfish and horrible?"

We have this conversation all this time. Poppa and Muti want me to be meaner. They think it'll help me fit in.

"Well," I tap my chin dramatically. "I called Nicolianus, the tree naiad, a name."

"Good!" Poppa grins, showing off his missing front tooth. "What did you call her? Dumb as a stick?"

"That's an insult, not a name," corrects Muti. "Maybe wooden head? Tree scum?"

"Not exactly."

"When what?"

"I called her…" Pausing, I force on a terrible scowl. "Nicola."

Muti scrunches up her face. "That's not a mean name."

Poppa shakes his head. "Oh, my poor Calla."

"Hey," I counter. "I have it on good authority that Nicola is a super-huge insult on Earth."

Which is a total lie. However, Poppa and Muti have never been to Earth. It's an easy all-purpose excuse. I've visited a few times, but I always end up at the same boring spot. Long story.

"Well, humans." Poppa sniffs. "They have a lot of strange ideas. I hear they eat babies named Ruth."

Muti nods quickly. "And drink their own pee on something called a television."

Poppa joins in the nodding routine. "I don't think they're mean so much as nuts." He knocks on the wall. "No insult intended." That's a good move. Our oak has its own naiad, Jolly. Despite the name, Jolly is anything but *happy go lucky.* Tick him off and you'll end up stuck to your bed with a pile of sap. No lie.

Muti lets out a long-suffering sigh. "So, back to our question. What have you done lately that's evil?"

At last, the obvious answer appears in my mind. "My latest pranks, of course. There's the Macarena Caper as well as my Hairless Elf Council Adventure." I give my pranks formal names; it helps me keep track of things. Pausing, I wait for the inevitable comeback from my parents. This will be something like, *pranks on the council don't count.*

That's not what happens.

Poppa smacks his thin lips. "Ever since Muti and I adopted you from the Ley Queen, we've only wanted what's best for you."

I frown. Nothing good ever comes out of a parental speech that includes, *we only want what's best for you.*

Muti leans forward, setting her elbows on the tabletop. Normally, she's very anti-table-elbows, so this is serious. "Both Poppa and I have come to a dark conclusion. Namely, we suspect your pranks are only done for *good reasons*." The way she says the words *good reasons*, it's like I pooped in her dinner bowl.

This is seriously bad news. My pranks are the only thing giving my parents hope that I'll turn into a regular fae one day. You see, the lands of Faerie and Earth are connected by cords of power called ley lines. As in, there are literal blue lines of magic waiting underground. Using those cords, fae can travel about. And if you're human and live near a major ley line? Then, watch out. You might have a fairy for a kid. Which is my story, by the way. After my human birth parents gave me up, Poppa and Muti took me in.

Voila. *I'm a faeling.*

According to rumor, we faelings have soft hearts. In my case, those rumors are spot-on. I need to fake some evil here.

All of which is why I put on my most innocent face, which involves widening my eyes while pursing my lips. "Whatever do you mean? All my pranks are filled nothing but cruelty." I hold up my hands in a claw-like way and say *grr*, just for emphasis.

"Let's consider that prank about losing hair," says Poppa. "Isn't that what Summer Fae do to changelings? Bring those humans here from Earth, put them in brown robes, and then shave their heads?"

I raise my pointer finger. "Winter fae don't do that."

"You know what Poppa means," presses Muti. "Were you trying to show the council how a changeling human feels?"

I open my jaw wide in what I hope is a convincing show of shock. "Wow, I never thought of it that way, but you're right. It would have given that experience."

"And the dancing prank," adds Poppa. "The revels require that humans dance themselves to death."

Once more, I raise my pointer finger. "Winter fae only ask for human volunteers."

I tried that route, by the way. My goal was to find a super-old human who wanted to kick the bucket while dancing. But the council got bullied by Lazare, the Protector of the Summer Realm. Lazare hates me for some reason, so he insisted I find some unwilling human to kill. Which I did.

Sorta.

Kinda.

Not really.

Griff volunteered in exchange for Macarena fun. Not that I'll ever tell Poppa and Muti that.

"Don't try to fool us," warns Poppa. "You were giving the council a taste of how it feels to be abducted into the revels, weren't you?"

"No, I was just acting super-evil with Griffin, my totally kidnapped human." *Lie.*

Muti drums her fingers on the tabletop. "And you just happened to pick a prank that gave the council a—*what do the humans say again?*—taste of their own potion?"

"It's *medicine,*" I say.

"What's medicine?" asks Poppa.

"Calla needs to answer the question," insists Muti.

I press my lips together while bobbing my head. This is my classic *thinking face.* Namely, I'm wondering if there's any way out of this conversation.

Nope.

I throw up my hands. "You got me. If I'm pulling a prank anyway, why not give it a double purpose?" I hold my thumb and pointer finger an inch apart. "Just a little bit of good. Barely noticeable. And all while I'm being super evil at the same time."

Muti sighs. "You can't be nice, Calla. Ever."

"Why not?"

"You're already a rarity," says Poppa. "How many faeling are there right now?"

This is a depressing topic. "One," I reply. "Just me."

Muti gasps. "What about that troll, Finster?"

"He's been around for six thousand years," adds Poppa. My parents are big into Finster the troll. He's their example of faeling who made it.

"Died last month in a freak bridge accident." Sadly, the death is totally sketchy. But after six thousand years in Faerie, you're bound to have a bridge fall on your head at some point, right?

"This is bad," groans Poppa.

"Terrible," agrees Muti.

I slap on a grin. "Look, it wasn't always this way, right? When good King Tristan ruled the summer fae, he wasn't all pro-selfishness. He said we need a balance. Fairies like me were fine."

Muti raises her shaky fist. "And look what happened to Tristan! That evil winter prince, Reiver, stabbed the good king through with a magical blade."

"And now Tristan lays trapped in an enchanted sleep," adds Poppa. "Lazare will run the summer realm for all eternity."

All of which is true. Depressing, but valid.

I've only one argument left. "My point is, the winter fae aren't as dedicated to evil. Reiver's little brother, Dare, is a nice guy." I can't help but blush as I say Dare's name.

"What good does that do?" asks Muti. "The winter fae aren't as numerous or powerful as summer. Never have been."

"You need to work on being more genuinely evil," says Poppa earnestly. "Can you do that, Calla?"

Time to fib my face off. "I'll try."

"That's all we ask." Muti twiddles her craggy fingers over the table. A cascade of silver fairy dust falls down. Seconds later, my parents' bowls fill with goopy pre-chewed dinners. Which makes sense; the situation with their teeth is pretty sketchy.

As for me, I get a bowl of galla root with cashew dressing. My favorite. Happy for the distraction, I dive into my nutty feast. After dinner, I'm super sleepy (galla root does that). So I kiss Poppa and Muti good night and flutter off to bed. That's where I am right now, by the way. And I'm basically ready to snooze when it happens.

I notice a small white box on my bed stand. It wasn't there a moment ago. *Magic.*

Plus, there's even a card on top. I open it.

Calla, Here's a gift for you. - Dare

Oh, my.

This is huge. I get one gift from Dare each year on my birthday. That's how Dare works. But the *Great Festival Of Me* remains a week away, so this isn't a birthday present. It's something more.

Breathe, Calla.

~

Dear Diary,

I'm breaking this out into its own section ~~because I'm obsessed with Dare and will want to easily find this bit later.~~ For no reason.

-Calla

DAY FIVE AND A HALF (NOT SURE THE 'NEW ME' STUFF IS WORKING OUT)

*D*ear Diary,

For a long minute, I just stare at the box. *This is it.* Dare's eighteen. That's makes him of age to marry. In other words, Dare could name his future bride any second now. Sure, princes of the winter realm normally marry other elves—and royal ones at that—but I'm both a faeling and super-awesome. That puts me in a separate category.

Why *wouldn't* Dare pick me?

Sure, the guy still thinks of me as a kid, but that can't last forever. And I'm totally fine with waiting until I'm eighteen to marry. Considering how I'm now basically sixteen, eighteen is pretty much around the corner. I can handle a long engagement, no problem.

I nod once to myself. *Yes, this is the moment.* Inside this box, there's definitely a commitment ring along with another note asking, *marry me?*

My pulse speeds. Little by little, I pull the top off the box. Leaning forward, I check out the contents.

What's inside isn't exactly a ring.

Nope.

It's a tiny yellow snake.

Which is a totally odd gift.

Okay, this is a little weird, but Dare's a winter fae. They do strange stuff all the time. It's true that snakes are more of a summer fae thingy, but there must be snow-friendly snakes, right?

I lift my chin. *This might still work out.* Maybe the snake has the ring on its forked tongue or something. That would be skewed but acceptable. I'm not picky.

The serpent slithers out of the box, down my bedside table, and onto the floor. From there, it expands in size, all while staying an annoying shade of yellow. I frown. The colors of the winter realm are black and white. Time was, summer fae loved red (that was Tristan's favorite color). But Lazare adores yellow, so everything summer has been that shade for ages.

Long story short, it's not a good sign that this snake remains the same color as sunshine. That said, my room is lit by candles. Yellow could be a trick of the light. My snake present might actually be winter white.

Yes, that's it. *Winter white.*

The serpent coils higher. Once we're at eye level, a hood expands behind its head. Now it's clear this isn't just any serpent. It's a cobra. Even worse, there's a definite sun symbol on the back of its hood. I pound my fists onto my coverlet.

What a disaster.

Still, I'm girl enough to admit it. This isn't a proposal from Dare. Nope. It's some kind of assassination attempt from Lazare.

So disappointing.

The sun cobra sways from side to side.

I hold up my hand in the universal movement for *stop*. "I need a sec."

The snake halts in place. I think it's more out of shock than anything else, but I'm still glad for the break. This is a definite bummer. Even so, I must move on. A killer snake now slithers around my bedroom. I'm not shocked—Lazare is a total creep who hates me—yet still. The serpent must be taken down.

Time to focus.

Straightening my shoulders, I glare at my scaly assassin. "Look, I'll give you a chance here. Take off. Slither back into your little cosmic box and go home." *Seriously.* Sun cobras are a level one spell. I could kill this thing in my sleep. "You've no idea who you're dealing with."

The cobra opens its overlong mouth. "Pixxxxxie."

"Yes, I am a pixie but I'm also faeling. That makes me really-really-really powerful."

"Liesssss," hisses the snake.

Crud. My snake assassin has a point. Most faeling are super weak in the magic department. I was hoping this cobra would be uninformed. No such luck.

Which leaves one last thing to try.

I raise my right hand. Magic whirs within me all the time. Now I focus that power into a sphere of pink light that hovers over my palm.

"Last chance. No namby pamby fairy dust here. This is a magical orb, dude. Slither off."

"No! Ugly pixxxxxie will die!"

"That does it. Nobody calls me ugly."

I picture what I want my magic to do. Instantly, the sphere whizzes across the room. As the sun cobra lunges for me, my magical orb slams right into the serpent, freezing it in place.

Sun cobra, meet freezing time.

Now for the good stuff.

I imagine my next spell. Another sphere appears. This time it morphs into my favorite magical creature. It's a little spell of my own design, too.

My little bunny-saurus.

Sure enough, a tiny bunny T-Rex appears on my upturned palm. Pink, of course. It comes complete with a furry head, bunny ears and a mouth that's lined with razor-sharp teeth. From the neck down, it also has a T-Rex body that's covered in pink fur instead of scales. And as a final touch, there's a fluffy cottontail.

Cute and deadly, just like me.

My little bunny-saurus focuses its beady red eyes on me. "What you want?" it asks in a gravelly voice.

I nod toward the cobra. "Kill the snake."

Bunny-saurus growls. "Too easy."

It takes me a second to realize what the creature means. Then, I get it. The sun snake is still frozen in place, mouth open, fangs out, and ready to attack. Bunny-saurus likes a challenge.

"No problem."

I snap my fingers; the sun cobra springs back to life. Fast as a heartbeat, the snake lunges for me. Bunny-saurus is much faster.

My creation leaps off my hand and latches onto the cobra's tail. Bunny-saurus shakes its head from side to side, whipping the cobra across my room.

Wham! The serpent's head slams into the wall.

Thud! Its skull mashes into the floor.

Whump! The ceiling.

Boom! My bedside table.

In short order, the sun cobra serpent is limp. And by that, I mean it's totally dead.

Now comes the yucky part. *Dinnertime for Bunny-saurus.*

This is ugly stuff, so I silently whistle while staring at the ceiling. Sadly, there's no missing the slurpy-chomping noises as Bunny-saurus munches away. A little burp sounds, which is the signal it's all over.

I refocus on Bunny-saurus once more. "Thank you."

My creature lets out another little belch. "Yummy snake."

"That was a lot of information. Thanks, Bun!"

I snap my fingers once more; Bunny-saurus disappears. Sadly, my room is a total disaster. The side table's overturned. Scales lie embedded in the wall. Entrails cover the floor.

Eew.

Pulling on my magic, I summon another pink sphere of power. This time, I imagine the magic becoming pink birds and some matching mice. When it comes to mess removal, I straight-up follow *fairy tale* tradition. Birds and mice clean up everything.

A knock sounds on my door. "What's wrong?" It's Muti.

I pop my hand over my mouth. *Dang, I forgot all about her and Poppa.* Whipping a sun cobra around my room must have caused a major racket. My parents sleep really soundly, but even that has limits.

"Nothing," I reply brightly. "Just practicing some magic."

Poppa's reedy voice echoes in from another floor. After all, it's an oversized sprite house, but it's still an acorn.

"What's she up to?" calls Poppa.

"Calla says she's practicing magic," cries Muti.

"Tell her she's supposed to do that at the citadel."

Muti's voice echoes through the closed door. "You're supposed to do that at the citadel."

"Got it. You can both go back to sleep now."

I hear Muti's creaky wings flapping as she takes off. Then, Muti pauses. "Were you practicing anything evil?"

"Sure. My bunny-saurus."

When Muti speaks again, there's no missing the joy in her voice. "Oh, that's so cruel and bloodthirsty of you. Have an awful night, dear."

"You as well."

By this point, my little bird and mouse friends have finished their work. Snapping my fingers, I make them vanish a puff of pink smoke. In fact, I'm ready to fall asleep for reals when the scar on my palm glows white.

Like snow.

The winter court.

And the color of Prince Darius's magic.

This is an old signal between us, by the way. Basically, Darius is saying, *may I appear to you?* We have matching scars on our palms that empower us to talk over distances. The spell has a catch, though. You have to accept the other person in order to see each other and have a magical chat.

This is another big decision.

Before approving Dare's visit, I must check something very important: *How I look.* Fortunately, I'm wearing cute pink pajamas with a matching silk robe. Totally Dare-ready.

I whisper onto my palm. "You may visit."

~

Dear Diary,

The last time I started a new page was a bust because ~~it wasn't a proposal from Dare~~ the snake thing happened. So this time I'm starting another fresh sheet for the sake of neatness. It definitely has nothing to do with Dare.

-Calla

DAY FIVE AND THREE-QUARTERS

*D*ear Dairy,

When we last left my life, I'd just accepted a magical visit from Dare. Now a small sphere of white light materializes in my bedroom. The shape expands until it turns into what I call Ghost Dare. Technically, this is his astral body projecting for a visit.

Ghost Dare is just catchier, in my opinion.

For a moment, I drink in the sight of him. Even though he's semi-transparent, Ghost Dare is still rather attractive. Like all winter elves, the prince is crazy tall and ripped with muscle. As always, Dare's longish dark hair perfectly highlights the straight cut of his jawline. Chunks of white mix within all the black strands—that's is a super-cute look. Today Dare wears his standard black armor and a fur-trimmed cloak. It's really a shame that the winter realm is so cold. I never get to see the guy in shorts.

Dare's teeth turn super pointy while his nails stretch into extra-long claws. That's a winter elf thing; it means he's upset. "I just left a meeting with the summer court," Dare says in his rumbly voice. "I have terrible news."

"Let me guess. Lazare is sending an assassin after me."

"Yes. How did you know?"

"I'm incredibly wise about a lot of things. It goes along with being grown-up and mysterious." *There, that told him.* "Anything else?"

"I'll be at Lazare's court for some days." He raises his hand, showing off the scar on his skin. "I may not be able to acknowledge your palm line summons. At least, not right away."

Huh. Two things can happen when I use our palm line connection. First, Dare might accept my visit. Second, Dare could just acknowledge my request. In that case, the palm line will pulse like a busy signal. And Dare always, always, always acknowledges my palm line summons.

This news is el strange-o.

"Anything I should know about?" I ask.

"Perhaps." Dare rakes his fingers through his messy hair. That's a sure sign he's hiding something.

"Let me guess. Does it have to do with naming your bride?"

"Calla." Even as a ghost, I can see him blush.

The pieces fall together. For Dare to ensure I'm his future wife, he must meet with Lazare. After all, summer fae are more powerful than winter. Most likely, Lazare thought Dare would wed one of his yucky daughters.

Ick. What a horror show those three are.

Dare must offer concessions so Lazare will accept a different choice of wife. Magic wands, most likely. Those store power and are crazy expensive. I nod once to myself, confident I have it all worked out. And once everything is set with Lazare, Dare will spring his surprise proposal on me.

What a sweetie.

"I completely understand." It's an effort not to blab my discovery, but I don't want to ruin Dare's plan. "I'll be fine while you're gone."

All signs of blush leave his face. Ghost Dare fixes me with a serious look. "Listen to me carefully."

I shift in my bed and lean forward, as if I want to hear better. Which is *sort of* true. However, the movement also gives me the change to rearrange my blankets in a way that best shows off my pretty PJs.

"Go on," I say solemnly.

"Lazare won't stop trying to somehow ruin your life. Be on your guard. Summon me if you need me." Ghost Dare raises his hand once more. The scar on his palm glows white with power. "I will always find you."

Sweet, but not a proposal. I slap on a fake smile. "How nice."

"There's more, Calla." Ghost Dare float-walks even nearer and—*at last* —I know this is it. His heartfelt confession.

All of a sudden, it's hard to pull enough air into my lungs. "Yes?"

"I've always noticed you," says Ghost Dare.

"Of course." I look up at him through my lashes. According to my kissy novels, this particular glance works well for romance. "You see me as—"

"The little sister I never knew I wanted," finishes Ghost Dare.

"What?" *I can't believe this.*

"You're the only trustworthy person in my life. As an elf prince, you've no idea what that means. Especially in my family. You know about my brother."

Heck, everyone's heard about Reiver. Dare's older brother tried to murder Tristan and failed. Instead of killing the king, Reiver knocked Tristan into an eternal sleep, murdered the king's guard Halycon, and ended up getting his own nasty self offed along the way.

Clearly, I'm getting the better brother.

In fact, the only good thing Reiver ever did right was to die while Dare was still a toddler. I can't imagine growing up around *that* piece of work.

Speaking of Dare, my future husband leans in closer. "No matter what happens..." My heart pitter-pats while my favorite prince takes in a long breath. "I'll always protect you."

"Oh." Words echo through my mind.

Protect.

Not love.

Not marry.

Protect.

With that, it's official. My life sucks. Pulling the covers over my head, I scrunch lower on the mattress. "Got it," I say through the comforter. "I'll stay safe."

"Am I being dismissed?"

"I ate galla root for dinner and you know how filling that is. Bye, Dare."

"Rest well, little hob."

Sheesh. Little hob is a nickname from when we were kids. Like I need reminding that Dare's *frosty pea brain* has me stuck at six years old. To show my displeasure, I pull down the covers and stick out my tongue once more. *That will show him, part deux.*

Ghost Dare grins, and it's a great look on him. Who am I kidding? Every expression works on this guy. A moment later, Dare's cloudy self dissolves from the room. Which is fine. Now I can get some rest. Only trouble is, the more I think about it, the more I keep wondering about Dare's visit to the summer elves.

Fat chance of falling asleep now.

-Calla

DAY SIX

*D*ear Diary,

It takes me forever to get to sleep, mostly because—*surprise, surprise!*—I obsess over Dare. What's he doing at the summer realm anyway? Eventually I do drift off, though. Once I awaken, I'm majorly groggy. Three reasons for this. I shall list them in their very own area because I'm super-accurate and motivated.

Why I, Calla, Am Super Sleepy

One. It's early morning, or what passes for early to pixies. 11 AM.

Two. After much contemplation, I decided that Dare is definitely visiting the summer realms for my benefit.

Three. I therefore spent my wee hours concocting a plan to eavesdrop on Dare. Sure, my prince wants to surprise me with his proposal, but I have rights, too. It wouldn't hurt to know a *little* bit more.

Here's what I'm thinking. Lazare's palace is carefully tracked, so it's not like I can fly into the guy's backyard without being detected. However, there are secret doors in the basement of each citadel. Those were built to allow magical workers to share knowledge faster. The only working citadel left is in Pixieland, but that's beside the point.

The citadels and their connecting doors still exist.

And did I mention that there's a link between the Pixieland Citadel and its summer counterpart... which just so happens to be right by Lazare's super-protected palace? There is.

Long story short, I'll use the door from my home citadel to magically transport over to the one near Dare, get some intel, and skedaddle on back. No one will be the wiser.

My plan is so perfect, I can't stand myself.

With all this decided, I magically change into a cute pink mini-dress and flutter downstairs for breakfast. After last night's excitement, I expect Poppa and Muti will still sleep all day long. That's not the case, though. Both wait at the breakfast table. Fresh bowls of mush lie before them. Neither have touched their food.

I slide onto my usual spot. Muti sprinkles more fairy dust onto the tabletop. This time, I get a bowl of inkus leaves. Not my favorite, but still pretty yummy. I take a few bites before asking the obvious. "What's wrong?"

"Your father and I feel terrible," moans Muti.

"Why?"

"You were acting evil and selfish last night," explains Poppa. "We should have encouraged it."

Poppa and Muti look so mopey, I can't leave them hanging. "No, I made all that noise because you totally encouraged me toward evil. That was really mean and selfish of me, right?"

"I suppose," sighs Muti.

"As a matter of fact, I plan to do more evil things today." *Namely, eavesdrop on Dare.*

"At the citadel?" asks Muti. She knows I study there most days. "You can't upset Bilge."

"Not at the citadel, but somewhere else." I bob my brows. "It'll be a surprise."

That answer seems to make my parents happy, since they now dive into their mush. For my part, I take the chance to finish my breakfast extra-fast. Within minutes, I'm saying my goodbyes and zooming over to the citadel. Speaking of which, it's a tall and round tower that's topped with I call the *upside-down ice cream cone*. The citadel is also pink because that's the best color ever. I fly in through a low window.

Hmm.

Saying I *fly in* doesn't do me justice. It's a rather complex move, actually. I shake my bum, let off a ton of fairy dust, shrink down, spin into a barrel roll, and then whip right through a skinny window-hole. Once inside, I pop back to regular size. It's really advanced magic and I totally nail it.

As planned, I land smack in the main reception hall. This is a tall space made of pale pink stone and covered in tapestries of pixies, dwarves, and sprites. Bilge, the Master of Potions, is also here. He's a squat green hobgoblin with a bald head, tiny eyes and pointy ears. Tusks jut up from his lower lip. Today he wears a short black robe and sandals. His little green piggy, Oinky, snuffs around his ankles.

I wave. "Hey, Bilge!"

"It promised to help us with potions at dawn," snaps Bilge. By the way, Bilge always calls everyone *it*, except Oinky. That's a hobgoblin thing.

I take a second look at Oinky. Sure enough, Bilge already strapped a basket thingy to the pig's back. Plus, the carrier's loaded with small vials of *who knows what*. Bilge is great at creating potions. It's his labeling and storage skills that stink.

A memory appears. I totally promised to meet Bilge at dawn. Yet I now have a Dare-related secret mission at the exact same time.

Crisis!

There are a number of things I can do here. First, I could tell the truth about my *Dare spying extravaganza*. Unfortunately, that would end in Bilge lecturing me to avoid the winter prince like the plague. No fun.

Which leads to the second option. *Tell a little white lie.*

Sold.

I grin at Bilge. "Of course, I remember. I just asked some of my friends to help you out instead. If they didn't show, then I'd come back later today."

Bilge's pointy ears twitch. The move is hard to miss, considering how those organs are like a pair of antennae. "But it has no other friends," announces Bilge.

Which is also true. The whole *reputation for trouble* thing limits my social life. I clutch at my chest. "Ouch."

Bilge wags his stubby finger in my direction. "It wants to see that snow prince. It plans to sneak into the basement."

"I was NOT going to sneak." *My plan was to march right in.*

"It schemes to use the secret doors to other citadels."

"I do that all the time, Bilge."

Poppa and Muti are citadel workers, although they rarely show up these days. Still, my parents brought me to the citadel tons when I was little. By age six, I'd mastered the secret basement doors to other realms. Which meant I also figured out ley magic. What can I say? I had a lot of time on my hands and very little adult supervision.

"Secret doors are secret," says Bilge. *This is one of his favorite lines.*

"And I keep it that way, don't I?"

"No one must know that it uses ley line magic."

I set my hand over my heart. "No one does, either. Only you, Bilge."

Which is true. I haven't even breathed a word of my ley magic to anyone, even Dare. Everyone thinks I use wands.

Bilge huffs out an angry breath. "It shouldn't go to see *that prince,* even if he is in the summer realm."

I pause. *Wow. Bilge is super-sharp this morning.* He must have downed a truth-detecting potion.

Time to regroup.

I think through my options once again. Cast some spells? Not on Bilge and Oinky. Lie some more? I already tried that. Pranks? I only use my skills for positive stuff, not to weasel myself out of a bad situation with good friends.

At this point, there's only one thing to do. *Ask the question.*

I set my fist on my hip. "Will you tattle on me, Bilge?"

"Never." The hobgoblin lifts his itsy-bitsy chin. "Bilge is no snitch." Oinky lifts his snout as well. They really are the best of buddies.

"Thank you." I flap my wings, ready to zoom past. "If you'll excuse me, I'm off to the basement."

Bilge moves to block my way. *Annoying.* "It has a check-in with the High Council in two days."

"So?"

"Sneaking into Lazare's realm will only cause it trouble." Bilge lowers his voice. "Rumor is, Lazare wants to assassinate it and—"

"I know, I know. A sun cobra tried to kill me last night. Not a problem."

"It did not let me finish. Lazare wants to hurt those it loves as well."

"Bah. Lazare would never go after you and Oinky."

"We are too powerful to attack, and we protect Poppa and Muti too." To emphasize this point, Oinky does his version of an angry pose, which involves scraping at the ground with his front hoof.

"So? Everything is fine."

"And it will remain so. It will not visit the Summer Realm until after it sees the High Council. Oinky and I have put our cloven feet down."

I roll my eyes. "Bilge."

"It shelves potions now." With that, Bilge huffs out a breath through his wide nose. A cloud of snot-spray cascades to the floor.

Boo.

I could push this, but Bilge can—*and will*—block the basement with a border potion. If my hobgoblin buddy says I won't enter, then that's not happening.

Not today, anyway.

Plus, I did give my word. "I will help you, absolutely."

"That's what's best for it."

Bilge and Oinky slowly march up the stairs. Taking to the air , I zoom up the staircase and arrive first. The second level of the citadel is entirely dedicated to storing potions. Keeping with the theme of the building, the shelves are laid out in concentric circles.

Once we're all ready, Bilge lifts a small vial from Oinky's basket. He reads the label aloud. "Evil scheme detection serum. Just made a pot this morning."

"Thought so." I swipe the vial from his hand.

Together, Bilge and I march past the various shelves. Oinky prances behind us. Once we find the right spot, I set the vial in place. I take care to go slowly, mostly so Bilge has time to share local gossip. The winter and summer realms are run by elves, who—as everyone knows—spend long periods of time sitting around and looking pretty, followed by short bursts of murder. So, so boring.

But Pixieland? That's where everyone else lives, and we have all the best action. I shall record three highlights for official purposes.

Totally Important Pixieland Gossip

One. The trolls have started making metal armor from human garbage. (Nothing with iron, mind you. That's poisonous to fae.) It looks terrible and smells worse.

Two. Turns out, Finster the troll had been cheating on his wife with a naiad (not Nicola, thank goodness). Mrs. Finster was the one who dropped a bridge on her husband's head. Serves him right, in my opinion. No one crosses a she-troll and expects to live.

Three. The orcs tried to raid the Ley Queen's palace. She choked a dozen of them with ley lines before they got within a mile. Bilge and I agree that orcs are stupid and the Ley Queen is a mean, mean, meanie.

We're having such a nice time, it's early evening when it hits me.

If Lazare wants to hurt someone I care about, there's only one choice.

Griffin.

Why didn't I think of it before? I must create a ley door and check on Griff. Sadly, Earth visits take time, and it's too late to start today.

Tomorrow is a different matter.

Unfortunately, Wednesdays are also when I practice spells at the citadel. I need to come up with an excuse here. As I set another vial onto a tall shelf, a plan appears.

"I forgot to tell you," I fib. "I won't be here tomorrow."

"It is supposed to practice orb magic with Oinky. Why won't it be here?"

"I must meditate and prepare for my visit to the council on Thursday."

"Lies." Bilge sniffs. "Meditate? It never sits still."

"Did I say meditate? That's the wrong word. What I meant to say is…"

Think fast, Calla.

"What?" Bilge gives me the side eye.

The perfect response appears in a flash.

"It's like this," I declare. "I'm keeping a diary for the council. They'll want to see it Thursday. So, tomorrow I'll record everything that happened today with you and Oinky." I fan myself with my hands. "You're both super important to me. It'll take all day to get it right."

Bilge beams. "Fine. It doesn't need to visit the citadel tomorrow or Thursday."

"Perfect." I spout my wings and speed-fly toward the stairs.

"It leaves now?"

"All the potions are shelved." And if I stay, Bilge might change his mind about tomorrow. He's tricky like that. I flit down the staircase at double speed.

"It will stay out of trouble," calls Bilge after me. "It will avoid that winter prince!"

"Will do."

And I'm not lying about Dare. I absolutely plan to ignore him.

Tomorrow, anyway.

-Calla

DAY SEVEN

Dear Diary,

It's Wednesday and I woke up at dawn. That's right.

Me.

A pixie.

Dawn.

That's just not how life's supposed to work. Maybe it's because I'm nervous about visiting Earth today. That doesn't feel correct, though. What awoke me was an itchy sensation at the back of my head, like I'm forgetting something. I snuggle under my covers before a few minutes before it hits me.

I didn't tell Poppa and Muti that I'd skip the citadel today.

Oops.

Bilge reports to my parents constantly, so there's no avoiding the truth. Poppa and Muti will discover that I was a no-show. In turn, that causes questions, uncomfortable situations, and creative truth-telling.

Time to stop writing and think up a plan. But not before I finish one little thing.

As part of the New Me plan, I cast a spell and got myself a new hat. I'm sick of wearing flowers all the time and this thing is all billowy fabric. Cute! So I'll do a super-quick drawing of that.

Then, I'll get back scheming. Absolutely.

- Calla

My New Hat

DAY SEVEN AND A HALF

*D*ear Diary,

After documenting my gorgeous headgear for all posterity, I craft a brilliant plan for Poppa and Muti. Brace yourself for the smarts, because here's what happens next.

Before leaving the acorn, I leave the following note on the dining room table.

Dear Poppa and Muti,
My council check-in is tomorrow. Therefore, I shall spend today at the Fens and write in my journal. By keeping an amazing diary, I will prove myself to be totally mature and (even more) awesome.
Kisses,
- Calla

Clever, right? Technically, everything I wrote is true. It's just that I skip over the *visiting Earth* part of my day.

You can't see this, my dear Diary, but I am now making crowd cheering noises while doing the *pushing up on the ceiling tiles* dance that's so popular with certain elves.

Sadly, I can't celebrate forever. Back to my day.

With my note complete, I take to the air. My destination? The bestest spot for opening ley doors.

The Fens.

Time was, the Fens were the nicest part of the summer realm. I'm talking green trees, chirping birds, and tons of elves romping around.

But then Lazare took over and a blight sickened the ley lines everywhere. Illness spread to the summer lands in particular.

Long story short, troll poop has more charm than the Fens these days. The trees resemble blackened skeletons. Swamp lands replace all the grass. Worst of all, the entire place smells like moth balls and old man farts. The only bright side is that the Fens are so crappy, the place is always deserted. No one's around to see what I'm about to do.

Yay for me.

Not that other fairies could stop me. It's more that Bilge made me promise to keep my abilities with ley magic on the down-low. Which makes sense. If people knew about citadel doors, they'd line up to use them. And if folks knew I could manipulate ley lines in general, they'd lock me up to leverage that power. I like my freedom.

After flying about for a little while, I find a relatively stink-free stretch of open ground. Kneeling down, I reach into the earth. At first, there's nothing—just a bunch of soggy dirt. Then I feel it—the tingle on my palms says I'm close to a ley line. Cool magic brushes against my skin. Gripping the line, I pull upwards. A hefty cord of blue power sits in my hands—more than enough for a trip to Earth.

And, eew.

This ley line is definitely struck with blight. Large gray splotches mark up what should be a solid line of glowing blue. All the ill bits are gooey and cold as well. A thread of unease winds up my spine. The blight looks way worse than last time I pulled a ley line. If this keeps up, what could happen next?

I set the thought aside, mostly because I've bigger things to worry about right now. Like Earth.

Avoiding the sticky and gross bits, I twist the ley line into a door shape. It's a lot like working with clay, only ley lines can zap your skin if you aren't careful.

Soon, I stare at a glowing door that hovers in the air. *Perfect.* I pull on the handle to reveal rolling green fields divided by a wide gravel road. A few yards away, there sits a heavy wooden sign:

Welcome to Glover's Hollow. Population 1400.

It's a view that's both good and bad. The nice part is that Griffin's nearby. The bad part is that whenever I visit Earth, I always get dumped to this same place.

Sadly, Glover's Hollow isn't exactly Thrill-A-Minute Land.

Before stepping through the door, I summon a sphere of pink power to my right hand. Releasing the magic, I press the energy into a cloaking spell. A moment later, I'm invisible. Hey, you never know what humans will do when confronted with a pixie.

After stepping through the door, I follow the main road to Glover's Hollow. The last time I was here, I basically ran over Griffin long before I got to town. For this visit, I'll need to use my amazing mental skills to track the guy down. The good news is, Glover's Hollow isn't exactly overflowing with people. I'll find Griff, no problem.

After reaching town, I stroll down the main drag (invisibly, of course.) There's a Headless Huntress Luncheonette, Headless Grocery Store, and even a Headless Huntress Library. No question about who's the local *legend-slash-tourist attraction*. Cheers echo down the street, so I follow the noise. Soon I find a small brick building called—*wait for it*—the Headless Huntress High School.

Getting closer.

Behind the building, a bunch of human kids kick around a checkerboard ball. I saunter my invisible self closer to the green. Sure enough, there's no missing Griffin's cropped red hair. I exhale.

He's safe.

There are a number of things I could do now. Top choices: chat with Griffin, discover more about Earth, and maybe even play a prank or two. Instead, a familiar hunger settles into my body.

These are humans.

And so are my parents.

I scan the faces of the adults encircling field. A bitter taste crawls into my mouth. My human parents handed me off to the Ley Queen, who then sent me off to the Winter Elves. The frosty fae asked Bilge for guidance on how to raise me… and that's how I ended up with ancient citadel workers for parents. Beyond hoping I fit in, Poppa and Muti aren't all that engaged. Even so, they show an amazing level of family love compared to most fairies.

Yet it's nothing next to these human parents.

The folks here watch every kick of the checkered ball with rapture. Some cheer. Others gasp. A lonely and empty feeling settles into my bones.

Do my human parents even know I'm alive? Would they care?

I force my spine to straighten. This stuff sin't worth worrying about. If anything, I should be happy the Ley Queen even handed me off to begin with. She's not the nicest of people, even on a good day.

All of which why I spend so little time on Earth. It's not because of the horror stories about drinking pee and eating babies named Ruth. It's the gap of my missing family.

Time to leave.

I summon a fresh sphere of pink power. This orb is invisible, same as I am. I toss the energy across the yard; it lands smack into the center of Griffin's chest. No one suspects a thing, even Griff. Yet now he's protected from attacks by predators, up to a level five spell. Considering how Lazare's only sent a level one killer my way, that should be more than enough.

Right after my spell sinks in, the checkered ball slams into a net. Everyone shouts with joy once more. For some reason, that makes me feel worse than ever.

After marching back to the welcome sign, I pull up a fresh ley line and return to Faerie. By the time I fly inside my home acorn, Poppa and Muti are already asleep.

I try to zonk out, too. Unfortunately, that doesn't happen right away. All of which is why, at this very moment, I'm spending extra quality time recording stuff in my diary.

And waiting for the High Council check in tomorrow.

Blech.

-Calla

DAY EIGHT

$\mathcal{D}$ear Diary,
    Council Check-In Time!

Note: I thought adding an exclamation point at the end of those words would make today seem less sucky. It didn't work.

After I wake up and eat my Pixie Os, I fly my sweet self over to the Pinnacle, which is a massive black castle where the council meets. The place is tall, windowless, and has lots of pointy things up top.

Subtle.

Landing on the drawbridge, I knock at the huge wooden doors. A small slot opens; a guard scans me.

"There's no one here," says a woman. Based on the musical quality to her voice, this guard is a summer elf. When no one else is around, summer elves are total smart asses.

I go on tiptoe and wave my hand. "It's Calla."

"Still don't see anyone," she snarks. Now I recognize the voice. *Monique, a senior guard.* She makes *short girl* jokes all the time. What she lacks in creativity, Monique more than makes up for by being hella repetitive.

"Oh, you don't see me because I'm so short. Ha ha. Now open up."

Monique isn't dropping the joke, though. "Wait. Perhaps it's a child. A mischievous little one who went and turned the council bald."

"That's me, the bringer of baldness." I thump my fist against the door. "Hurry up already. I'm late for my check-in." Now, I shouldn't let the 'child' crack get to me, but I'm a curve-free teenager and a pixie to boot. That means everyone thinks I'm nine years old.

Don't say it.

Don't say it.

I can't help but say it.

"By the way, I'm almost sixteen."

The door swings open. A line of guard faces appear in the break. Of course, they all have golden hair, high cheekbones and pointy ears. And they all appear eternally twenty-one or whatever. Stupid elves.

"You're really not nine?" asks one.

"She looks eight to me," snarks another.

"How can someone be so little… yet cause so much trouble?" That's Monique. I'm starting to hate her.

Raising my right hand, I summon a sphere of pink power to appear above my palm. "You want a piece of this?"

The guards laugh, but there's a nervous ring to it. *Good.*

"You're free to go home," says Monique. "There's no check-in today."

That's a shocker. "When did this happen?"

"Just now. A new initiation is taking place instead. Lazare caught a fresh changeling to serve him." There's an evil gleam in her eyes that I don't like at all. I think about Bilge's warning. A chill rolls across my shoulders.

"Who's the changeling?" I ask.

"A human boy. What do you care?"

"Does he have freckles, red hair, and sparkly eyes?"

Monique grins. "Why, yes. It's your human, Calla."

Taking to the air, I fly over the guards' heads and toward the council reception hall. The guards don't follow, but that's no surprise. Everyone knows Lazare wants me dead, exiled or imprisoned. The fact that I'm flying into the council chambers unannounced? That breaks about ten different rules. These guards are happy to set me up. In fact, Lazare might give them all medals.

Seconds later, I zoom into a huge space made from shiny onyx. Time was, this chamber would be crammed with hundreds of elves, along with other kinds of fae, like goblins, trolls, naiads, and pixies. But that was years ago. Now, only a handful of elves represent everyone.

Long story long, it takes ages for me to fly across the council chamber. Why can't they meet near the doors? Sheesh. That said, there is a bright side. I can fly in interesting patterns and leave pink dust trails behind me.

At last, I reach the far wall and the summer and winter courts. It's easy to tell who's who. Summer elves all wait to the left. They're totally gold: hair, gowns, armor, everything. Winter elves stand to the right.

They have way more variety when it comes to hair and skin color. Plus, winter elves have talons for nails, pointy teeth, and dark leather armor for clothing.

I scan the faces carefully. No Dare today. *Le sigh.*

A figure lies crumpled on the floor. I spy a shaved head, tattered robes and shaking limbs. No doubt about it.

That's Griffin.

A weight of guilt settles in my stomach. Sure, I cast a spell to protect this human from assassination attempts, but that wouldn't stop Griff from being abducted and brought into Faerie. Why didn't I cast more spells? What was I thinking?

I kneel beside him. "Griff, are you okay?"

His blue eyes fix me with a glazed look. "Is this a dream?"

"Absolutely," I lie. "Just stay quiet and I'll get you out of here." I round on the council. "Who claims this human as their slave?"

Lazare drums his fingers on the arm of his golden throne. Like always, the guy looks like a blond teenager with pointy features, and I'm not just talking about his ears. Lazare's nose and chin seem like they could puncture metal. I guess it's attractive in an elfy sort of way.

"Others find you entertaining." Lazare gestures across the room. Many nod their agreement, even some of the summer elves. "You're their miniature court jester."

I roll my eyes. "Whatever."

"For my part, I loathe you. You charmed all my underwear to give wedgies… enchanted my eyebrows to run away… and even transformed my shampoo into hair remover. Because of you, I waste time on needless frippery. This cannot continue."

I stifle a grin. I'd forgotten about the Great Wedgie Happening. As for my Brow Freedom Project, Lazare has massive eyebrows that are way too dark and bushy. Those things were crying out to become charmed and free.

Final point. Who uses *frippery* in a sentence? Only Lazare.

Narrowing my eyes, I give the protector my most serious look. "Not continuing the frip, got it. So… do you claim this human for slavery or what?"

"Elves don't keep slaves," intones Lazare.

"You know what I mean. Slave, human changeling, whatever. Who claims Griff?"

Lazare smiles. "Why, I do. Of course. I brought him here this morning."

"You can have any human you want. Why pick my friend?"

"Why, indeed?" asks Lazare. "I think we both know the answer to that question."

Which we do. *This is all one big Calla-shaped trap.*

"Set the human free," I demand.

"Happy to," retorts Lazare. "Let's make a bargain of it."

This raises a basic rule of survival in Faerie. *Never bargain.* I don't even respond to Lazare's question. Pulling on the magic inside me, I draw in fresh power. A pink sphere of energy hovers above my palm.

"I made everyone dance the Macarena for three solid days. Do you really want to test what I can do?"

Queen Saita—that's Dare's mother—shifts in her onyx throne. She's tall and pale with long black hair. Her white gown glitters like fresh snow on a winter morning. "Perhaps there's another option. How about you forge a bargain with me?"

"The faeling already refused my deal," grumps Lazare. "Now the human must serve me forever."

"Forever? Really?" I scan the room. No one says a word. That's a bad sign. At last, Saita speaks up.

"I've never received an answer on my offer," states the queen.

"I'll pass." My sphere of power still hovers above my right hand. Whatever Lazare has planned, I can cast a counter-spell.

"Then let's get on with it." Lazare pulls a wand from the folds of his golden cloak.

At this point, it's important to restate how wands store magic. Using them means you're either weak or lazy. In Lazare's case, I suspect that he's both.

Still, fighting the summer fae is going to suck. Mostly because there are twenty summer elves here and just one of me. Not great odds. Plus, Queen Saita won't lift a finger to help yours truly. In her mind, I'm free entertainment, nothing more.

Not to mention the big magilla here. Once I attack, I've basically written my own ticket to exile or prison.

My throat tightens. In cases like this, there's only one person I can rely on for help. Focusing my power, I send magic to my palm line. The mark flares white against my skin.

Need you, Dare.

Usually, the light blinks to show Dare got my message. But this time? No response. Ick.

Counter spells flicker through my head. There's my piggy-conda, which squeezes people in classic snake-style. But that only works on a single opponent. I could also go for my killer kitty horde. That's a level seven spell and works best against a group. However, killer kitties require an incantation. Since Lazare is using a wand, I won't have time for long speeches.

All of which means I'm probably best off with an orb of protection. That will block Lazare's magic while keeping Griffin safe. But then what? I can't hide in a sphere forever.

Suddenly, a deal doesn't sound like a crap idea any more. I focus on Saita. Sure enough, she catches my gaze. There's a knowing look in her gray eyes that says, *bargain with me.*

I lower my hand. "All right, I'll make the bar—"

～

Dear Diary,

What happens next involves Dare, so I'll start a new page. Since we're almost engaged and everything, recording this kind of thing separately is pretty much my job now.

-Calla

DAY EIGHT AND A HALF

*D*ear Diary,

When we last left my life, I was about to fight Lazare, the Protector of the Summer Elves.

That doesn't happen.

Instead, the back doors of the meeting hall swing open. Prince Darius marches into the room. Even from a distance, there's no missing how the firm angles of his face are tight with rage. Dare wears his black body leathers and silver crown. A fur-trimmed cloak flows off his wide shoulders.

"Calla is under my protection," calls Dare. "No magic touches her."

If I had a gold coin for every time Dare announced this to the council, I'd be a rich pixie. Before, worry had been coiling inside me. Now that knot of anxiety loosens as a massive yelling match begins. This is familiar stuff. And, if I'm being honest, it's also more than a little entertaining.

Lazare freaks out on Dare.

Queen Saita scolds everyone.

All the summer elves howl at their winter counterparts.

In fact, there's so much chaos that no one notices the wine steward come in. His tray overflows with a decanter and goblets. The steward is a human, and his gaze automatically locks on Griffin. They share a look that overflows with misery. And that's when an idea appears.

The best prank of all time.

I shift my weight from foot to foot. This is such a perfect scheme. But how can I do it? I'm already treading on thin ice. There's no way I can pull another prank.

I really shouldn't.

Griffin does that guy-thing where he wipes away a tear with his knuckle. That settles it.

One new prank, coming up.

As the steward passes by, I send a little thread of magic into the wine. Then I inspect the room. Did anyone notice my spell? Doesn't look like it. There's still way too much yelling going on. Some diary-worthy highlights.

"Shred her!" cries one summer elf.

"Tear off her wings!" That's another rando blond stooge.

"We hate you, Lazare!" Those are Lazare's eyebrows talking. They must have sensed my magic and shown up for some fun. Turns out, it's a really great idea to give enchanted facial hair squeaky voices.

Lazare rises from his throne. Throwing his arms in the air, he bellows above everyone. "Watch me destroy her forever!"

Queen Saita waves at him in a way that says, *sit down already.* "Calla is an amusement, nothing more. You must calm yourself."

Lazare plunks back onto his throne. "I'm trying." He points right at my face. "Only this one is too much."

Another random summer elf steps forward. "How about a refreshment, my Liege?"

Now I have no idea who this summer elf is, but I could kiss him.

"Steward!" cries Lazare. "Bring me wine."

Which the steward does. It takes everything in me not to rub my hands together and go *mwah-hah-hah.*

Once Lazare's glass is full, the steward circulates the room, offering drinks to other elves. Using maximum casualness, I stroll closer Dare. To be even trickier, I take care to speak from one side of my mouth.

"Don't drink that," I saw in a low voice.

Dare gives me the side eye. "None of my elves were planning on it. We've seen how you work, Calla."

Sure enough, drinks are handed out, yet the winter elves don't take so much as a sip. I guess my sneakiness is getting somewhat predictable. I'll have to work on that.

"Now that we're all calm once more," states Saita. "How about Calla reports her progress?" She looks to Lazare. "You were the one who wished to question her today."

"Quite right." Lazare downs his entire goblet in one swig. And because they follow their master blindly in all things, the other summer elves finish everything in a single gulp as well.

This will be so awesome.

I pretend to cough, just to have an excuse to hide my laughter.

"How have you been improving yourself?" asks Lazare.

All eyes focus on me. "Well, I keep a diary. It's supposed to help with my maturity and self-awareness."

Not today, obviously. But in general.

"Really?" asks Lazare. "Where is this journal?"

I tap the locket around my neck. "It's enchanted into this necklace, so don't get any ideas."

Dare turns to me. His gray eyes are so intense, it makes my insides flip around. "You still work at the Pixieland Citadel, do you not?"

This is an easy question, which I totally appreciate. "Yes, I volunteer and help the potions master, Bilge."

Gurgle, gurgle. A gentle noise echoes through the chamber. Someone has an upset tummy.

One guess who.

If Saita hears the noise from Lazare's belly, she doesn't show it. Instead, she raises her pointer finger. "Before I forget, please tell Bilge I require a new tonic for my ice garden. His growth serum was most effective."

"Will do, your Majesty." I curtsey. "Bilge will be thrilled to know it helped." Saita's really into her ice garden. She grows all sorts of winter stuff, like holly and pine. Guess everyone needs a hobby.

Lazare fidgets in his chair. "What else have you done?"

Another positive thing occurs to me. "I also care for Bilge's piggy familiar, Oinky."

Lazare's face flushes red. This is a really powerful spell. Honestly, I have no idea how Lazare is still here. "Do you really think that aiding a pig is a sign of personal improvement?"

At this point, a super loud noise reverberates through the room.

GURGLE, GURGLE!

Everyone else heard it, too.

Queen Saita rises. "I believe that is enough for today." She looks to Lazare. "Is it agreeable to cancel the rest of our time?"

"That's fine," says Lazare quickly. "This session of the High Council of Elves is hereby called to a close."

"Bathroom is at the end of the hall," whispers Saita. Although she doesn't really whisper it, since we all heard her anyway.

At this point, it's important to restate how summer elves are indeed more powerful than their winter counterparts. Does Saita enjoy how I take Lazare down a peg or two? Absolutely.

"Court dismissed!" Next Lazare does that thing where you walk away really fast, all while clenching your butt cheeks. Sighing, I watch all the summer elves all file out behind their leader. Most are doing the poop-walk as well. Sadly, it won't be long before their magical doctors run a tracer spell and find out I was behind everything.

I'm in deep trouble, but it's totally worth it.

Dare leans in closer. When he whispers, it's magically enhanced so no one else can hear. "I'll cast something to block the tracer spells."

Now, I know Dare can't *really* read my mind. But that came pretty close. "How did you know what I was thinking?"

"You forget. I've known you since the Ley Queen first brought you to our palace." The hint of a smile winds his wide mouth. "Even as a baby, you were a sneak."

"What about the human?" I ask. "He should go back to Earth now, right?"

Dare inhales a long breath. "I don't understand why you care."

I fold my arms over my chest. "You know I won't back down, though."

Evidently, Saita had been eavesdropping on our chat. She gestures toward Griffin. "Has anyone claimed this mortal?"

Silence is the only reply.

"Excellent," says Saita. "I shall send him back to Earth immediately." She pulls a wand from the folds of her robe and flicks it at Griff. A coil of blue smoke surrounds my human friend. When the haze vanishes, Griff is gone as well.

I bow low. "Thank you, Queen Saita."

"Most welcome."

Dare focuses on his mother. "I'd like to speak to Calla alone."

In realty, beams on sunlight don't flood the chamber at this point. No elf choir materializes in order to sing love sings with the plinky-plink of lute music. Still, I can imagine it all in my wee little brain.

New section coming up.

-Calla

DAY EIGHT AND THREE QUARTERS

*D*ear Diary,

This mini-story about Dare should be fun to write. It's not. In fact, it's almost painful to record what happens next. Why? Because here's where Dare transforms from a badass protector into a no-fun loser. Good thing he's cute or I might call off our engagement.

Not that we're officially getting married.

Yet.

Anyway, everyone's well and gone when Dare turns to me. "Call-la," he says in a sing-song voice.

The moment I get that particular tone, I know.

This won't be good.

Sticking out my hip, I glare, glare, glare. "What's the bad news?"

"Why should you say that?" While Dare asks that question, his features transform into the picture of gray eyes and gooey handsomeness. A distraction.

He can kiss my pixie butt. I still know something's up.

"Remember when we found that Pegasus puppy?" I ask.

Dare nods. "Princess Pampertoes."

"Right. We snuck her into your wing of the winter palace and she piddled everywhere."

"Pegasus hounds fly, so that was a real mess. The servants were scrubbing the walls for hours." Dare opens his mouth, ready to go on about puppy clean-up. For a prince, he over-explains the process of sanitizing stuff. Not today.

"Hey!" I interrupt. "Telling a story here."

"Apologies." Dare bows slightly. "Pray continue."

"You'd give that puppy a very particular look and say, *time to go outside.*"

"My palace is surrounded by a tundra. Princess P required a heads-up in regards to the change in temperature."

"Exactly. That's the face you're giving me now. The *time to go outside* look."

"Funny you should say that. Remember when we were kids, how we'd talk about traveling? I believe you might benefit from touring Faerie. Now."

At this point, I'm trying not to get excited. It isn't working very well, though. Mostly because Dare said *touring* and I'm assuming this is some kind of invitation here.

For us.

Rosy images flicker through my mind: Dare and Calla, flying across the mountains, hand in hand. Well, not holding hands because we'd end up steering each other into a cliff wall, but it's the idea that counts. The pair of us would travel together. My head turns fuzzy with the possibilities.

Yes, yes, yes!

I bite my lower lip, which is another sure-fire look according to my kissy books. "Who am I traveling *with*?"

Dare sets his fist over his heart. "An honor guard of my best lady warriors." He grins. "I look forward to receiving your postcards from the road."

"Because I'm going alone."

"Look, Calla. It's better than being exiled. Taking a tour would also give the council some breathing room. Meanwhile, you'll enjoy an adventure."

I kick at the floor. "I don't want to visit Faerie."

Dare frowns. "When did that change?"

I open my mouth, ready to share where I always wanted to visit, *really*. Earth. Mostly to find my human parents. And I've tried to visit, but I keep getting bummed out and heading back to Faerie. But I don't say any of this aloud. Dare would never understand why I'd seek out my parents in the first place. Most fae see humans as one tick above pond scum.

"I changed, that's all. I'm a grown-up woman of many moods."

"Calla." The sing-song voice returneth, only it's even more sugary this time.

Danger zone!

I gesture across Dare's general face area. "I know that look. It's the one you gave Princess P when you told her she was going on a puppy vacation."

"It *was* a vacation. We sent her to live on a lovely farm with many other happy canines."

I gasp. "You're sending me to a puppy farm?"

"I'm protecting you from the council."

This is a stunner. I can't help thinking that's it's hard for Dare and I to get married if I'm traveling around with lady warriors and he's stuck in the winter realm.

Huh. There is most definitely something else going on here. Dare is of the age to get married. He's not asking me at the moment.

That makes me one pissed-off pixie.

All of which leads to the thing I do best when angry. Scheme. The first part of this process involves asking more questions. Dare is overly trusting when it comes to yours truly.

"If I did leave, how long should I travel for?"

"Six months would be enough time."

I tap my cheek and debate my next move.

Just ask him, Calla. Spit it out.

"Are you getting married?"

And it's out.

"No. It's as I said before. I simply plan for your safety."

My thoughts whirl through this answer. Fairies can't lie. And elves are a type of fairy. However, they can twist the truth around.

Only this is Dare. He wouldn't do that.

Unless he's relying on *me* to be overly-trusting, the same way I'm relying on him. That's a definite possibility.

It's so confusing to be in a relationship.

"I'll think about it," I say at length. "Talking hypothetically, when should I leave? "

"How about tomorrow?"

I gasp. This time, the inhale comes complete with setting my hands on my throat and everything.

"Dare! My birthday is coming up."

"I'm sorry." And he does a very good job of looking apologetic. Dare has these long lashes that enhance the sad factor. "There's been so much going on, I forgot."

"What *has* been going on, exactly?"

"I'm trying to get access to King Tristan."

"Why? All he does is sleep."

"Lazare is out of control. Trying to assassinate you? He's lost touch with reality. And the blight is growing worse by the day. Some summer elves have actually fallen ill."

My eyes widen. "That's serious."

"We only had blight like this once before in our history, and the person who ended it was Tristan. Yet I can't end the blight or get rid of Lazare if I can't awaken and reinstate Tristan. That's hard to do when the king has been placed in some secret spot. No one will tell me where."

"That makes sense." I picture elves with that gray goo on their skin. Not good. And Dare has other things to do now than worry about my sorry butt. "I'll think about the traveling thing."

"Thank you, little hob."

Dare gives me a nuggie.

I'm talking fist to the skull.

Messing up my hair.

Total humiliation.

I wiggle out from under him. "Goodbye, Dare."

There's no avoiding the truth. Dare still sees me as a kid. Which is awful. I take to the air and speed away. Even the long line of summer elves outside the bathroom doesn't cheer me up.

Sometimes, it's not easy being me.

-Calla

DAY NINE

*D*ear Diary,

After yesterday's action-packed check-in with the High Council, today started off pretty slowly. First of all, there was no one to greet me at the breakfast table. Bummer. Normally, Poppa and Muti rally their old bones for my return. At the very least, they sleep at the dining room table in a puddle of their own saliva.

No such luck this morning.

So I conjure myself a bowl of Pixie Os and make a super-mature list in my diary. After my conversation with Dare yesterday, I still haven't made my decision about traveling.

Reasons to Stay in Pixieland

One. Keep playing pranks on the High Council.

Two. Spend quality time with Bilge and Oinky.

Three. Continue giving Poppa and Muti something to live for.

Four. Find out what His Royal Sneakiness Prince Darius is up to (because it's something!)

Reasons to Travel

One. Find my human parents on Earth.

Two. That's about it.

I finish my list just as Poppa and Muti flit in for breakfast. About time.

"Here I am!" I point to my face for emphasis. "I'm sure you were worried."

"No," says Poppa. "Prince Darius told us about your day yesterday."

"He did?" I scrunch up my face in confusion. "How did that work?"

"The prince sent us a letter," explains Muti. She starts casting bowls of sloppy goop for her and Poppa.

I hold out my hand. "May I see this letter?"

"Nope." Poppa speed-smacks his lips, which is a sure tell that he's making up a lie. Or he lost another tooth. "We, uh, destroyed the message after we read it."

"There was nothing important in it anyway," adds Muti. "Unless you count the part how he said you're thinking about traveling across Faerie. Is that true?

"I'm thinking," I reply. "As in considering."

Poppa and Muti exchange a long look. I've seen that glance before. Dare's message held other information; Poppa and Muti won't tell me what it is. Good thing they're both a lot old and a little slow. I'll get the truth out of them.

I finish off my bowl of Pixie Os. "What do you know about my parents?"

"Those worthless humans?" asks Muti. "Why would you care?"

"I'm a curious pixie."

Poppa shrugs. "It's as we told you. Soon after you were born, you sprouted wings. Your humans became overwhelmed dropped you off at an orphanage. Eventually, you became ours."

I tap my spoon against the tabletop. "Nothing else?"

"Nope," says Muti. "Oh, there is one thing we forgot."

"What?"

"Your friend is outside," answers Poppa.

"You mean Bilge?"

"Not him," says Muti. "Another friend."

I slump in my seat and think through who this could be. Apart from Bilge, I've got no one. "What does this person look like?"

"Oh," says Poppa. "You know. Not too fat, not too thin. Not too tall, not too short."

"And a lady," adds Muti.

I tap my spoon more quickly. "This can't be a friend. It must be an assassin."

Muti fans herself with her weathered hands. "You've made an enemy, that's wonderful."

Energy streams through me. I haven't used my killer kitty spell yet. This could be the perfect opportunity.

"I'll just step outside and say hello," I announce.

"Be nasty!" says Muti.

"Lose your temper and kill things," adds Poppa.

If the sun cobra was fun, this promises to be even better. All of which is why I'm breaking it out onto a new page.

- Calla

DAY NINE AND A HALF

*D*ear Diary,
Assassin, here I come.

Shaking fairy dust off my butt, I quickly change into pink battle leathers because that's what you wear when kicking ass.

Shrinking down, I fly through the acorn's cap. Once outdoors, I retake my full size and—WHAMMO—there's my target.

An assassin stands by our oak. The sun rises behind this mystery attacker, leaving their face in shadow.

It's such a dramatic moment, I can't even. I soak in the green vista of our pasture. My towering oak. The rising sun. And me, a badass pixie warrior in pink leather. It's tempting to cast a spell of background music for the occasion.

Raising my right hand, I summon a sphere of pink magic. "Who goes here? Or *there*? No, definitely *here*."

Not my best opening.

The shadows shift, revealing my opponent.

It's a young girl. Strangely enough, she's just as Poppa said. Her features are both bland and shifting. Whoever this really is, they're cloaked in a glamour spell.

"Show yourself," I call.

That was much better than the *who goes here* line.

The edges of the girl's body morph and stretch. My heart sinks. I know this visitor.

It's the Ley Queen.

Now, I'm ready for a battle but I'm not cuckoo. No way am I making the first move against someone as powerful as the Ley Queen.

"Walk with me." The Ley Queen strides through the open field behind our tree. I don't get to see her often, so I really take a closer look. Hair, gown, and wings… Everything about the Ley Queen is blue. Darker lines of blue power twist across her skin in a constant dance.

I follow beside her. She's got super-long elf legs, so it's hard to keep up. "May I ask you a question?"

"You have my permission."

"Why are you here?"

"Faelings are important to me." She pauses and looks me over carefully. "I protect what the ley lines create."

I'd point out her that her protection wasn't much help to Finster the troll, but I'm not pushing my luck.

"I am not pleased," continues the Ley Queen. "Living with Poppa and Muti should have kept you separated from the rest of Faerie. That did not happen. I do not blame your parents, however. It was Bilge who failed."

"Hey. Bilge has done a great job of protecting me."

"He's kept you away from ley lines and citadel doors, but that is all."

I stare at the ground and try not to look guilty. I broke Bilge early.

The colored marks on the Ley Queen's face swirl more quickly. Seems like that happens when she's angry.

"And there is more," snaps the Ley Queen. "Bilge was supposed to keep you from the Elven High Council. In that, he has also failed. Miserably."

"Are you planning to do anything to Bilge? Because I don't know if that will work out well for you."

A ghost of a smile rounds Blue's mouth. "I shall do nothing to Bilge. It is *you* that I came here to warn. If you cause more trouble, my hand will be forced. For your own protection, I shall imprison you in a ley line."

I bob my head, thinking. *What's a ley line prison, anyway?* One way to find out.

"And what does that mean, exactly?"

"Suspended animation. You float within a blue sphere of time and space. Later, I'll remove you again if the opportunity arises." She taps her wand against her lips. "Perhaps once Lazare is dead."

I sniff. "That guy is immortal."

"I didn't say your stay would be short."

"And this suspended animation thing. I'm what? Asleep?"

"You're awake the entire time. It isn't ideal, which is why I placed you with Poppa and Muti in the first place. However, it is safe."

I tap my cheek and think things through. "I've been a bad girl for a while now. Is there anything in particular that's causing today's warning?"

"Clever." The Ley Queen smiles, and it's like the sun peeping out from behind storm clouds. "My visit does indeed have a specific purpose. Whatever you do, you must *not* go the summer palace for the next two days. Can you do that for me?"

"Yeah, sure." That isn't a convincing answer, even to me.

The Ley Queen scowls. "Do not try to run away or second guess me. I've more magic than you know." To emphasize this point, the Ley Queen lifts her arms and sprinkles a bit of blue fairy dust in my direction.

Instantly, my chest constricts. Pain like I've never known shoots through every nerve ending in my body. I crumple onto my knees.

"Thwart me and that agony will be your eternity. Do you comprehend ?"

"Completely." *And do I ever.*

"Good enough." The Ley Queen flicks her wrist; all my pain ends. "What will do you now?"

"Go to my room and record all this in my dairy." I set my hand to my heart. "I swear, I will do everything in my power to change. Writing everything down will help."

"Very wise." The Ley Queen waves her arm. Fairy dust cascades around her in pretty swirls. She vanishes.

With the Ley Queen gone, I fly straight back into my acorn and get to work. Which brings me to this very moment and my most solemn vow of all time.

For the next two days, I shall not go to the summer realm, let alone the summer palace. This is a new day and an all-new Calla. Really-really-REALLY.

And to keep temptation to a minimum, I plan to stay in my room and practice spells.

- Calla

DAY TEN

*D*ear Diary,

Turns out, Poppa and Muti don't appreciate experimental spells inside their acorn. Personally, I thought the horde of killer leprechauns were cute. And in reality, our little green friends would never have actually choked Poppa and Muti with rainbows. But I do agree that the way they constantly chucked coins at us was annoying.

So fine. I get sent off to the citadel to practice. Totally fair.

After downing my bowl of Pixie Os, I fly off for the Pixieland Citadel. As I close in, one thing is clear. Or rather, hazy. And that would be the smoke billowing out of the skinny window-holes that surround the pink tower. Based on the yellow and purple colors in the air, there's no question what happened.

A potion went wrong.

I hover out side the window-hole to the Bilge's cauldron room. Using my magic, I make my voice echo extra-loud. "Bilge? Are you in there?"

"It is visiting us," comes the reply.

Yup, Bilge is here, all right.

"Is everything okay?" I ask.

"Messy." Bilge's green face appears in the window hole. "*Someone* kicked over three of my cauldrons."

Sad little snuffles fill the air. No question who the *someone* is in this scenario. Oinky. This has happened before. Oinky knocks over one cauldron, gets over-excited, and rushes around, toppling even more over.

"I know you didn't mean it, Oinky." Another snuffle follows, and this one lands on a happier note. "Do you need help with your mess, Bilge?"

"No, I need *it* out of my way."

"Poppa and Muti don't want me in the acorn."

"Then it uses the citadel door in the basement." Bilge waves his arm. "Scat!"

I don't need to be scatted twice. After flying into the citadel proper, I speed down the corkscrew staircase that leads to the basement. There I find a small room made of pink stone. The place holds nothing but a wooden door and a thatched welcome mat. I land in the chamber's center.

Here it is.

The door that will take me anywhere in Faerie.

Kneeling, I pull up the welcome mat. Underneath, I find a gap in the floor and within that open space? Dozens of ley lines. Some are merely threads. Others are hefty as my arm. Most stay still—a low pulse of blue light is the the only sign of magic inside. A few flip about like fish on a dock.

I brush my fingers along the ley line for the Winter Citadel—it's a thin cord that drips with tiny icicles. The barest chill soaks into my fingertips.

Visiting the Winter Citadel is always a good time. Sure, the tower part got obliterated when Reiver tried to kill Tristan. Even so, the catacombs below remain intact. There's lots to explore and no one to stop me.

Another ley line catches my eye: the fancy braided cord for the Summer Citadel. I can't help but recall how the Summer Citadel rests near the summer palace. In reality, those are two totally different places.

In fact, the more I think about about it, the more I'm convinced that the Ley Queen *only* meant for me to avoid the palace itself. The citadel is fine. Plus, it's packed with tons of awesome stuff, like dust and yellow sheets. Totally educational.

As a side bonus, the trip would also help me test my resolve. By visiting summer territory, I'll prove that my vow to avoid the palace is indeed unbreakable.

This idea gets better by the second.

Without further ado, I pull on the ley line for the Summer Citadel. Once the cord is raised, it's craft time as I press the line around the basement's physical door. From there, the cord melts down the wood, turning into an intricate blue mural of the citadel itself.

Done, done, and done.

Stepping through the door, I find a familiar sight, namely shadows, dust, and lots of furniture draped with yellow sheets. Once Tristan got knocked out, all the citadels were shut down except for Pixieland. This particular building has been deserted for years. Stepping inside, I close the door behind me.

My pulse speeds with excitement. Here I am, Calla the pixie, hanging out in the Summer Citadel. Behold, for I display exceptional inner strength and vow making ability.

Thirty seconds tick by.

Then I realize the sad truth.

My vow is toast. I'm totally sneaking into the summer palace.

Here's my reasoning. Sure, I've been told not to go. Yes, it's absolutely dangerous. But I'm tired of everyone protecting me by wadding me up in cotton balls and terror. I'm a powerful pixie who can take care of herself. Whatever's in that palace, I can handle it.

With the decision made, I step toward the citadel's back door. I don't get two yards before it happens.

White light appears on my palm.

I do a combination eye-roll and snort. This light can only mean one thing. Dare wants to chat. Normally, I'd be happy to talk. Not this time. I don't even acknowledge him with a busy pulse.

Knowing Dare, he won't wait too long to track me down. Best to hustle.

I speed-walk through the back door and into the Buttercup Forest. Here the trees all have yellow leaves. Morning sunlight dances through the colorful branches. On the ground, sunshine yellow cats scamper about in packs. For whatever reason, felines love the Buttercup Forest. Beyond the woods, there looms a golden palace whose exterior glimmers with murals of dancing elves.

Bands of anticipation tighten around my throat. I've snuck in this particular section of the palace complex before. It's the main preparation chamber for big events.

Time to snoop around there again.

On reflex, I check my palm. The white line has vanished. Maybe Dare's given up. Nice.

Dragging open the door, I march inside. While the building's exterior is all gilded, the interior has all the charm of an empty box. The gray walls surround me. Supplies of all kinds line the floor. I catalog piles of dishes. Great wooden trunks that overflow with linens. And a cluster of greenery which looms by the far wall.

Stepping into the space, I also discover a painted sign.

Welcome to the Summer Masquerade Ball.
Tonight only! On the Eve of the Summer Moon.

I frown. The eve of the summer moon? This masquerade takes place tomorrow night.

Ahhh-HA!

So this is what the Ley Queen wanted me to avoid—a summer realm party? I've never broken into an elf thing in my life. Who wants to be ignored while getting looked down upon?

Of course, now I absolutely must attend. I'm in too deep to back out.

A line of paintings lay stacked against a nearby wall. I step closer, finding that all the images show previous masquerades. In one, a group of summer elves order around a bunch of changeling humans in brown cloaks. *Charming.* Another picture shows elves in costumes. No one wears much. In my opinion, its more beach party than masquerade. A final painting depicts a young boy in a crown who stands beside a tiny llama. This is young King Tristan and what looks like his favorite pet. I smile.

Masquerading means going in costume. I totally know what I'm dressing up as, and it's not little King Tristan.

Hello, baby llama.

Pulling up a small sphere of pink magic, I chuck it into my own face. A moment later, I am an adorable pink llama with purple eyes and pointy toes. I prance about in a circle.

"I looo awwssss," I announce.

What I meant to say is that *I look awesome*. It will take some practice to learn how to speak through a baby llama mouth.

Ending the spell, I return to just being Calla in a pink mini-dress. Baby llamas and masquerades? No question about it. This is my best idea ever.

A group of potted trees grabs my attention. Some are topiaries from Lazare's collection. Others come from Queen Saita's winter gardens.

Crossing the room, I slowly step around the greenery. Queen Saita's offerings are lovely. Tiny red berries decorate the pines in intricate patterns. That said, Lazare's topiaries are truly amazing. They look like real humans. One of them rustles.

I step even closer.

The topiary shows an older human with short hair, glasses and a business suit. I scan him carefully, wondering how a tree like this could rustle without any wind.

The face moves. The topiary seems to whisper a single word.

Heeeeeelp.

On reflex, I take a half-step backward. *Am I seeing things?*

I lean in again, wondering if the topiary will mouth something once more. He doesn't.

A new voice booms from the main doorway. "What is this?"

No question who's arrived. Swinging around, I find a familiar form standing in the doorway.

Dare.

And he's got his grumpy face on.

New page, here I come.

- Calla

DAY TEN AND A HALF

*D*ear Diary,

Dare stalks into the chamber with wary steps. For him, this means swinging his head from side to side while making no noise despite his mega boots.

"What is this?" he asks.

"What is *what*?" If in doubt, always answer a question with a question.

"You're in the summer palace. Did you follow me here?"

I lift my chin. "I could ask you the same thing."

Good one, Calla.

"This is the preparation room for summer elf parties. What's the interest?

"I'm a snooper. It's what I do."

Dare chuckles. "True."

A question rattles around my head. Me being me, I come right out and ask it. "Are you working with the Ley Queen by any chance?"

"No, the Ley Queen speaks to no one, not even Queen Saita and Protector Lazare. Why would you ask?"

"No reason."

Dare stalks nearer. The interest in his eyes says that he has zero clue about my visit from the Ley Queen. *Yay.* That said, Dare also suspects I am holding back something from him. Which I am. *Boo.*

Time to change the subject.

"Guess what? I'm considering that traveling thing."

Dare's shoulders slump with relief. "Good."

"Well, you better get back to whatever you're up to." Unfurling my wings, I speed-fly toward the door. "And I'll return to Pixieland."

"Wait," orders Dare.

Still hovering in mid-air, I slowly flit around. "What?"

"If you leave for these travels, when will you go?"

"After my birthday party." *Which is two days after the masquerade ball, but who's counting?*

A forced smile flickers on Dare's mouth. "Of course."

"Bye now!"

This time, I take no chances and fly my ass out the door at triple speed. In no time, I'm back in Pixieland. And my room. All while not casting spells.

This gives me way too much time to think.

As the hours roll on, anxiety charges my limbs. To pass the time, I draw a portrait of Dare. Turns out, that's better than a soothing spell. The eyes are super tricky—it takes me an extra long while to get them just right.

Once art time is over, I circle back to worrying. My concern isn't about my costume. What's got me in knots is the masquerade ball itself. I've never been to any fairy gathering other than the Elven High Court.

This could be great.

Or a disaster.

Guess I'll find out tomorrow night.

-Calla

Prince Darius

DAY ELEVEN

$\mathcal{D}$ear Diary,
     Masquerade night!

Note: this time, the exclamation point totally works.

All day long, my skin feels too tight. Nervous energy zings through me. Time ekes by as I wait for the masquerade to start.

What a bummer that summer elves are nocturnal.

It seems to take forever before Poppa and Muti fall asleep (actually it's more like eight o'clock). Once they're snoring, I sneak off to the summer palace and magically transform change into my costume. Dang, I look amazing.

Behold, for I am Calla the pink baby llama.

Joining the crowd, I sashay through the front door. As the paintings showed, the summer elves don't wear a lot. On the other hand, the winter elf guys sport fitted black shirts, matching trousers, and half masks. The ladies are in shimmery dresses of winter white. I can't remember the last time I saw Dare when he wasn't wearing full body armor and enough fur to choke a grizzly. This'll be great.

Goal for the evening: check out Dare.

Who knows? Maybe he's super gross under all those layers. Unlikely, but this is a scientific thing. I must be certain.

My llama self prances through the crowd. With every step, my little enchanted feet hit the floor in a loud rhythm. I have two toes her leg, complete with pointy nails. So cute!

The party itself is huge. No matter how many rooms I explore, there are more to check out. The chambers are packed with fancy furniture, hefty drapes and thick rugs… every last inch of them decorated in gold. It's a little monotonous, to be honest. In my opinion, summer elves are more about gardens and growing things. This obsession with metal is a little odd.

Then again, so is Lazare.

Finally, I reach the main gathering chamber. Here the walls are lined with the trees from Saita and Lazare's gardens. The different arbors combine into a scene of happy folks dancing through a piney forest. It's more fae-like and comfortable in here, which is probably why the place is so full.

My pulse speeds. I bet Dare is nearby.

My gaze catches on something. It's the same topiary guy I saw yesterday in the preparation room. He mouths a single word once more.

Heeeeelp.

I step closer. Topiary guy does it a third time.

Heeeeeeeelp.

I am totally *not* imagining anything. And this can't be part of a spell. Who would cast something just to play a prank on a llama?

Strike that. When it comes to yours truly, everyone in Lazare's court wants a little payback in the prank department. The real question is this: who in the summer court is *smart enough* to play a prank on me?

That would be no one.

Most likely, this topiary guy is a human under an enchantment. It's like turning a prince into a frog, only with elaborate greenery. There are a number of spells that could release him. I catalog the options in my head.

Someone gently yanks my little llama tail, interrupting my thoughts. Turning around, I find Lazare's eldest daughter, Lotti. She looks like her father, too, what with her blonde hair and oversized nose. In honor of the party, Lotti's wearing some kind of bikini outfit with a see-through kimono deal.

"Shall we talk… Calla?"

"I am an anonymous llama, thank you very much."

How excited am I about how clear that sounded? Very much, indeed. Take that, llama mouth!

Lotti eyes me from head to toe. The crinkle around her mega nose says she doesn't like what she sees. "Your costume is very… creative."

"Yours is very… not there. How is that even dressing up?"

"I am Azemorphia, First Queen of the Summer Elves."

"Wasn't she a warrior who always wore full body armor?" I paw at the ground. "Not sure how that works." A question appears. "And how do you know my name?"

"Please. I've seen you at the Elven High Council. Don't you remember me?"

"Not really. You attended every council?"

"I'm Lazare's oldest daughter and heir. I join every session, I can assure you." The way she says *I can assure you*, it's clear that someone's not too happy with my history of high jinks.

"Oh, right. Too bad about your hair."

Lotti waves her hand in a dismissive gesture. "It grew back."

"And the Macarena."

She fake-laughs. "I enjoyed it."

"And the poop drink."

"That was annoying, but I've moved beyond. In fact, I'd like to talk."

Now it's my turn to scan Lotti. Certain summer elves give the word *nasty* an extra-harsh meaning. The look in Lotti's eyes says she could bite through my rib cage, chomp down on my liver, and then spit said bloody organ across the room, all while having zero regrets.

"I don't think so."

"Won't you please reconsider?" asks Lotti. "I would love to get acquainted. How many royal elves have you socialized with? Perhaps we could become friends."

Much as I hate to admit it, Lotti brings up a good point. When Dare and I get married, I'll have to chat up snobs like her all the time. It can't hurt to practice.

~

Dear Diary,

I'll break out this next bit separately so I can read it over later.

Turns out, Lotti is a real piece of work.

- Calla

DAY ELEVEN AND A HALF

*D*ear Diary,
     A long time ago, I promised Nicola the tree naiad that I'd be super-specific in my diary. More importantly, I promised myself. Therefore, I shall now craft this super-accurate and unbiased description of both Lotti and our conversation, starting with an amazing title.

Profile Of An Elf Chick

Name: Lotti-insert-twelve-syllables-here-silva, eldest daughter of Lazare, Protector of the Summer Realm. (Elves are overly-aggressive in naming, so I won't encourage that by recording every little detail. Plus, I never paid close attention at Elven High Councils when she was introduced.)

Appearance: Crazy-tall and skinny as a bone. Blonde hair. Pointy elf ears. Evil gleam in her green eyes.

Costume: Azemorphia, warrior queen of the Summer Elves, who in Lotti's version wears a bikini for some reason.

I am most definitely not recording this because of what happens later. I've moved on from that life-ending nightmare.

Absolutely.

Mostly.

Not at all, but that's beside the point.

Back to the masquerade.

As I said before, Lotti sports swimwear and some kind of see-through lace kimono. Though it pains me to admit it, she looks fabulous.

Lazare's eldest daughter settles into a little seating alcove filled with overly-puffy pillows. All golden, obviously. Lotti situates herself in the best way to show off her bikini ensemble. It's hard to sit when you're a pink llama, so I just hang nearby.

"This is us," I say. "Chatting." Her liver-eating stare is downright creepy.

"Did you know I was sweethearts with Halcyon?"

"I didn't. Sorry about Dare's brother killing him and everything."

If Lotti is upset about Halcyon's death, she doesn't show it. "My sweet lover gave me a nickname, Calla."

"M'Kay."

"Halcyon called me Lotti the… can you guess? It rhymes."

Now things are getting fun. "Oh, I can totally guess." I prance about in a circle because that's fun to do as a llama. "He called you Lotti the Dotty."

"No."

"Lotti the Potty."

"No."

"Lotti the Snotty."

"NO!"

"Lotti the Snotty Potty."

"No, no, no! Halcyon called me Lotti the Body." She stretches out over the pillow-pile. "Because, unlike pixies, I have curves."

Ugh. Anti-pixie bias is a real thing. That said, I think her catchphrase is totally wrong, so that's exactly where I go next.

"Your nickname sucks," I say.

"What? How can you possibly believe that?"

"Wait, let me look." I make a great show of sizing her up. "Elves are not curvy, and neither are you. Take it from a llama. Your best bet is to work the waif angle."

"What do you know? I'm a woman and you're a little girl."

"Hold on, there. Are you trying to intimidate me?" I chuckle. "That's good." I prance around some more. "Here I am, so intimidated. Lotti the Snotty Potty totally got me!"

This isn't mature, but I'm a pixie. We're supposed to be obnoxious.

"You're impossible."

"I've heard that before."

"Why do I waste my time? You're not really one of us, faeling. Lazare made me speak with you tonight. Count yourself lucky I was forced to befriend you at all."

"M'Kay."

Lotti makes a *grr* sound and stalks off into the party. At this point, I'm having the best time, ever. I just verbally shredded a mean summer elf. I still look fabulous. And Dare roams somewhere nearby, ready to be dazzled by my llama-ness.

Everything is perfect. Who says I should avoid the summer palace? I have this nailed.

Then, it happens.

My world ends.

I shall not ruin the beauty of what I shall forever call my Lotti Shedding Adventure by placing a total catastrophe on the same page.

Moving on.

- Calla

DAY ELEVEN AND THREE-QUARTERS

*D*ear Diary,

I promised to be honest in my diary.

Here goes.

With our little chat over, Lotti strolls across the chamber. As she glides along, her see-through kimono sways behind her. The room falls silent. All eyes focus on Lazare's eldest. Excitement fills the air. Squiggly feelings twist through my stomach.

What does everyone else know that I don't?

Lotti ascends onto a little stage by the far wall. From her new height, Lazare's daughter surveys the room with that same predatory edge. In her world, everyone in this room is nothing but a bag of bloody organs, ready to be bitten open and spat out. More partygoers stream into the gathering chamber. Soon we're standing so close, I've got nothing but the backside of elves before me.

Behold the dark side of little llama-hood. Elf butts.

That fidgety sensation returns to my stomach with more force. Across the room, Dare steps up onto the platform to stand beside Lotti. Sure, he's wearing a mask over his eyes, but I've memorized every square inch of that jawline. Despite my nice llama coat, my skin chills over.

"Greetings, everyone!" Dare pulls off his mask. Dang, but he looks so cute in his black shirt and straight pants. Turns out, there really is no reason for him to wear all those layers constantly. He's got plenty of muscles to show off. Why not help the female population and display them more often?

Lotti slips closer to Dare's side. Jolts of rage charge through every muscle in my llama body. Dare is *my* friend. Why is Lotti pretending that my guy wants to smell her stink?

A little voice in the back of my head points out that Lotti doesn't, in fact, smell badly. I ignore that voice. Instead, I focus on the what Dare said before about negotiating access to King Tristan. There's a blight on the land. Only Tristan knew how to fix it, and Lazare is hiding the sleeping king.

Whatever this is, it's about Dare and King Tristan.

I smack my llama lips and contemplate. Maybe the winter prince will announce they're about to wheel the old king out for show-n-tell. That would be a total Dare move. My future husband is notorious for putting together bargains and telling no one about it, not even his mother. I think through all the faces I've seen tonight. Queen Saita and Protector Lazare aren't here.

That settles it. This definitely one of Dare's infamous *side deals*.

Saita's always saying Dare is too independent. For the first time, I think she's right.

"I have an announcement to share before you all." Dare turns to Lotti and smiles. I gasp. His dimples are on full display and everything. My little llama eyes cloud over with fury.

Dimple-smiles are mine. No one else's.

Dare gets down on one knee. All of a sudden, it's like I'm floating above the party, looking down at this fiasco from on high. Every inch of me turns numb.

For his part, Dare gazes into Lotti the Snotty Potty's eyes. "Lotti Manare Solaris Beauchamp La Silva, first born daughter of Protector Lazare, would you do me the honor of becoming my wife?"

He pulls out a commitment ring and lifts it toward Lotti.

Whoa.

That's my ring.

As a matter of fact, that's my Dare.

Lotti gazes out across the crowd. Somehow, she finds me. Okay, I'm not all that hard to discover, considering how I'm a pink llama and everything. She stares right into my shocked and fuzzy face as she five words.

"It would be my honor."

My mind unhinges. There's a lot of screaming about Dare being a lying liar. I realize that the person who's yelling is me.

Next I transform back into my pixie self, conjure a bunch of power spheres, and go to town. Orbs of pink magic ricochet off the furniture and guests. Elves scream. Vases topple. At some point, the palace walls explode, sending partygoers flying. No one is hurt—not even the topiary people—but I feel like I've made my point.

Total silence follows.

In that quiet, I march away from the ruins, return to the Summer Citadel, and open the door to Pixieland. Bilge waits for me on the opposite side.

Bilge is all smiles. "Greetings! Did it have a fun?"

"No."

"What happened?"

"I went to a party at the summer palace. Dare got engaged to Lotti."

Bilge's grin fades. "And then what did it do?"

"Did you hear what I said? Dare got engaged to Lazare's eldest daughter!"

Bilge grabs my hand. "What did it do, my Calla?"

It's the *my Calla* part that breaks through my brainless fury. I didn't know Bilge could string those two words together.

"I blew up the summer palace. Everyone wants me to be evil. That was evil. Aren't you going to throw me a party?"

"There is a celebration tomorrow. For its birthday."

"Well, now it can be a birthday-prison party because I'm pretty sure that's coming."

Bilge's lower lip trembles. "My Calla."

"I've got to go."

"I cannot explain this to Poppa and Muti."

"It's not your job; I'll do it. Bye, Bilge."

Unfurling my wings, I fly home and into bed. My head is a total mess at this point. I absolutely plan to explain everything to Poppa and Muti, but that needs to wait until the morning when I'm (hopefully) not hysterical. For now, just writing it all down is enough.

~~Good~~ bad night.

- Calla

DAY TWELVE

*D*ear Diary,

Worst birthday ever. No exaggeration. It all starts when I wake up to a bunch of unpleasant noise.

Stomp! Stomp! Stomp!

Next comes a gentler sound.

Knock, knock.

"Calla?" It's Muti, calling to me through the closed door.

I yawn. "Yeah?"

"Why is our tree surrounded by thousands of elf warriors in golden armor?"

My eyes widen. That would be the stomping noises. I scamper out of bed and whip my door open. "Morning, Muti."

"What happened?" Muti's face is all big eyes and worry lines.

My thoughts race through possibilities. *Is there any way to soften the blow here? Not really.*

"It's like this," I declare. "I blew up Lazare's palace yesterday."

Muti exhales. "Oh."

I do a double-take. "That's it? Oh?"

"Well, it's not like Poppa and I haven't seen this coming." She pats my shoulder. "We'll talk about it more over breakfast."

And so we do. I shall now record the conversation highlights as this is important stuff.

Things Calla Explains

One. Dare is engaged to a psychotic blonde elf. He is also a lying liar.

Two. As a result, I lost my temper and blew up the summer palace. In my defense, it was too gaudy anyway and no one was hurt.

Three. Because of what I'm now calling the Palace Explosion Incident, the Ley Queen will likely imprison me inside a ley line.

Four. Since the High Council meets tomorrow, that's probably when I'll get magically locked up. No doubt, the elf troops are here to escort me to the Pinnacle.

Five. I still want a birthday party.

How Poppa And Muti Reply

One. They saw this coming (this gets repeated a ton.)

Two. Imprisoned in a ley line sounds like a safe choice for yours truly. They suggest bringing along my diary locket so I have something to do in all my spare time.

Three. Bilge and Oinky will join us for cake later today.

Overall, my impression is that Poppa and Muti are very old. Having me around has been a big strain on the little energy they have left. While they find it super sad that I'm getting imprisoned in a ley line, they also appear half-glad it's all over, one way or another.

Not gonna lie. This entire conversation is super depressing. It takes a force of will, but I remind myself that for fairies, Poppa and Muti are positively overflowing with parental affection. The fact that they've put up with me for this long? That's some kind of fae record.

Our chat goes on for a while. At some point, Bilge and Oinky stop by with a cake that reads, *Happy Birthday and Imprisonment!*

It's the thought that counts.

Still, I don't eat a bite.

Jolly pipes in to announce that he's always wanted me off his tree. He doesn't drip any sap on my head, so I guess that shows some affection.

With every passing hour, my heart sinks lower. One way or another, all my life's being torn away. Poppa and Muti are relieved that the terror of raising me is done. Dare is a lying liar who's marrying a snotty potty. I'm about to be imprisoned in the most boring way ever. I could cry into my banishment cake, but that's not my speed.

Instead, I make another vow.

I'll get way out of this, one way or another.

-Calla

DAY TWELVE AND A HALF

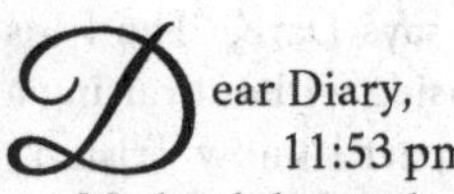ear Diary,
 11:53 pm.

My birthday is almost over.

All of a sudden, my palm flares with white light. I don't even check to make sure I look cute because who cares what a lying liar thinks?

"I accept your visit," I whisper.

A moment later, Ghost Dare stands in my bedroom. "You're angry with me."

"You think?"

"Know this. I did not lie to you. Lotti and I have a bargain. In exchange for offering her the commitment ring, I receive Tristan's location. I have no plans to actually wed."

That does help a little. And I did release a lot of my anger when I blew up the summer palace.

"Why didn't you tell me?"

"Because you'd show up in an outrageous costume and blow up the place."

He's got me there.

Ghost Dare sits on the edge of my mattress. "You'll be taken to the Pinnacle tomorrow. The Ley Queen will determine your sentence."

I pick off bits of thread from my blanket. "She already told me what'll happen. I'm to be imprisoned in a ley line."

Dare's mouth quirks into a smile. "And how will you fight back?"

"That's a work in progress."

"You won't be alone. Whatever that prison is made of, I'll fight to tear down its walls."

I force a smile. "Thanks."

My jaw gets all wobbly. A sob constricts in my throat. Still, there's no way I'll spend my last night of freedom boo-hooing to Dare.

Giving him trouble is more my style.

"I'm still mad at you," I state.

"Are we changing the subject?"

"We are. After all your lying lies, did Lotti tell you anything useful?"

Dare nods. "King Tristan is being held in the catacombs underneath the Fens Citadel. Lazare is unaware I know this."

I sit upright. "The Fens Citadel. That's a good place to stash Tristan."

"And how would you know that?"

"Bilge can be a chatty hobgoblin." I don't get into the rest of the story, though. Secret doors stay secret and all that.

"I've looked at this a hundred different ways," says Dare. "The Fens Citadel is surrounded by an orc army. I can't get inside without raising a force of my own. And if I do that, Lazare will suspect I know Tristan's hiding place. The Protector will move the good king before I get a chance to find him. Still, I need to get past that army." Dare's gray eyes fill with sorrow. "And I'm out of ideas, Calla."

It's those big gooey eyes that snap me like a twig. Before, there wasn't a great reason to break my promise to Bilge. But now? Lazare is a freak who's trying to kill me. His blight is poisoning the land. Surely, I can make just one exception.

"Okay, you totally broke my spirit. I'll blab. There are ley doors in the basement of each citadel. All of them connect, if you know how to use them."

Dare rubs his neck, his eyes lost in thought. "Are you certain?"

"Oh, yeah. I've used them for years."

Every line in Dare's body pulls tight with interest. "So you use ley wands to open the doors?"

"Nah. All I do is go to the basement, pull up the mat, and the ley lines are right there in the floor. I pull up the cord for the Fens or whatever and the door opens to that citadel."

"Can you show me?"

"Not really. There's an army of summer fae outside my tree. They're accompanying me to the High Council tomorrow. I don't think any side trips to the citadel will be wise."

Another option appears. Perhaps I can pull a ley line out of the floor. I've never done that before, but doesn't mean anything. Everything I know about ley lines I learned from trial and error. Slipping out of bed, I kneel and set my palms against the wooden slats. Sadly, there's no sense of ley magic anywhere nearby.

A crushing sense of pressure builds around my rib cage. I've felt this sensation before. It's the Ley Queen. Somehow, she can tell I'm monkeying with magic that might help me escape.

Dang, that hurts.

Rising, I quickly return to bed. The pain in my chest vanishes. Lounging atop my comforter, I keep my body splayed like a starfish.

"I can't believe I'm going to jail," I gripe.

Dare scooches closer. "Hear me, Calla." His mouth thins to a determined line. "I shall find a way to set you loose."

"Not if I beat you to it." I meant for that to sound badass, but my voice got all wobbly instead.

"And so you will." Dare's face softens. "Until then, let's get you some rest."

"I'd been trying before you showed up. Not happening. My plan is to spend the night alternating between writing in my diary and staring at the ceiling."

Dare pulls up chair beside bed. "In that case, I'll keep you company. And I won't peek at your diary, either." He sits down and kicks his legs forward, which is Dare body language for *I'll be here for a while.* Not an easy thing to do while in ghost form.

I slip back under my covers. "I'd say you're wasting too much magic by hanging out here—which you are—but I really appreciate it."

"Not to worry, little hob. I'll remain right by your side."

Normally, the *little hob thing* bugs the crap out of me. Tonight, I totally appreciate it. Which brings me to this moment.

My eyelids feel so heavy, I can barely stay awake.

- Calla

DAY THIRTEEN

Dear Diary,

Yesterday, I woke up to the sound of boots stomping. Today, I awaken to a lyrical voice.

"Callllaaaaaa!"

Turns out, it's an elf warrior named Captain Solei. She leads the more than one thousand troops hanging out around my tree. For an elf, she's got a powerful set of lungs.

Eventually, Jolly made an appearance to shut her up. "Calla will be down in a minute. Now get off my moss."

I get ready extra fast. Once I finish breakfast—a final meal of galla root, naturally—all that remains is a lot of hugging and crying with Poppa and Muti.

"We shall miss you," says Poppa.

"Write to us from your enchanted prison," adds Muti. "If that's even possible."

"Of course, I will." I tighten our hug. Poppa and Muti always smell like old scrolls and new mold. I'll miss that when I'm floating in my evil ley prison.

"Do you think you'll escape?" asks Poppa in a low voice.

"I'll try."

Leaning back, I break the hug. For years, my whole world has been Poppa and Muti. Their wrinkly faces take on a dream-like quality. I'm flying out of their acorn and lives, possibly forever.

"How likely do you think escape will be?" asks Muti.

"Why do you ask?"

"Poppa and I were thinking about converting your bedroom into conversation pit. Lots of pillows, a wet bar, that kind of thing."

My mouth drops open with shock. "Are you serious?"

"Why shouldn't we have fun?" asks Poppa. "We've still got ten or twenty thousand good years left in us."

Both stare at me for what feels like forever. That's when it hits me. They're not kidding.

Before, the kitchen had a dream-like quality. Now reality returns in a heartbeat. Fairies aren't naturally nurturing, as a rule. Poppa and Muti are no different.

"Calllllllaaaa!" Solei calls again.

"I better go." That's what I say, but I don't exactly leave.

Poppa and Muti get back to the table and their breakfast. "Bye now," they say in unison.

It seems that *tear-filled goodbye time* is over. I can't help but notice the latest copy of Party Sprite Magazine on the tabletop.

That's more than I needed to know.

Taking to the air, I zip out of the acorn, land on the grass outside, and scan what should be familiar surroundings.

Everything has changed.

A neat column of warriors stretch off to the horizon. All of them wear golden armor with matching pointy helmets. That stuff can't be comfortable.

Captain Solei marches up to me. She looks the same as the other summer elves, namely tall, lithe and gorgeous. The only way I can tell her apart is that her helmet is covered in swishy patterns.

Solei raises her hand. A long loop of rope dangles from her fist and —*of course*—the thing is golden in color. "Lift your hands."

I can see where this is going. Not a happy place.

"Are we flying to the Pinnacle?" I gesture toward the rope. "Because winging around with bound-up wrists? That's a recipe for crash landings and general mayhem."

"You shall march," declares Solei.

I scrunch up my nose, as if I'm really considering this idea. "Ah, no."

"No?"

"No." I pretend to flick some dust off my wings. "My fate is in the hands of the Ley Queen. So I'm flying over on my own."

This is a total fabrication. One of my best, actually.

"I was instructed to have you march with your hands tied." Solei frowns. "Perhaps I should send a messenger to the Pinnacle and confirm."

"Let's not drag this out," I counter. "I'll walk with my hands tied. Just remember what I said."

With that, I've planted a seed. For the next few hours, I plan to watching it grow into a nice flower of prankster-ism.

In the end, I march in the middle of a thousand elves in golden armor. Along the way, all the roads are lined with spectators, which I guess is part of Lazare's revenge plan.

Ick. Everyone in Pixieland must have gotten the day off because the roadside is packed. Many feel they need to shout out nasty statements in my direction.

"Always knew you'd come to a sorry end."

"Faeling have no place here."

"I hate pink!"

Whatever.

Time to kick my plan into action.

I stop. "Ouchie! I totally stepped on a rock."

Behind me, the columns of army elves pause as well. Or try to.

"Oof!"

"Yow!"

"My toe!"

A lovely chorus sounds as the eld warriors slam into each other. A few tumble over.

"Oh my," I say innocently. "Perhaps if we flew, this kind of thing wouldn't happen."

Solei's glare flickers between the rope on my wrists and my very sneaky face. No question what she's thinking here. Solei wonders whether to yell at me for causing the elfy log jam.

And here is when my Ley Queen lie pays off. Solei already thinks she's pushing it by not letting me fly. Yelling at me while I stomp along might be too much.

"Soldiers!" calls Solei. "Give the prisoner some space while we march."

We take off again. For a short while, the warriors give me room. But there are a thousand of them and one of me. And I keep changing my pace. Soon enough, they're all scrunched up behind me.

I stop once more. "Oh no! I dropped something!"

"Yow!"

"Ouch."

"My foot!"

It's beautiful.

I scan the ground carefully. "Guess I was wrong."

Thus begins my project for the morning. I keep a tally of how many warriors I get to tumble onto their butts.

Thirty-nine.

Not bad.

I then declare that the Ley Queen demanded that I take regular breaks to write in my diary. That's where I am at this very moment. Solei stands nearby, fidgeting with her swirly helmet and worrying that we'll be late.

As mornings before imprisonment go, I'm having a blast.

- Calla

Captain Solei

DAY THIRTEEN AND A HALF

$\mathcal{D}$ear Diary,

Eventually, I reach the lair of all things Elven High Council. *Pinnacle ahoy.* I'm led inside with an honor guard of fifty warriors.

The council chamber is packed for the occasion. Everyone is there, from Lazare and his trio of daughters… to Saita and Dare. I'm glad Poppa and Muti stayed home for this. Some things they just don't need to see.

Lazare launches into a long speech. I try to pay attention, but for an elf, the guy has zero charisma. Here's what I remember.

Lazare's Big Anti-Calla Speech

One. According to Protector Bossy Elf, I am a bad, bad baddie. In fact, I'm the absolute worst creep since Dare's older brother Reiver tried to kill Tristan while actually murdering Halcyon and then getting his terrible self dead. This part of the speech gets repeated at least four times.

Two. I can't help but notice how Lotti doesn't so much as flinch whenever Lazare mentions her dead boyfriend Halcyon. For a summer elf, that's some cold stuff.

Three. The Ley Queen will imprison me and it won't be a fun experience. This is also repeated way more times than is necessary.

Four. Lazare will block all my fae magic using the infamous Scepter of Summer, which is the most powerful wand in all of Faerie.

Five. Without my magic, I'll never escape my prison.

Once anti-Calla speech time is over, Lazare raises his big-ass golden scepter. This is no skinny wand. It's a huge stick, thick as my arm, and topped with a massive golden ball. Lazare could beat me senseless with it, no magic involved.

The protector points the scepter in my direction. A beam of crimson power careens out of the top and slams straight into me. Every inch of my body feels like it's being torn apart and put together again, over and over.

Lazare keeps blasting me with the scepter. Pain radiates through my limbs. I sway from foot to foot. If nothing else, I won't let him see me crumble.

And I don't.

The beam from the scepter dies out. Lazare shakes it, like you would a quill that might have a little more ink remaining.

Lazare lowers the scepter. "It is done."

I search inside myself, trying to summon up some fairy dust or fae power for a magic sphere. The power that normally courses through me had dried up. I debate about pulling in ley magic, but the last time I tried that, it ended with some *rib cage crushing action*. I'll pass on that, thank you very much.

I've no magic. Zip. Zero. None. This is a disaster.

The Ley Queen steps forward. "And now, the punishment will be delivered." She raises her arms. the palace floor rumbles.

BOOM!

A great line of blue power bursts through the marble floor. It's four feet around and heading right for me. The azure cord engulfs me from head to toe. The council chamber vanishes. Instead, blue light surrounds me.

And everything becomes nothing.

As in, all I do is float around in blue space. It's quiet. Empty. Weightless. And so boring I want to poke out my eyes with a fork.

I pull out my diary from my handy locket and get to recording all of today's unpleasantness. That's where this particular diary entry comes to an end.

Now that I'm out of stuff to record, I think I'll float around and ball my eyes out for a while.

- Calla

DAY SOMETHING

Dear Diary,
  I float in a blue haze.
And float.
And float.
Time for a new list.

Benefits of Being Imprisoned In A Ley Line

One. Unlimited napping.
Two. Writing in my diary.
Three. Not much else.
I've given up on crying, by the way. Nothing is worse than stuffing up your nose when there are no tissues around. Plus when I sneeze, a snot blob floats around for a while before disappearing. It's really gross.

To pass the time, I try for my magic again. That's a big failure. Lazare really did a number on me.

Next I work on grabbing Ley magic. Nothing happens there, either. Yes, I'm inside an actual ley line but can sense none of its power.

Thank you, Ley Queen.

I see if I can perfect some circus style flips in zero gravity. That doesn't work, either.

Guess I'll take another nap.

- Calla

DAY SOMETHING-SOMETHING

*D*ear Diary,

Today I felt the pulse of a ley line. It was just a low thing, but it was definitely there.

My theory: As a faeling, I have access to typical fairy magic, obviously. But somehow I also have special access to the ley lines themselves. That power wouldn't have been crushed by Lazare and his phallic scepter of stupid. And maybe it's something even the Ley Queen can't control by chucking me in here.

Getting my hands on some ley magic.

It's worth a try.

- Calla

ANOTHER "DAY" (AND YES, I MAKE FINGER QUOTES WHILE WRITING THAT)

*D*ear Diary,
    I have no idea how long I've been floating around in my blue prison, but I can tell you one thing. I just had a major *yay* and *boo*, respectively.

First, the *yay*. I tapped into the ley lines for a hot second.

Second, the *boo*. Touching that power hurt like you wouldn't believe. As in, it feels like my skin's getting peeled off.

Still, ley power might my only way to escape. I'm sticking with it.

- Calla

YET ANOTHER DAY... WITH FINGER QUOTES

*D*ear Diary,

Behold my new purpose in life, which I have since given a formal name as follows.

Grabbing Onto Ley Magic Until It Hurts Too Much And I Let Go

As a title, it's not my best. In my defense, having this many owies so close together does something to your head.

As does floating around in space with no one to talk to.

Which is why my latest attempt at grabbing ley lines was so unbelievable.

Here I was, grabbing onto ley line and screaming in agony. An image appeared in my mind. I saw the Fens as they were when I was little, before the blight turned them into the Land of Yuck.

Red light flashed and I saw—or at least I thought I saw—another person in the ley prison with me. She was an older elf, dressed in blue, and wore a crimson blindfold.

Seeing her should have seemed odd, yet it felt natural somehow. It's very possible that I've blown out my brain past the point of no return.

I might need a new hobby.

Drawing. That's the ticket.

- Calla

My New Hobby

GIVING UP ON THE DAY THING

*D*ear Diary,

Drawing isn't working out.

All I do is scribble circles and think about how this activity isn't helping me escape.

I'm back to grabbing ley lines. Lately, I can hold on for five full minutes before I give up and let go. Sure, that feeling of my skin falling off grows more intense. Yet the last time I grabbed a ley line?

More strangeness.

It looked like my skin really peeled away. And not in a gross sense, either.

What was left behind was me, only taller and with bigger wings. This marks the second time I'm seeing people while causing myself unthinkable levels of ouch. First was the blue lady with the blindfold. Second, I got an altered me.

Once again, I have a theory.

Humans believe that angels find you after you die. In my case, these visions might be winged death fairies. Ley magic could be telling me I'm about to kill myself with all this line grabbing.

Perhaps I should listen.

After all, the Ley Queen promised to set me loose if she could. There's no reason to keep grabbing onto magic and be in agony.

Besides, there are worse things than floating around and writing in a diary. Going forward, I promise to enjoy my *blue space girl life*, not try to destroy myself with escape.

A new vow.
Even I'm not sure how long this one will last.
- Calla

THE END - MAYBE

*D*ear Diary,

I tried to enjoy life as a floaty blue bubble girl, but it's just not me.

Perhaps I have a death wish.

I prefer to think of myself as too badass to contain.

Whatever the reason, hanging around while watching my snot float away is not how I plan to spend my future. Next time I lean into the ley magic, I'm not letting go. I'll hold onto the power until I pass out or die.

Therefore, this may be my last diary entry. If so, I want Poppa, Muti, Bilge and Oinky to know I love them.

And Dare: if you really do marry Lotti the Snotty Potty, I will haunt you blind. Plus, I'll make sure Lotti gets crushed under a bridge or something.

- Calla

DAY THIRTY (I CHECKED A CALENDAR)

*D*ear Diary,
    Guess what? I made it!

When we last left my life, I was about to lean into ley magic until I died or passed out.

Passed out looks to be the winning option.

After the pain, I wake up to find myself sprawled on my back on a stretch of green grass. A familiar sign looms nearby.

Welcome to Glover's Hollow. Population 1400.

Once again, I've returned to this same spot. No complaints, though. I'm alive and no longer floating in blue space.

This is a good day.

For a long time, I just lay on my back and feel completely wrung out. Every inch of me feels empty.

Eventually I run a quick check on my fae powers. Starting small, I try to shake out some fairy dust. Nope. Next I work to summon a sphere of power. That doesn't happen either. Seems like Lazare and his scepter still block my fae magic.

That said, it wasn't traditional fairy magic that got me out of prison.

That was ley lines.

I roll onto my hands and knees. Even that motion is a lot of work for me at this point. Reaching out with my senses, I check for ley lines under the earth.

A pulse of magic greets me. *Yes!*

Reaching into the soft soil, I search for a line of power. A cool cord of magic brushes against my hands. Gripping the line, I yank it upward, pulling so hard, the cord snaps into a wriggling thread. It isn't easy, but I wrap the line up into an orb of power. The sight reminds me of a ball of yarn, only glowing and blue.

Closing my eyes, I picture the sphere transforming into a nice bowl of galla root. Cool magic churns across my palms. When I open my eyes, I hold my favorite meal.

Sighing, I soak in the moment. Sunlight dances across my face. Wind rustles the trees. I've casted a power orb spell with ley magic. No one is crushing my rib cage in punishment. Sweet.

This opens a lot of possibilities, none of which should be considered on an empty stomach.

Sitting down, I chomp down on my galla root and consider my situation. I am now Calla the Outlaw, considering that I just broke out of jail and everything. And what is the cause of all my trouble? Who turned me into a convict while also transforming the beauty of Faerie into a blighted mess?

Lazare.

So far, I consider that I've been a pretty reasonable. Taking down Lazare was more of a nice to have. But after getting my skin literally shredded a ley prison, I am done being Little Miss Nice Pixie.

Lazare is going down.

And I won't just defeat that pointy-nosed creep, either. I'll put good King Tristan back on the throne while I'm at it. Nyah.

Time for a quick list.

Taking Down Lazare — My Allies

One. Me. I'm pretty awesome.
Two. Dare. He's already on the case.
Three. Bilge. Potions, baby!
Four. The Ley Queen? She says she protects faelings like me. And it's no secret that Lazare is filling her precious ley lines with the magical equivalent of sewage.

Also-*also*, the Ley Queen is the most likely person to find out that I've escaped. If I want her on my side, it's better to approach her versus get caught.

Also-also-*also*, I want everyone in Faerie to think I'm still in prison. Okay, mostly Lazare. The Ley Queen is my best chance at having that happen over the long run.

Good list, me.

Confronting the Ley Queen is a huge deal. I can't just break out of prison and open a ley door smack-dab into her castle. I'm outside Glover's Hollow. It would be better spend some time roaming the countryside. Perhaps even take a little jaunt into town.

There's no need to rush into anything.

- Calla

DAY THIRTY AND A HALF

*D*ear Diary,

I ended up waiting a good two minutes before I decided to visit the Ley Queen's palace right away. I'd say the move was strategic, but the truth is that I just get antsy. Plus, Glover's Hollow is a snore.

Back to the action.

Reaching down, I pull up more ley lines. This time, I press the cords into the shape of a door. As the lines take shape, I picture where I want to go next.

The Ley Queen's castle.

Beyond it being blue, I don't have much to go on. Hopefully that'll be enough.

My creation solidifies until it's a blue door hanging in empty space. My fingers shiver as I grip the handle and pull. When the door swings open, I find myself looking into a castle's interior. There are heavy rock walls, an arched ceiling, and tapestries lining the walls. Everything is colored in various shades of blue.

Yes!

Threads of ley power wind up from the floor, their thin forms climbing and combining until they line up into a humanoid shape.

"Welcome to the Ley Queen's castle," says someone I've decided to call Spaghetti Man. His voice has a slurpy tone to it, too. *Good name.*

"Hello, I'm—"

"We know who you are," says Spaghetti Man. "I shall take you to the queen."

I exhale. "Thanks."

Whatever's about to happen, no one is tossing me right back into prison, so I'm counting this as a win.

Stepping through the door, I follow Spaghetti Man down a curly flight of stairs and into the castle's basement. Like the Pixieland Citadel, it's a round and empty space.

"Wait here," orders Spaghetti Man. Stepping out, he closes the only door behind him.

A pang of worry moves through me. Did I just let Spaghetti Man lock me into a new prison?

Maybe this wasn't such a good idea after all.

Suddenly, a pulse of magic moves across the floor. The force is so strong, my teeth seem to vibrate in my head.

Ley magic.

Kneeling down, I touch the ground.

The blue stones vanish beneath me. It's reflex for me to unfurl my wings and avoid falling. I hover mid air as a great chasm opens beneath me. The bottomless pit is filled with more ley lines than I ever thought possible. Cords shoot and dive across each other. Every so often, a handful blast upwards, where they disappear into the ceiling.

So cool.

The door swings open. The Ley Queen swoops in, her great blue wings pumping behind her in a calm rhythm. Whatever this chasm really is, it doesn't bother her in the slightest.

"Welcome," she says.

"What is this place?" I'm pulling for *not-a-prison*.

"One of my workrooms."

Another handful of threads stream up from the pit on a direct path toward the ceiling.

"One moment," says the queen. Flying forward, she catches the upward threads in her fist and scans the group. "These are threads of the future. The present is in the floor."

My body turns numb with awe. "Ley lines do more than transport you around?"

"Infinitely more." Reaching into cords, she plucks out one that is gray. "Take this thread of time, for instance. It could cause trouble down the road." She crushes the thread in her free hand. A withered line tumbles into the pit. "Now that possibility is gone."

"Wow." *And that's all I can say right now.*

The queen opens her hand. The rest of the threads stream toward the ceiling once more. When the colored cords hit the rock above, they vanish from view.

"I just made a bowl of galla root with ley lines. I thought that was some advanced stuff."

The queen shoots me a sly look. "Oh, you've no idea with ley magic can do."

"What happens when the threads hit the ceiling?"

The queen gestures to the open space below. "Then those threads join the pit of the present. There are relatively few actions we do in the present that affect the future in a serious way."

In all honesty, I could spend all day chatting up ley lines. Not a good idea, though. Straightening my back, I force myself to refocus. I'm here to take down Lazare.

"I escaped your ley prison."

"Clearly." She flits over the churning ley lines, scanning the mass of cords with an expert eye.

"I could have hidden from you but—"

"You wouldn't have lasted long." The queen pauses and shoots me a look that could freeze white-hot flames. "Give me one reason why I shouldn't punish you with death."

I totally have this one.

"Because we have a common enemy. Lazare. I plan to take him down and bring back King Tristan. That way, Tristan can end the blight that's ruining all the ley lines." I flit closer. "Will you help me?"

"I can aid you, but you must do something for me."

I battle the urge to twist my mouth into a grumpy face. Honestly, I don't fight too hard. "A deal?"

"Yes. Find me the ultimate source of fae power, and I will bring you to King Tristan."

"Where is this ultimate source? I'll be honest. I'm hoping for a map."

"The future is a complex weave. I must choose the best thread for the right outcome. Therefore, the most direction I can provide you is not a map. It's a clue."

"M'Kay." *This is so sketchy.*

"The clue comes from me, and you will find it in the town of Glover's Hollow. That is all."

"Huh. So the clue is not a map?"

"No."

"Does this clue maybe lead to a map?"

"Let me make one thing clear. You will not be receiving any kind of map."

"Oh." I was really hoping for a map, obviously.

"And my clue has conditions. Only you may pursue its answers. No other fae."

This so-called help is getting worse by the second. First, it's just a dumb clue in a town that's the size of a postage stamp. Now I have to hunt it down solo? How boring is that? There must be some way around this condition.

"What if my helper fae is royal?"

"No, Calla. That is my condition. And if you break it, your attempts to solve my riddle will prove fruitless. Do you understand?"

"Mm-mmm." It's a non-committal sound and that's because I am so not agreeing to this crap deal.

The Ley Queen flicks her hand slightly. I catch only a small cascade of fairy dust tumbling from her fingers. Another spell. Sadly, it's a familiar one. Instantly, pressure binds my rib cage until my chest feels ready to give in. Pain radiates through me.

It's an effort speak. "No fae help. Got it."

The queen waves her hand once more. The pain vanishes. "Glad we are agreed."

"Peachy."

"You must be tired."

I rub at my chest. *That really sucked.* "Not too much."

The Ley Queen raises her hand once more. The threat is silent but clear. *Want me to break a few ribs?*

"On second thought, I'm totally exhausted."

"As I suspected," says the queen. "You may leave my castle once I deem you are fully rested and healed."

No way am I giving her any more lip. "M'Kay."

The door swings open again, revealing Spaghetti Man. "Come with me," he says in his slurpy voice.

I step out into the hallway. The moment I pass out of the work room, the door shuts with a slam.

This isn't my week for tearful goodbyes, I guess.

"This way," announces the Spaghetti Man. "I shall take you to your chambers."

I follow Spaghetti Man through the castle's maze of passages. Eventually, he leads me to a large room decorated with all blue furniture. The bed appears especially puffy and comfortable. I tuck myself under the covers and write in my diary. That's where I am now.

And I'm not sleepy.

Much.

Fine. I'm barely keeping my eyes open.
Good night, dear Diary.
- Calla

DAY THIRTY-ONE

*D*ear Diary,

I ended up sleeping for two days straight. We pixies love to snooze, so that's not too alarming. Unlike dwarves, for instance, who only nap once a year. If a dwarf conked out for two days, you'd want to go casket shopping.

Once I'm up and lively, I try to leave. Spaghetti Man stands right outside the door, blocking my exit. With his yarn art face, he declares that I must remain in my chambers until the Ley Queen approves my departure.

I nod, say that's fine, and return to my room. After that, I scheme on how to break Spaghetti Man like a wet noodle. Mostly, my scheme is to complain so often, Spaghetti Man will just give up and allow me to leave.

My Spaghetti Man Whining Plan

One. Ask for new meals every ten minutes. This has backfired a little. Now Spaghetti Man just opens the door every ten minutes and tosses in a box of elf wafers (which taste like sawdust).

Two. Twice an hour, I ask for a books with the words *blue, string* or *pasta* in the title. Spaghetti Man always says no. So far, my favorites are *War and Pasta, A Tale of Two Blue Men,* and *A Midsummer's Night Pasta Dinner.*

Three. I repeatedly ask for permission to leave. This happens more on an ad hoc basis than a set schedule. In reply, I always get more excessive use of the word *no.*

Four. At the same time, I ask for a full explanation about why I can't leave. Here the Spaghetti Man states that the Ley Queen is concerned for my health. I don't buy that for a second. Spaghetti Man also declares that his mistress will crush my rib cage like a walnut if I try to escape without her approval.

This I totally believe.

All in all, this is a lot like the ley prison, only my snot doesn't float around. One bright spot: I can draw here. To kill some time, I create the image of a sleepy dragon.

However, I am *not* drawing yawning reptiles because I'm still tired and recovering from my prison escape. The Ley Queen is very much wrong on that score. I am Calla the Outlaw and I don't need rest.

Although one more little nap wouldn't suck.

- Calla

Sleepy Dragon

DAY THIRTY-TWO

*D*ear Diary,

What a revelation today! A total epiphany, I tell you!

Here's what I figured out. I don't need to prank Spaghetti Man for entertainment. I have my super secret way of summoning Dare! It's so obvious, I can't believe I never thought of it before.

Maybe I did need some extra sleep, because it's not like me to forget anything Dare-related.

I make my palm flash white. Sure enough, Ghost Dare soon materializes in my room. He looks all tough and grumpy in his armor. The second he spies me, Ghost Dare beams. And his grin has two dimples, which is a big deal.

Overwhelming happiness... I do have that affect on some people. Others decide to assassinate or imprison me, though. Life is confusing that way.

Ghost Dare keeps working his dimples. "You're free."

"Sort of. I'm in the Ley Queen's palace."

"How did you escape prison?"

I sigh dramatically. "I suppose I shall have to tell you one of the many super cool secrets I've concealed all these years."

Ghost dare's dimples get deeper, if that's possible. "I can't wait."

"I know how to manipulate ley magic."

"Beyond opening the ley doors in the citadel?"

"Yes."

Dare's face goes slack in a genuine look of shock. "No."

"It's true. I can grab raw ley lines from the ground." Here I kneel down and mine gripping cords of magic through the carpet. "Then I can then twist them into a door."

"Wow." The Dare-shock continues. My day is totally looking up.

"There is more I can do, though." To accent the drama, I slowly rise. "I twist up bits of ley line into little power spheres and chuck them around." Here I mime twisting up a ball of ley line and chucking it across the room. "It powers all higher-level spells."

"Breathtaking. And how did you acquire this ability?"

"There are ley lines in the basement of the citadel. I just played around with them a lot as a kid. Maybe Poppa and Muti should have gotten me a doll or something, but there you have it."

"Verily, you carry many secrets."

"That's what I've been trying to tell you."

Ghost Dare steps around me in a slow circle. A little line forms between his brows. "Huh."

"Huh, what?"

"You've grown." Ghost Dare pauses beside me. "You used to come up to here on me." He touches chest. "Now you're here." He gestures to his upper arm.

"You're right." My mind spins through this very important revelation. "When I was escaping the ley prison, it felt as if my skin were getting peeled off." I shiver at the memory. "Maybe the ley magic did something to me."

"It appears to be so." Ghost Dare keeps working his super-intense stare. My knees get watery.

Something strange happens.

Instead of working my eyelashes or positioning my clothes, I full-on panic. Before my relationship with Dare was something else. He called me little hob and I planned our wedding. that was familiar. Comfortable.

This feels like uncharted territory.

I may be Calla the Outlaw, but even we badasses know when we're in too deep.

Breaking our eye lock, I gesture around the room. "Guess what? The Ley Queen and I have a deal. She's helping me take down Lazare."

For a moment, Dare opens his mouth, as if about to say something. For some reason, I contemplate hiding under my bed. Dare inhales a long breath before speaking once more. "That's excellent news. What can I do to aid you?"

"Nothing." I sigh. Dare and I are back to planning adventures. *This is familiar territory. Whew.*

"And why not?"

"The Ley Queen was very specific that I have to do this alone." A memory appears. I snap my fingers. "How's your search going with the Fen Citadel? The Ley Queen didn't say anything about *me* helping *you*… just *you* helping *me*."

Ghost Dare raises his brows. "My name came up?"

I blush bright red. Stupid pixie skin. "Just answer the question."

"I found a wand to work the ley doors. I can now enter the Fens Citadel from its Pixieland counterpart."

"So how did that go?"

"It hasn't yet. Orcs are tough opponents. They have strong senses of smell and they move fast in a fight. And that's just one orc, not an army. Bilge is brewing me potions for my visit. If I step into the Fens Citadel without additional protection, I'll be discovered and killed in short order."

"You can tell Bilge to brew an extra batch, because I'm going with you."

Dare winks. "Perfect."

A knock sounds on my door. Only one person visits me: Spaghetti Man. I open the door a crack and peep through. Even so, I can sense Ghost-Dare looking over my shoulder.

"What is it?" I ask.

"The Ley Queen says your visitor must depart."

"Who is that?" asks Ghost Dare.

"My Spaghetti Man."

"I am not a Spaghetti Man. I am a ley golem with a name: Octaosirus Ne Regillius Fortesquillarum."

Like I said, Spaghetti Man.

I whip the door fully open. "And this is Prince Darius who is visiting me in astral form."

"Humph," says Spaghetti Man.

I set my fist on my hip. "Is there a problem?"

Ghost Dare stalks up to the door. "You cannot hold her against her will. I forbid it."

Wow. I totally should have summoned Dare earlier.

Spaghetti Man lifts his chin. "The Ley Queen says the faeling may depart in the morning. But *you* must leave now."

"M'Kay. We'll get right on that." I go to close the door. Spaghetti Man stops it with his noodly foot.

"He leaves now."

Sighing, I turn to Ghost Dare. "You better go. The Ley Queen does this chest-squeezy thing to me when she gets cranky."

Ghost Dare frowns. "Once you're released, will you return to Faerie?"

"I'd share my destination, but that would break the conditions of the Ley Queen."

Ghost-dare's frown deepens. "I don't like this."

"You remember that changeling, Griffin? He didn't like it either."

That was a hidden clue, by the way. Dare knows all about Griffin and how he came from Glover's Hollow. Dare also knows how my sneaky mind works.

"Understood," says Ghost Dare smoothly. He bows slightly. "Until we meet again." He vanishes with a puff of smoke.

Once Ghost Dare is gone, I come to another momentous revelation. I didn't get called *little hob* this time. There wasn't even an attempt at a nuggie.

That shouldn't make me nervous, but it does.

- Calla

DAY THIRTY-THREE

$\mathcal{D}$ear Diary,
  This morning begins with Spaghetti Man leading me back to the same spot where I entered the castle. My very same ley door is hangs in the air.

"Fare well, faeling. I shall miss your attempts to irritate me."

"Thanks, uh, you." He doesn't seem to like being called Spaghetti Man, so I avoid that name. And there's no way I can pronounce the other thing.

Yanking open my ley door, I step right back onto Earth. Before me stands the familiar town sign for Glover's Hollow. The Ley Queen's words appear in my mind.

Your first clue will come from me, and you will find it in the town of Glover's Hollow.

I march off to town. Last time I was here, I stayed invisible. On this visit, I remain in all my visible glory, from my cute minidress to my sweet pink wings. Calla the Outlaw doesn't hide because a human or two might be afraid of our pixiefied awesomeness.

It's a short walk to my destination. The town itself consists of a few dozen wooden buildings flanking a thin strip of road. At the end of the street, there stands a tiny park with a tall statue. I step along the sidewalk. Once again, I spy the Headless Huntress Luncheonette, Headless Grocery Store, and even a Headless Huntress Library.

My stomach rumbles—no way could I down any more elf food—so I march into the grocery store.

Inside, I find a snug space whose walls are lined with shelves and colorful cans and boxes. The place is empty, except for middle-aged man with round glasses and ebony skin. He looks up from behind a counter, a movement that highlights the flecks of gray hair framing his face.

"Hello, young lady," he says. "I'm Arnold. How may I help you?"

Planting my feet apart, I do my best Calla the Outlaw stance. "I demand food."

"You've come to the right place," says Arnold. "Let me guess. You're here for the Headless Horsewoman Festival. everyone dresses up." He eyes me slowly from head to toe. "What a great costume. Those wings look real."

I lift my chin. "They *are* real."

"Staying in character. Love it!" Arnold shakes his head. "You're early, though. The festival doesn't happen until next month." He flashes me a smile. "Halloween weekend."

"Halloween." I turn the word over in my head. The summer elves always hold revels on that night. If I were a human, I'd never leave my house for the whole month of October.

"What would you like to eat?" asks Arnold.

"That depends. What do humans like you enjoy?"

Arnold winks. "This early in the morning, everyone likes my apple blossom pastries." He gestures to platter by his register. Small round shapes sit atop it. "See, they look like the apple blossoms from my orchard. Each flower there carries seven petals. No more, no less."

I inch in closer. "Are those edible? We don't have things that shape in Faerie."

Arnold shakes his head. "Still in character. You're a cosplay superstar."

Bending over, I sniff at the circular food. *Not bad.*

"Sorry you came all the way out here on the wrong weekend." Arnold pushes the plate closer. "Take one for free. My treat."

I worry my lower lip with my teeth. Those look good, but who knows? Human food could kill faelings like me.

Or not.

I got this far, didn't I? Calla the Convict fears no pastry. I grab the treat and bite down. Deliciousness overtakes my taste buds.

Whoa. This is amazing.

I decide that Calla the Convict would be nice to someone who introduces her to apple pastries. Fluttering my wings, I bow to Arnold.

"Thank you!" My mouth is full, so I spray the guy with some pastry bits, but Arnold doesn't seem to mind. Still stuffing my face, I march out of the grocery store. Touring the town doesn't take long. Soon, I reach the end of the street and the statue.

I freeze.

The statue is supposed to show the Headless Horsewoman astride a rearing steed. There's nothing atop her neck all right. In her left hand, the woman holds her horse's reins. In her right fist, she grips her own head by the hair.

And I know those features.

After all, there's no forgetting that face. The Ley Queen. I read the plaque.

> *Find your family*
> *Align your power*
> *Explore the line*
> *Live with magic*
> *Investigate all seven*
> *Never doubt yourself and when in doubt, always...*
> *Go underground*

This statue and inscription aren't new to me. Only, I've never noticed one key thing about them before. The first letters of this inscription spell F-A-E-L-I-N-G. Based on the general tone of the words here, it's clear that I need to follow a ley line from this spot.

Is this the clue the Ley Queen told me about? I'm going with *yes*.

Kneeling down, I touch the ground. A heavy cord of ley power pulses beneath my fingertips. I smile my face off.

Bite me, Lazare.

At the end of this line lies the ultimate source of fae power. Once I get that to the Ley Queen, I am owning your elfy butt.

- My Bad Self

DAY THIRTY-THREE AND A HALF

*D*ear Diary,

I'm at the statue.

The riddle of the inscription is solved.

Next up? Yank on this ley line and find my way to the ultimate source of all fae power. I'm guessing it's a wand, but it could also be a ring or something. You can jam magic into anything, really.

It's habit to reach under the soil and search around for the cords of blue power. For a moment, I find nothing. Then, I sense the energy pulse. Magic dances across my skin. Grabbing it, I yank for all I'm worth.

The blue cord breaks free from the soil.

Now comes the last line of the inscription-n-riddle. *Go underground.* It takes some wrangling, but I force the ley line into a sort of human manhole cover that rests atop the grass. Then I speak my request.

"Go underground."

The ley lines swirl, whirlpool-style, before sliding out into the middle of the human street. For a second, the magical circle flashes more brightly. Next it disappears, leaving a massive hole yawning right the middle of the asphalt.

I step up to the edge. Some humans in their metal boxes zoom about. One yells that I'm a crazy lady and need to use the sidewalk. Another screams that I can't go making potholes.

Sad, sad, humans. They don't understand the beauty of magic.

I look down into the pit, which connects to a passageway beneath the street. This must be what the Ley Queen was guiding me toward.

The ultimate source of all fae magic.

I jump in.

Underground, I find a thin corridor made of rough hewn rock. I navigate the underground maze. With each step, my pulse speeds faster. *I am doing this!*

Then I see it.

A brick wall.

Literally.

A voice echoes though the stone hallways. "Calla? Is that you?"

That tone is familiar. I spin around. "Griff?"

Sure enough, Griffin turns a corner and steps into view. He grins. "It *is* you."

I shake my head, not believing what I'm seeing. "You know who I am? But Queen Saita wiped out your memories."

Griff shrugs. "I live by ley lines. Rules don't work here."

I shift my weight from foot to foot, considering this news. I suppose that makes sense. After all, my pixie magic is gone, but I can still access my ley stuff. Maybe the something similar is happening to Griff.

"We've got issues, Calla."

"M'Kay."

"You tore up my town."

"That was just a little hole in the street."

"There are six camera crews around it."

"Not my problem. So you know, I am now a terrible outlaw. Besides, you just said everyone here knows about fairies."

"Not ones that tear up main street with magical blue swirls."

"Trying to care." I frown. "Nope, not happening."

Calla the Outlaw wins again!

I refocus on the brick wall. Touching the masonry, I search for any sense of magic. Zip. Still, the Ley Queen sent me here. there must be something supernatural going on.

I turn to Griff. "What's behind this?"

"It's a vault from before Glover's Hollow was founded. Supposedly the Headless Horsewoman built it herself."

I point upward. "What's above this? I've been walking around for a while."

"My high school."

I tap my chin and consider. "This opens possibilities, especially for an outlaw like me."

"Look, I don't mean to be disrespectful. After all, it's amazing to just speak with an actual fairy. But all of Glover's Hollow is going on lockdown. The governor is sending in the state militia. No one will be able to leave their homes."

I set my fists on my hips. "That won't work. Not if I'm going to school with you."

"You are?"

"Sure. I need to get into this chamber, and it looks like that won't happen here without getting your human digger machines involved."

"That would be bad."

"Not to worry. Once we return to the surface, I can access my magic and fix your human problem. It'll probably knock me out for a little while, though."

The wail of a siren echoes through the tunnels. Griff frowns. "We don't have a lot of time to decide here."

"Fine, I'll do it." I fly out of the tunnels and back to the Earth's surface. Griff crawls his way out behind me.

Once outside, I find that everything is indeed a mess. There are sirens. Big red boxy things with the words *fire engine* written on the side in huge letters. Humans holding smaller boxy things on their shoulders. Griff calls these TV cameras.

Speaking of Griff, he fidgets beside me. "Can you fix all this?"

"Maybe, but it'll be a big effort for me pull up that much magic. I'll be a little useless afterwards."

As I speak, more angry humans fill the sidewalks. Many point in my direction and scowl. No point waiting. Sighing, I set my hands on the ground. Fresh ley lines pulse beneath me. I pull them up like before. Some bystanders stop to take pictures.

"This isn't good," whispers Griffin.

"Please remain quiet," I state. "I am an outlaw who is concentrating." I mold the blue cord into a circle, picture the spell I want, and set the power loose.

The blue orb ricochets through the town, smashing into buildings and people. Beside me, Griff makes a lot of yipe-yipe noises. When the ball finally vanishes, everything is back to normal. There's no hole in the street. No fire engine box. The humans are gone, even the ones with their camera.

Every cell in my body feels drained and empty. White spots cloud my vision.

"What did you do?" asks Griff.

"Reversed time." I grip Griff's upper arm. "I need to sleep. Take me to the forest."

"I'm not dropping you off under a tree, Calla."

The next part is a little fuzzy. I get laid down on something that smells of dead cow—a leather seat, perhaps? There are vrooming-noises. Griff carries me into a human dwelling.

I force my eyes open. "Where am I?"

"You'll stay with me while you recover."

"Is this house filled with babies named Ruth? I'm an outlaw, but not evil."

Griff chuckles. "No, I'm more of a Mars Bar kind of guy."

"All right. Then I shall sleep here."

Griff sets me in a human bed. It takes all my concentration, but I'm able to write this diary entry before sleep takes me over completely.

- Calla

DAY THIRTY-FOUR

Dear Diary,

When I wake up, I'm still in the human bed at Griff's house. My head's still pretty woozy.

Roooooar!

Ominous cries echo through the bedroom door. I've heard such things before.

An orc.

Images appear. I picture the sun cobra attacking me right before my birthday, as well as my little bunny-saurus striking back.

That was fun.

No question in my mind. This is another assassin of some kind. Maybe not from Lazare, but Earth is full of monsters.

Whatever this terror is, it's going down.

My heart thuds. The problem is, how do I get more ley magic? Kneeling on the fluffy carpet, I set my palms against the floor. Ley magic pulses under the house.

I scratch at the floor, wondering if I can pull up the power through the carpet.

That doesn't work.

So I try something else.

Closing my eyes, I picture my hands reaching into the soil under the house. My fingers can almost feel the chilly ground.

I grin. This might be working.

Shifting my hands, I look for the ley lines. Energy pulses by my skin.

Yes! I clasp my hands around the cord, feeling it solid in my fists. I yank upward and open my eyes.

A section of ley line sits in my hands.

My heart soars with joy. It worked! I'm getting this stuff down.

Roar!

That monster is still on the loose, roaming through Griff's house. Calla the Outlaw is on the case. I twist the cord of magic into a small sphere. Excitement streams through my limbs.

I steal toward the exit. Pushing on the door, I force it to swing open, inch by inch. Out in the hallway, I see the trouble. A tall mechanical orc attacks a human woman.

Not on my watch.

I send out the sphere of power, aiming it right toward the orc. Once the ball of power moves inside the beast, I turn it into a little spell I like to call *the bitey biter*. A set of blue teeth chomp through my metal enemy. With each bite, more of the orc vanishes. Soon the whole beast is gone. I snap my fingers, making they bitey teeth disappear.

The human woman looks between me and the vanished mechanical orc. Her eyes are wide with terror.

I step into the hallway. "Do not worry, human. The enemy is vanquished."

She screams and runs to safety. *Poor human.* That orc really shook her up.

A door swings open across the hall. Griffin steps out, a towel wrapped around his waist. His hair drips from his hair and down his chest. "What's going on?" he asks.

I lift my chin. "I saved the human and killed the mechanical orc."

Griff scans the hallway. "Calla, you scared my cleaning lady and destroyed the vacuum."

I roll my eyes. "That's what you think, human." I picture about the frightened look on the woman's face. "I hope she's all right."

"Mrs. Brillig will be fine. She's used to strange things happening around here."

"Ley lines, right."

Griff glances away. I catch an odd look on his face. Was that guilt? Hard to tell. I'm a terrible outlaw, not a mind reader.

"Look, let me get dressed and we can talk about this some more. Plus, I'm sure you must be hungry."

My stomach growls its agreement. "And thirsty," I add.

"Be right out." Griff closes the door. A minute later, he emerges in sweats and a t-shirt. "The kitchen is this way."

As I follow him through the massive house, we pass a lots of paintings, potted plants, and unused furniture. A wall of golden trophies catches my eye. Most show a small metal man kicking a ball. I stop. "What's this?"

"My soccer awards. I've been playing for years."

Pursing my lips, I eye the display. "This gives me an inspiration. When I create my new home, I shall add a hall of conquests to celebrate my victories, too."

"What?" Griff's face turns slack with shock. "You're leaving?"

"I must build a fairy home. It took my Poppa and Muti two years to craft their acorn. they built it by hand. By using magic, I hope to finish more quickly."

Griff shifts his weight from foot to foot. "I was hoping… I mean, I was thinking…"

"What?"

Griff gives me a lopsided smile. "Why not stay here?"

I consider this offer. What if I dragged a human home to live with Poppa and Muti? Not good.

"Are your parents okay with that?"

"My family founded the Hollow." He stares at me like those words means something.

"The Hollow, huh?"

Griff chuckles. "The Hollow is a huge company. We make everything from sneakers to baby food. My great-grandfather Glover founded it here."

My eyes widen. "That's why the place is called Glover's Hollow."

"And it's how I got the name Griffin. My father is George. Right now, my parents split their time between our estates in Milan and Paris. I'm the only one who stays local. After all, I'll inherit the company one day. I want to be near our roots."

A certain painting catches my eye. Undoubtedly, this is Griff and his parents. All have the same red hair and blue eyes.

I step closer. "Something about George seems familiar."

"Beyond the fact that we look almost identical?"

"Yes," I reply. "I can't quite place it."

"Enough about me and my boring family," says Griff. "Are you still thirsty?"

I fold my arms over my chest. "I do not drink my own urine."

"Good to know. I've given up on it myself."

"I can cast my own food and drink now. There is no need for your kitchen."

"Even if there are apple pastries?"

"Show me this place."

I follow Griff into his kitchen. There, another mechanical hum sounds. This one is lower, but the metal beast making the noise is even larger. Worry tightens every muscle in my body. I point at the latest assassin. "Another mechanical orc!"

Griff plasters himself with his back against the orc. "No, this isn't an orc. It's a fridge. It makes noises sometimes. No magic."

I narrow my eyes. "You're certain?"

Griff touches a handle on the orc's belly. "Look inside."

Stepping forward, I grip Griff's wrist. "No, allow me. You are too frail and easily killed."

"Okay, just don't destroy it. Unlike the vacuum, I care about this one."

I pull the metal orc's belly open. Inside lies cans and boxes. "I've seen these in Arnold's store."

"See? It's all good."

"It could be a glamour. I need to test." I open and close the contraption a dozen times. The interior doesn't change. I exhale slowly. Worry seeps from my shoulders. "It is safe."

I take a seat at the nearby table. This reminds me of the one I used with Poppa and Muti, only it's shiny metal instead of wood. A weight of sorrow settles into my bones.

I miss my parents.

Setting my hands onto the tabletop, I picture grabbing fresh ley lines. Sure enough, it works again. When I open my eyes, I hold new blue cords in my fists. Twisting them, I create the rough shape of a bowl, fork, and cup. With a flash of blue light, the magic transforms into some galla root and hocus juice. Comfort food. While I chow down, Griffin makes something called a sandwich. He plunks down to sit beside me at the table.

"We didn't get to talk before," says Griff.

"About what?"

"It's just so exciting to be speaking with an actual fairy. I want to know everything." Griff takes another mega bite of sandwich and swallows. "Why are you back on Earth?"

"I was imprisoned. I escaped. Now I'm trapped here."

Griff's eyes get all blue and sweet. "I'm sorry to hear that, Calla. Like I said before, you're welcome to stay with me."

"No, I'll find a nice tree. I need to build a new lair." I stuff in my own bite of galla root.

"Any other plans?" asks Griff.

I point my fork at his face. "You have a lot of questions."

Griff holds his hands up, palms facing me. "You're just so interesting, that's all. And you won't tell me why you're staying in Glover's Hollow." Griff puffs out his bottom lip a little. It is a cute face.

I down another bite of gallow root and think this through. I could tell Griff about my quest from the Ley Queen. That feels like a lot of sharing, though. And humans can be evil, end of story.

That said, I do have another project while I'm here: finding my human parents. It could help to have an insider around.

"I'm a faeling," I begin. "Do you know what that is?"

Griff shakes his head.

"It means I was born from human parents who lived near a ley line. Over the years, magic soaked into them and they had a fairy for a child."

"How often does that happen?"

"There was one other faeling around when I was back in Faerie. Now, there's just me. So not too often."

Griff leans back in his chair. "That's why you're here on Earth."

"Partially. I wish to attend your school. Will you help me?"

Griff leans forward until we're only inches apart. "I could never refuse you anything. My family got Principal Tothes his job. Fall session just started. I bet you can start next week, if you like."

"I do not like. I must build my lair first. My new magic is rather tiring. It may take me some time."

Griff finishes off his sandwich. "That seems like a lot of work."

"Of course." I don't expect Griffin to understand about lair building. Real fairies simply do not live in human houses.

I polish off the last of my galla root and hocus juice. Snapping my fingers, I make all signs of my meal disappear. "If you'll excuse me."

"You just woke up after using a ton of magic. How about taking some time off to watch television with me?"

I scan the empty house. "You're lonely here." It isn't a question.

Griff clutches at his heart and blinks a lot. "Horribly." He's playing it up, but it still works.

It seems Calla the Outlaw has some soft spots. "M'Kay."

We leave the kitchen to sit on a couch and watch a small mechanical plate that Griff calls a wide screen television. It displays sports shows, which are exceptionally boring. We then switch to watch something called *Arctic Survivor.* Unlike sports, this is very interesting. Who knew humans had to act so strangely in order to stay alive? In the end, Griff and I engage in what he calls an all-day binge of seasons one through six.

Turns out, humans do drink pee.

I stay one more night in the human bed, which is about all I can stand. Drawing helps me fall asleep, so here's one of Griff.

- Calla

Griff

DAY THIRTY-FIVE

*D*ear Diary,

I spend the morning meandering around the forests in search of a spot for my new home. My goal is to find a nice tree, boulder, or lake. Once there, I'll create a permanent ley door to what's called a pocket realm, which is little fantasy world that's completely formed via magic. Sure, creating and maintaining this will be a constant drain on my powers, but I don't plan on keeping my new home forever.

And the castle I plan to make is so cool, I can't stand myself.

After roaming about the woods for a few hours, I discover a nice maple that dominates a small clearing. As I approach the tree in question, a wide circle of mushrooms sprout up from the ground. It's a good sign —this spot clearly welcomes my magic.

I build my new home in record time. Here are the highlights.

My Castle of Badassdom — The Coolest Parts

One. The main ley door. The entrance to my castle is set directly onto a tree trunk. It's invisible to humans, but I can both see and open it.

Two. My pocket realm. This miniature world is a land created in the sky. I'm talking a bunch of grey clouds that churn around at night. There's no ground, just a long and thin walkway from the tree trunk door to the castle's main gate. Lighting strikes all around. It's perfect stuff for Calla the Outlaw.

Three. My Secret Door. The main entrance is obviously a very dangerous way to get into my home, so I build a smaller, secret ley door on the side of the trunk that will lead directly into the castle proper. The main entrance is more to foil and frighten my enemies. The secret door will open right onto my bedroom.

Four. The Castle Itself. My creation looks like the Pinnacle, only bigger and more evil looking. Inside, there's a massive dining hall, ball room, and weaponry. I also set up an entire hall for statues of my battle conquests. So far, there's only one to the metal orc vacuum, but no doubt I'll get more soon.

Five. My Bedroom. I created a massive chamber with dark curtains that open onto a view of my dark clouds and lightning bolts. Low rumbles of thunder mark the passage of time.

In all honesty, I may have overdone it. I end up conjuring a little chamber in the basement that looks a lot like my old acorn bedroom. That where the second tree door opens onto. And it's where I am now.

Tomorrow, I'll start my new life as Calla the Outlaw in her Castle of Badassdom. For now, I'll pretend I'm still at home with Poppa and Muti.

- Calla

~

Dear Diary,
My hand just pulsed with white light. Dare alert!
- Calla

DAY THIRTY-FIVE AND A HALF

Dear Diary,

I receive a late-night summons to chat from Dare. Thankfully, I already conjured some cute PJs. This style used to be loose—now not so much—but they still work.

"You may visit," I say into my palm.

Ghost Dare appears. He's in casual clothes. Don't get me wrong; he still looks like a ninja. Only one in a fitted shirt and pants. So more of a tailored ninja.

"Hello, Calla." Dare's voice rings with that deep and growly tone that I like.

Maybe I obsess about it a little bit.

Okay, a lot.

"Hey, Dare. How are things with the Fens Citadel?"

There. That was smooth and casual. I'm just hanging out in my cutie-pie PJ set, not acting odd over Dare's voice or anything.

"As a matter of fact, I'm here in the Pixieland Citadel with Bilge and Oinky. We'd like to try out my new wand and see if it can open a ley door from the citadel to somewhere else. Want a visitor?"

My mind blanks. Every ounce of cool in my soul evaporates. "As in you?"

"Yes."

"Coming to see me?"

"Correct." He gives me a sly grin. "I can check if you've grown again."

"Sure. Fine. Yes. That's great. Visit."

Stop talking, Calla.

Ghost Dare looks down. "Fine, I'll tell her."

I roll my eyes. No question who Dare is talking to. *Bilge.*

Ghost Dare meets my gaze once more. "Bilge says, *it must not spend too much time with the winter prince.*" An amused gleam shines in Dare's eyes.

A pause follows. I cross my fingers behind my back, hoping Bilge doesn't say anything embarrassing.

"Are you sure you want me to say that?" asks Ghost Dare.

"You know what, why don't you visit tomorrow or something?" I speed-yawn. "I'm super-tired."

"Fine," says Ghost Dare to the unseen Bilge. "I will tell her."

I fight the urge to run. "Tell me what?"

"*It will remember to wipe its bum-bum.*"

"Bilge did not say that. Once when I was six, I forgot to... and now Bilge... you know what? Forget it. I'll go hide now."

Dare bites his lips together. "I'm on my way, Calla."

A moment later, the ley door in my bedroom glows blue. That's Dare activating the connection from his side.

At this point, I really should run for the hills. But it's Dare. And my Castle of Badassdom is really lonely. I pull open the door.

Dare strides through. He looks so tall and perfect with his dark locks, cut jawline and gray eyes. Even so, I just can't face him right now. With my left hand, I push against his chest. My right grabs the door handle.

"Test is successful," I announce. "You can leave now."

Bilge pops his head in. "You got the message about your bum-bum? Poppa and Muti mentioned it as well."

"I got it, Bilge. Good night."

I push harder on Dare's chest. That's a mistake. The guy is like a muscly brick wall. "You can leave too."

"No." He slowly closes the door behind him.

At this moment, I realize I'm touching Dare and we're all alone. This is awkward. I lower my hand. "You should know I don't want to see you."

"Did I ever tell you about my first summit with Lazare? I was six years old."

"And it went perfectly?"

"No, it did not. We met at a town on the edge of summer and winter realms. The place was a frozen city called Oasis then. Now it's an icy pile of sludge, thanks to the blight."

"What happened?"

"I took a sledge over and got a little motion sick. When I met Lazare, I barfed right on his shoes."

"You did not."

"I most certainly did."

I try not to grin, but I don't work too hard on it. "That's a terrible story."

"We all do strange things when we're six. Now let's see if you've kept growing."

"I don't wanna." Having these *my how much you've grown* conversations is almost as embarrassing as the bum-bum thing.

Dare shuffle-walks to align at my side. It's a little silly and makes smile broaden. Dare moves his palm between the top of my head and his upper arm. "You've grown another inch."

"No way."

"Quite." He steps back. "Since I'm here, would you mind giving me a tour? I'd love to see what you've built."

My eyes widen. "That would be awesome." I stretch my arms wide. "To begin with, I call this place, the Castle of Badassdom." I scan the chamber. "Okay, this room is pretty much a recreation of my home with Poppa and Muti. But the rest is really something."

I take Dare on a guided tour. He likes the armory. I don't use a lot of weapons and stuff in battle, so most of the swords are just blank and pointy. We go on to the hall of conquests. Dare is appropriately impressed with my statue of the evil orc vacuum. We then sashay on over to the ballroom.

"This is rather large," says Dare.

"It's also very dark and ominous, like the rest of my castle." I step around in a slow circle. "In creating this, I thought of the rooms in the summer palace. There are a lot of them, but they're all pretty small. I wanted something huge."

Dare winks. "And you've met your goal."

"How *is* the summer palace, by the way?"

"Lazare has asked Master Mab to cast him a new building."

"No. That fairy is old as dirt. Asking him to give up that much magic could kill him."

"It did."

"Oh." Cold seeps into my skin. "I didn't mean for that to happen."

"You didn't do anything. If Lazare were a legitimate ruler, he'd be able to use the Scepter of Summer to cast himself a new palace easily. It's not your fault."

I decide that now is a great time to fidget with the tie on my robes. It's much easier than making eye contact with Dare. "And how is Lotti?"

"Determined."

"Are you two… you know?"

"Still officially engaged? Yes." Dare steps closer. "I told her I wanted to find King Tristan in order to discover evidence that could clear my brother's name."

"Is that even possible?"

"Sadly, no. Reiver is very guilty. That said, if Lotti figures out that I really wish to place Tristan on the throne, things could get tricky. Right now, I allow her to think the engagement is real. It keeps her from contemplating the larger picture."

I nod. "That makes sense. King Tristan stopped the blight before. We need him back. And if that means Lotti gets her heart broken, then *it is what it is.*"

Dare moves even nearer. We're only a few inches apart now. "I don't care about Lotti's heart."

All of a sudden, I can't seem to breathe easily. "Not sure she has one anyway."

Dare gives me one of his dimple-grins. "I've an idea. How about we use the ballroom?"

Must. Get. Air. Into. Lungs.

"For what?"

Dare lifts his hands. A sphere of white magic appears between his palms. Dare extends his arms apart, and the orb of power splits. A cascade of white sparkly stuff fills the room, reminding me of fresh snow on a winter morning. When the magic settles, the dark chamber walls are now decorated in a pattern of massive snowflakes. Tiny bits of magic swirl through the air like so much glitter. An orchestra of ice players now wait against one wall.

It's really pretty, and a super show of power to boot. A single thought echoes through my head.

"I don't dance."

Dare kneels before me. He touches each of my slippers with his fingertips. The shoes gleam with the same snowflake patterns as the walls.

"Perfect," says Dare. "You are now the proud owner of enchanted shoes. You may now flawlessly perform any dance you choose."

"No way." I lift each foot in turn to check out my new gear. "How about Swan Lake?" *We pixies love ballet.*

The orchestra strikes up the tune. Instantly, I am on my tippy toes and doing those little baby ballerina steps across the floor.

"That's it!" Dare tosses another sphere of power at the opposite wall, where it transforms into a massive mirror. Now I can watch myself do those leapy-things where my legs are all straight and stuff.

"I look awesome."

"That you do," says Dare. "How about some swing?"

"Not familiar with that," I reply.

Dare snaps his fingers and the orchestra changes its tune. Now the drummer strums out a deep rhythm, followed by all sorts of trumpets.

"It sounds amazing. What's this song called?"

"Sing, sing, sing," replies Dare. "It's part of a human style called swing music."

"All right. I'm game."

My shoes do their thing. This time, Dare and I dance together. Turns out, swing involves getting tossed around. Dare swoops me up into the air and down between his legs. Next he bouncing me off each hip. After that, we hold hands and kick back and forth to the fast rhythm. My heart soars. This is beyond anything I'd ever imagined.

I recall all the times Dare and I leapt into fun as kids, like when we rescued Princess Pampertoes. It's the same and different, all at once. I smile my face off.

The tune ends. Dare and I are breathless and staring into each other's eyes. Dare cups both my hands between his. "Lotti means nothing to me, Calla. Believe that."

"M'Kay." Not my best response, but I mean it.

"Would you like to dance some more?"

"Yes. This swing stuff is great."

And so we dance until my legs feel all gooey and I forget Lotti the Snotty Potty ever existed.

Dare walks me back to my bedroom before leaving for the Pixieland Citadel again.

I collapse into bed, exhausted and happy.

What a good night.

- Calla

DAY THIRTY-SIX

*D*ear Diary,
          I wake up to hear someone calling my name.

"Calla! Calla!"

It's Griff, and he's really persistent. One might even call him border-line annoying. Then again, what I know about human men is zero. Maybe they all act this way.

Also, this brings up a possible design flaw in my Castle of Badassdom. I didn't put in sound barrier spells between the tree doors and my bedroom.

Something to fix later.

Rolling onto my back, I listen to Griff and frown. My brain is too sleepy to think about anything, though. I check my wall clock.

8 am.

Who wakes up this early anyway?

"Calla! Calla!"

Griff really has a set of lungs on him. Padding across my room, I open my ley door a crack. To Griff, this will appear as if the maple tree before him changes. Specifically, the bark gets all mushy and reforms into a small wooden door at the trunk's base.

"What?" I ask. And if my voice is a semi-snarl, so be it.

"I've been looking for you all morning." He gives me one of those grins where his blue eyes get sparkly. "You still want to attend my high school, right?"

"Sure."

"I heard from my principal. He can meet with you this morning."

"Why would I do that?"

"It's a human thing. You can't just show up. The principal has to let you in."

I narrow my eyes at him. It's true that I want to inspect the vault that's under Griff's high school, but something about this whole thing still feels off.

"How did you find me?"

"It's not that big of a forest, Calla." Griff gestures around. "The massive fairy ring was a dead giveaway."

"Okay, that makes sense."

"Great." Griff's grin gets even wider, if that's possible. "I'm parked not far from here."

"Parked? You mean in one of those metal box things?"

"They're called cars. Yes, that's how we'll get to school."

I purse my lips. "Ah, no. I'll fly there."

Griff frowns. "Look, you can't fly into school and expect them to enroll you. It's a school for humans."

Huh. I hadn't thought about that. Although I am still a little sleepy after building an evil castle yesterday, so I'm not at my sharpest here. I yawn, thinking that there's some gap in Griff's logic. Meh.

"And I have a box of apple pastries in the front seat. Not sure if you've tried this particular variety, but they're from the Headless Horsewoman Grocery store. Everyone around here loves the—"

"I'll be right out."

After slamming the door shut, I get ready in record time. Soon Griff and I are marching through the woods. It's a long walk to find what Griff calls a parking lot. Along the way, Griff shares how he used to go hiking in these woods all the time as a kid.

"Do your parents still do that?" I ask.

"What?"

"Hike in the woods. Or don't they have forests in Europe? I've only ever been to Glover's Hollow."

"Oh, sure. My parents march all around Europe. They love nature." Griff doesn't sound very positive about that point, though. I figure it's because he misses his parents. I get the feeling.

Griff approaches a small yellow box. I stop in my tracks. "That is tiny."

"It's a sports car."

"It's a deathtrap."

We then launch into a process of Griff luring me into the yellow coffin box with his apple pastries. I'm surprisingly easy to lure, as it turns out. The tiny leather seat quickly gets covered in crumbs as I polish off two treats in a matter of minutes.

Griff grips a round wheel in front of him. "Ready?"

After plucking the third and final pastry from the box, I decide that the metal boxes I've seen before were pretty slow moving. Flying through Faerie would be more exciting. I stuff a final bite into my head and speak through the yum.

"Sure."

The car careens off at neck-breaking speed. I lose my mind. Only one thought overtakes my head.

Escape.

Flying away is my first choice, but when I pump my wings, my face gets plastered against some glass. Next I work on burrowing my way free, but it's not as easy as it seems. There's a lot of metal and whatnot under the leather seats.

Griff stops the yellow box by the roadside. "What was that?"

"Out! Out! Out!" I reach down, ready to grab some ley lines, but there is a pesky metal plate in the way.

Griff rushes outside and pulls open my door. "Okay, here you go."

I speed fly out onto the side of the road. "I am never getting inside that again."

Griff picks through what remains of his front seat. "I just picked this up from the dealer."

"I don't know what that means and I'm not sure I care."

Griff rubs his neck while forcing in a series of slow breaths. "Okay, this isn't your fault."

"No kidding."

Griff keeps staring at the car's interior. "Guess I forgot about this."

"About what?"

"What it's like to be new here."

"New here? You're human."

"Did I say here? I meant to say being new *somewhere.* Like when I was taken into Faerie and forced to be a human changeling." Griff glances away. I catch an odd look on his face again, but I'm still too freaked out by the yellow death box to care.

"We aren't far from school now," says Griff. "Do you mind walking the rest of the way?"

"As a matter of fact, I do mind." I wag my finger at him. "You're acting really strangely. There is *no way* I want to meet your principal."

"Don't you want to go to my school?"

"I have my magic back. I can just sneak in."

"But it's my school. I can help you."

"Like how you tracked me down this morning and *helped me* into a box of apple pastries and death? No, thank you."

Griff's shoulders sag. "You're right. I'm so sorry. It's just that I'm really excited to have you here. You do understand that, right? You're an extraordinary woman, Calla. I guess it makes me a little crazy."

It's the *woman* part that slows me down. To most people, all I've ever been is a little girl.

"Here's what's going to happen," I state. "I'll go home now and use a tracer spell to find your school. I'll meet you there in the morning. No car rides. I'll just fly over while being invisible."

"Sure. Anything you want." He twists his hands at his waist. "I'm so sorry I screwed this up, Calla."

On top of being freaked out, now I'm on some kind of sugar high. After waving goodbye, I take to the air. Once home, I make a beeline for my cozy basement room, cuddle under my covers, and write everything down. After journaling everything out, one fact is clear.

I should use my magic to visit the school, but I won't. Every time I think about sneaking in, I picture those kids and parents at the playing field.

I want that.

Or at the very least, I want to see it up close, just once.

Back at it tomorrow.

- Calla

DAY THIRTY-SEVEN

*D*ear Diary,

The next morning, I wait in an asphalt field outside the Headless Horsewoman High School. Total shocker that I'm here in the middle of the night.

On pixie time, that means 8 am.

I cast a few knowledge spells last night. Even though Glover's Hollow is small, it's located in the middle of a bunch of far larger towns. Headless Huntress High School is the central school for tons of humans. Close to a thousand kids go here.

In terms of layout, the school is a series of blocky buildings connected by walkways. The place reminds me of Lazare's palace, only while that building is all gold, this structure is nothing but cement blocks.

Griff's yellow box careens onto the asphalt field. He screeches to a stop beside me. Maybe the move is supposed to scare me. Not happening. Being inside that thing was a surprise. Watching Griff tool around is a big snore. If he wants real speed, the guy needs to sprout some wings.

The side of the metal box dips open. Griff steps out. He wears a red sports shirt that matches the color of his hair. He's all glittery blue eyes, strong shoulders and a big smile.

"Morning, Calla!"

"Hey, Griff." I took time to hide my wings this morning. The rest of me is in my standard outfit: pink minidress with matching flats. My pink hair hangs in waves down my back.

Griffin pauses and eyes me carefully. "You've grown."

"What do you mean?" I pull on the edge of my minidress. "Is this too short?"

"You look great."

I debate about conjuring a new outfit. I did notice my dress was looking shorter on me. Also, the top is pulling a little. I'm getting a bit of an hourglass figure. Guess I'd just resolved myself that I'd always look like a pixie.

The idea of changing my clothes looms large in my mind. I picture myself wearing a sport shirt like Griffs.

And no.

I'm here to find the ultimate source of all fae power, not have a fashion show with Griffin.

"Where is this principal of yours?"

"Waiting for us," says Griff. "This way."

Griff and I walk through the maze of buildings that make up the Headless Horsewoman High School. Honestly? It's nice to have Griff by my side. This place is a little overwhelming. Everything smells like chemicals and stinky feet. Some walls are lined with tall, thin doors that lead nowhere. Griff calls them lockers. Sure, I could cast a spell to get around, but there's no magic to make transform the overwhelming into something familiar.

No doubt about it. I'll be able to find the Headless Huntress' vault more easily with Griff by my side.

We pause before a normal-sized door. The name Principal Tothes is written there in block letters.

Griff doesn't even knock. He just pushes the door open. "Hey, Tothes!" He gestures to me. "This is the friend I told you about, Calla."

Principal Tothes is a nervous guy with thick glasses and no chin. "Nice to meet you, Calla. Griffin is a new senior at the Headless Horsewoman High School. We're all so happy to have him here."

The words have a sing-song tone to them, like Tothes says them a lot. I guess that makes sense. Griff's family pretty much owns this town.

The principal gestures to a pair of generic wooden chairs before his clunky metal desk. Griff and I sit down. Tothes then sifts through a pile of what I can only assume is parchment.

"Griff filled out your paperwork," says Tothes. "It's a little light. Where are you from?"

The answer automatically falls from my lips. "Pixieland."

Griff winks. "She's from the city. That's what everyone calls New York these days."

"Ahh." Tothes shuffles the parchment some more. "You don't have a social security number."

"Oh," I say. "It's seven."

"Just seven?" asks Tothes.

"Yup. However many numbers there are, all of them are seven." *That ought to do it.*

"Then we're all set." Tothes shoves some sheets aside. "You start classes on Monday. Here's your welcome kit."

I take the packet from the principal's hands. "Thank you." Today's Friday, so I have all weekend to wrap my mind around this human stuff.

As we leave the high school, I make some quick goodbyes to Griff, turn myself invisible, and fly back to my Castle of Badassdom. I have a lot of work to do. There's no way I can rely on Griff to prepare me for everything to do with humans.

If this is going to be my only chance to see even part of families at work, I want to do it right.

- Calla

DAY THIRTY-EIGHT

Dear Diary,
I've just chosen the perfect spell to prepare me for being a regular human high schooler.

Then my palm lights up.

Dare.

I speak into my hand. "You may visit."

Ghost Dare materializes in my room. "Hello, Calla." He's working the dimples. That's good stuff.

"Hey. What's going on?"

"Bilge is working on those potions for us to sneak into the Fens Citadel. He needs us to stop by and give him things." Dare tilts his head. "You wouldn't know what those *things* might be?"

I bob my brows and look mysterious. "Maybe."

Ghost Dare steps around me in a slow circle. "You've grown again."

"Griff said the same thing."

"Your human?"

"He's not *my* human, but he's been helping me."

"With the secret quest from the Ley Queen that I cannot assist you with."

There's an edge to Ghost Dare's voice that I'm not sure if I like. Or maybe I love it tons. Life is confusing.

"That's the one." I yank on the bottom of my mini-dress again. "I'm not sure this really fits anymore."

"May I?"

Now I could ask for details, but Ghost Dare's gray eyes are all intense and stuff. It's impossible to say no. "Sure."

Ghost Dare touches my shoulder. A white orb of power appears on my shoulder, then cascades down my outfit. My pink mini-dress transforms into something that cinches at my waist and flares out at my hips. Ghost-Dare tosses another power sphere across the room. A full-length mirror materializes on the spot.

Stepping closer, I check out my new ensemble. It doesn't seem possible. I have curves. And a cute outfit that highlights my figure, complete with matching pink sandals. Who knew Dare had fashion sense?

"There now," says Ghost Dare. "Much better."

An electric silence falls between us. Finally, I'm able to speak. "Thank you."

"I'm in the Pixieland Citadel," says Ghost Dare. "Come over when you're ready. Only I'll suggest creating a ley door that leads directly to the potions casting floor. A lot of things have been happening in Faerie since you left. I don't want you distracted from the Ley Queen's quest."

"M'Kay."

"You're totally going to enter though the citadel's main door, aren't you?"

I shrug. "You know me."

"That I do." Ghost Dare bows and vanishes.

Now, I could say that I opened a ley door right away and went to the citadel. After all, future generations might read this and I don't want to come off as a superficial chick who got over-excited just because her crush got her a new dress that highlights her almost-as-new curves.

But yeah. I am that girl. I twirl before the mirror a few times. It's a total moment. I even do a quick sketch of my face using my handy-dandy new mirror.

This is one moment to savor.

- Calla

New Me?

DAY THIRTY-EIGHT AND A HALF

$\mathcal{D}$ear Diary,

With my drawing done, I open a ley door to the main floor of the Pixieland Citadel. Once there, one thing is clear.

There are new residents.

Sick elves, pixies, dwarves, and sprites lay in cots that cover the floor. All have the same gray boils that I saw on the ley lines in the Fens. No one even looks up as I materialize. The scent of sweat and desperation fills the air.

My heart cracks. I'd wondered if the blight had spread, but this is beyond imagining.

Taking to the air, I zoom through the citadel. Every room on the first floor is packed with sick residents of Pixieland. I want to comfort them, heal them, something.

Time to find Bilge.

Still in flight, I speed up to the cauldron room on the third floor. It's a shadowy space whose walls are lined with every ingredient imaginable. Bilge stands at his usual spot, churning an oversized stick through a massive cauldron. I land at his side.

"What's happening?" I ask. There's no point in adding the part about all the sick faeries. Bilge saw where I flew in from.

"Ley blight," says Bilge. "It's spreading."

I gasp. "What about—"

"Poppa and Muti are fine," says Bilge. "It is growing worse, but at a very slow pace. There is time, Calla."

"But you can brew a cure, can't you?"

"I try," says Bilge. "So far, I can only block their pain."

The scene downstairs suddenly makes more sense. "That's why the patients downstairs all seem so out of it. No one even noticed when I appeared." I refocus on Bilge. "Have we learned anything about what's causing it?"

Dare steps out from the shadows. "Lazare blames you."

I take a half-step backward. "Me?"

"The Protector thinks you played one last prank before leaving and it's killing us all. He insists the Ley Queen release you from prison so you may pay for your crimes. She has refused."

"But I didn't have anything to do with it."

"We all know it is innocent," says Bilge. Oinky trots out from behind the cauldron and nods in agreement.

"So what's really happening?" I ask.

"Only King Tristan knows," states Dare.

Bilge nods. "The sooner it finds King Tristan and restores him to the throne, the better." He churns his cauldron. "I need its help to finish the potions for the trip to the Fens."

I hug my elbows. This is getting serious. "What do you need?"

"On the count of three, it will spit into the cauldron." Bilge motions toward Dare. "And it will spit, too. Unified spitting, that's what the spell requires."

"Okay, give me a second." I rub my cheeks.

"What are you doing?" asks Dare.

"This isn't my first time spitting into a cauldron. You'll get better results if you rub your cheeks and then slosh the stuff around in your mouth a bit."

"It speaks the truth," says Bilge.

What follows is a lot of cheek rubbing and sloshing. Bilge starts the countdown.

"Three... two... one!"

Dare and I spit into the cauldron. I'd say it felt weird, but that ended after Bilge made me do this the first hundred times.

"Do you need anything else?" I ask Bilge.

"No, it has done well." Bilge looks to Dare. "And it has done well, too."

Dare bows slightly. "Thank you Bilge, for everything."

I focus on Dare. "How many of your people are ill?"

"Not many," says Dare. "I've brought them all here. But I do plan to cast some more healing spells on everyone. Perhaps it will help. So far, only Bilge's potions have any effect."

"I'll go with you."

"It needs to stay hidden," says Bilge. "No one can know it is out of the ley prison. Flying past is one thing, but staying for hours to cast spells? Someone is bound to notice it."

Sadly, Bilge is right. The best thing I can do now is focus on finding King Tristan. "When will the potions be finished?"

"In three days," answers Bilge.

I frown. "It seems like we should move more quickly."

"It goes quickly and bad things happen," snaps Bilge. "Palaces explode. Pretty girls end up in prisons. It will take time and be careful."

I nod. "That's good advice, Bilge." He really is a good friend.

Bilge grins. "Be ready in three days."

"I will."

I make some quick goodbyes and head back to the Castle of Badassdom. Once there, I try to figure out what is happening to my homeland. The blight is spreading. Everyone is at risk, including Poppa and Muti.

There's only one way I can help. Find King Tristan. Before, it was a matter of wanting to stop Lazare from being such a creep. Now, it's become something far more deadly.

- Calla

DAY THIRTY-NINE

*D*ear Diary,

This is another nothing-day before school starts. I really don't understand how humans do this whole weekend thing.

I keep picturing those ill fairies. The way their eyes sunk into their skin is nothing less than chilling. In the end, I decide that I simply can't wait to find King Tristan. After cast an invisibility spell, I zoom over to the high school.

Things do not go well.

The school is a maze with kids around, and even worse when it's empty. Although I cast a bunch of spells, none of them seem to go right. Truth is, I'm too worried to think straight. I must slow down and stick to my original plan—and that means attend school during daylight hours with Griff as my guide.

Plus, if I do some human-style homework, I may not even need Griff's help. With my new plan in place, I spend the rest of my weekend getting ready for high school.

To that end, I cast what's called an amalgam spell. This is where you pull together thoughts from living humans who can give answers. Specifically, I conjured myself a human teenager amalgam. I've been asking her questions all day long. Her appearance flips through the look of different people as my spell finds the right answer in various minds. Visually it takes little getting used to, but it's still super helpful.

Plus—although I supposedly shouldn't care about this—it doesn't hurt the humans at all.

Stuff My Teenage Amalgam Says

One. Classes are where you pretend to listen to the teacher but actually play with something called a hand-held device. I don't need human technology to ignore people, so I feel pretty prepared on this score.

Two. When it comes to outfits, humans have all sorts of odd names for things. It took a while to understand what a *hoodie* actually was. That said, my amalgam agrees that I'm fine wearing my new pink dress from Dare.

Three. We go through some basic terms. Lunchroom. Gymnasium. Schedule. Blah.

Four. There's a lot more my amalgam reviews, but it all starts to run together. I just don't want to stick out too badly.

After all, it's not like I'm actually going to attend high school forever.

- Calla

DAY FORTY

*D*ear Diary,

First day of school. Wow.

Way too early in the morning, I land on the edge of the parking lot. Headless Huntress High School stretches before me. A handful of humans walk around. Not too many, though. I got here pretty early.

Although I stand on the ground, my wings flutter behind me in a nervous rhythm. I'll see actual kids today. People who value something other than being mean. I can't wait to watch them.

First they need to see me, though.

Before I left my castle of Badassdom, I cast an invisibility spell. Now I pull in a new orb of ley magic to render myself visible again. To finish the human look, I retract my wings. At this point, I should blend in as a regular human.

Can't wait.

The parking lot only holds a handful of metal boxes. A small red one now opens. Griff steps out and runs over to my side.

"Good morning, Calla!"

"Your metal riding box matches your hair."

Griff looks over his shoulder. "I never thought of it that way, but you're right." He beams. "Are you ready for your first day of school?"

Nervous energy streams inside me. "Yes. I memorized my schedule and everything."

"Cool," says Griff. "I talked to Principal Tothes, and he changed my schedule to match yours. Isn't that great?"

I scrunch up my mouth and think. "You don't need to change your entire life around for me. I've been working all weekend. I figured I would do most on my own but have you for pointers."

"One weekend to learn everything about humans? Even you're not that smart… and you're brilliant."

I keep scrunching my mouth and wondering if this is a good idea.

"Please, allow me to do what I can to help you." Griff's eyes widen. "You saved my life, Calla. This means a lot."

"That's true. I did totally save your life."

"And my world is exceptionally boring," continues Griff. "You're the most exciting thing that's ever happened. Let's face it. You're the biggest thrill of my existence."

My resolve crumbles a little. Back in Faerie, everyone says how I'm a menace. In fact, I was just marched past crowds of people who screamed insults at me. Not gonna lie. It's nice to have someone see me as exciting or a thrill.

"Fine." I raise my pointer finger. "One class. We'll see how it goes."

Griff pumps his fist in the air. "Woo hoo!"

We step into the school. Griff guides me through the maze of hallways to a mostly-empty classroom. Like the rest of Headless Huntress High, the chamber is a lot of cinderblock and tile. Rows of desk-chairs fill the space. A blackboard covers the far wall.

It's all as my amalgam described.

So far, so good.

Humans file into class. There is surprisingly little chatter. Everyone looks sleepy and grouchy, not jacked up on excitement like me. I scan the faces, waiting for then to share smiles or stories from home.

Nothing yet.

Which is understandable. Seems like most human kids are about as much into mornings as pixies. I consider that a good sign. Griff sits in the desk-chair next to mine. When the teacher enters, Griff whips up, crosses the room, and whispers to her. She grins and they chat for a bit.

I can't help but feel a little ticked off. As part of my weekend preparation, I'd practiced what to say to my first teacher. I understand that Griff is only trying to help, but he's getting on my nerves.

His conversation over, Griff slides onto the seat next to mine once more. "All set."

"You didn't have to do that."

"I know." He winks. "I've got you covered."

"Don't take this the wrong way, but if I need your assistance, I'll ask for it. I appreciate what you're trying to do, but I'd like to work this on my own as much as possible."

A look flashes across Griff's face. Anger? Hurt? The expression passes gone too quickly to be certain. A moment later, Griff is all wide eyes and heartfelt sadness.

"Thanks for letting me know. I won't get in your way again." He slumps in his chair.

Ugh. Now I feel totally guilty.

The teacher claps her hands twice. "Good morning, class."

"Good morning, Miss Gyre."

My brows lift. This is one thing my amalgam didn't cover. Who knew humans spoke in unison sometimes? It's a little creepy.

"We have a new student with us today. Her name is Calla." She focuses on me. There's something blank in her expression, but I can't quite place it. "How unusual for you to start this late in the year."

I squirm on my chair. What do blank expressions mean from human teachers? If that comes from a fairy, it means they're about to crush you like a bug.

"Griff helped me."

That blank expression gets enhanced with a stomach-churning smile. "Griffin is a new senior at the Headless Horsewoman High School. We're all so happy to have him here."

Right.

My uncomfortable feeling transforms into something else. The little hairs on the back of my neck stand on end. An image appears in my mind.

Protector Lazare.

I shake my head. What would Lazare have to do with a rando human high school? I'm out of my element. My imagination is getting the better of me.

Miss Gyre scoops up a leather volume from her desktop. "Today, we'll dissect a poem by the nineteenth century writer, William Allingham." She opens the book and clears her throat.

> *Up the airy mountain,*
> *Down the rushy glen,*
> *We daren't go a-hunting*
> *For fear of little men*

Miss Gyre lowers her book. "Anyone wish to comment on these words?"

No one says a thing. I have a lot of opinions here, but it's my first class ever. I should wait a bit before speaking up.

"What do you think of the rhythm of the words?" asks Miss Gyre. "You can almost hear the little men marching along, right?"

And waiting time is over.

I sniff. "Little men."

Miss Gyre focuses on me. "What did you say?"

"The men aren't the ones to watch out for," I explain. "The lady fairies are the really nasty pieces of work. That is, unless you're talking about the bigger sorts of fae, like an orc or goblin." I pause, waiting for everyone to pipe up with their agreement.

That isn't what happens. The annoying silence continues.

"What?" I ask. "This isn't common knowledge?"

The humans squirm in their seats. A heavy sense of worry weighs down the air. I get the distinct impression that if they could slink out of the room, they would.

Griff pipes up. "Calla's from New York."

Everyone in the room sighs. "Ahhh."

Now that I've gotten started, it's hard to stop. The only time I have an audience, it's when I'm getting scolded by the Elven High Council. Having rapt listeners who aren't trying to imprison me is a rather nice change of pace. Perhaps they're a little frightened of me, but I can work with that.

"Plus, the Airy Mountains are nowhere near the Rushy Glen."

Miss Gyre pales. "What?"

Clearly, Miss Gyre is dazzled by this new information. Rising, I approach the blackboard. Bilge uses these for mapping out potion ingredients. I know how to write on them, no problem. Gripping a scrap of white chalk, I sketch out all of Faerie.

"The Airy Mountains sit on the left side of the summer realm," I explain. "The Rushy Glen is on the right. Only now, both those areas are hit with blight, so Protector Lazare has technically cut them off from the summer and attached them to Pixieland."

Suddenly, an insight hits me.

"Hold on." I turn away from the board and face my audience once more. "You wouldn't know any of this stuff if you were a hu—"

I cough to cover up the fact that I almost said the word *human*. Good catch.

"You wouldn't know this if you were from Earth," I clarify. "So unless this Allingham guy was taken into Faerie, he wouldn't know the landscape. And if he *did* get dragged out to Faerie, then watch out! Allingham would be a human changeling, which is—" I debate sharing the horrible fate of humans in the fae lands "—something that happens."

There, that statement is generic and accurate. Talking to humans is easy!

"Back on Earth, Allingham would be replaced by a fae changeling. This is an elf who looks just like the human. Which, come to think of it, explains a lot. This author was not a human but an most likely a changeling elf. Mystery solved!"

The bell rings. Everyone stands up so quickly, it's as if their desk seats just caught fire.

"Class dismissed!" announces Miss Gyre.

I purse my lips. That class went quickly. Must have taken me longer to draw the map than I thought.

Griff slowly rises. "That was interesting." His smile seems forced for some reason. I guess it must be hard to see me basically ace *question time* in class when he's been here for so long and didn't answer anything.

Oh, well. He'll recover.

"Gym is next," I explain. "You cannot follow me there." I notice a sticky something has gotten on the bottom of my shoe. It reminds me a little of Griff.

"Don't you need me to guide you?"

"No."

Hanging around might give Griff ideas, so I speed to my next class. This turns out to be interesting in the extreme.

In fact, this particular mini-adventure is so good, it deserves its own page.

- Calla

DAY FORTY AND A HALF

Dear Diary,
  The rest of my day is so kickass, I can't even.
And now...
Orchestra and choir kicks in. Ah-AHHHHH!
...The exciting tale of Calla the Outlaw And The Great Gym Class Banana Prank.
Applause!
It all begins when I enter a small and stinky chamber to change into what are called *gym clothes*, of which I have none. A human girl named Addie offers to lend me something called sweats. I refuse. Whatever games these humans plan to play, I can wear a dress.
Plus, we pixies do not sweat. We glisten.
Across the pungent chamber, a particular girl watches me with interest. The necklace around her throat spells the name Tory. She has shoulder-length black hair and smushed-up features. Beside Tory stands another human girl with brown hair and big sleepy eyes. I decide to call her Snory.
The pair pretend to talk only with each other, but their voices are far too loud for that to be believable.
"Did you see the new girl?" asks Tory.
"I know," replies Snory. "Going to gym class in a dress—What a weird-o!"
"I hear she's from New York," adds Tory.
"That explains everything." Snory giggles. "Don't get near her; you'll catch a disease."

The idea of seeing some nice humans do sweet things is super-interesting to yours truly. But I can hang out in Faerie if I want to see some mean meanies.

Therefore, I shall take you down, oh Tory and Snory.

Our group—about two dozen girls in total—head out to the gymnasium proper. It's a long rectangular box with a painted floor and odd equipment on either side. Our gym teacher, Miss Fran, announces that we are playing touch football today.

Not a problem. I saw this on Griffin's television.

Miss Fran is a pear-shaped lady whose gray hair is styled into a bowl cut. She has a deep voice and smells like some kind of smoke. She stomps up to my side.

"You don't want to wear sweats?"

"No."

Miss Fran eyes me from head to toe. "You're the new girl, eh?"

"That's right."

"Get regular gear next time. You're fine for today."

I like Miss Fran.

We file off into different positions. The nice girl, Addie, shows me where to stand and what part I'll be playing in this little performance. I am something called a line backer and my job is to flatten people.

Not a problem.

Miss Fran blows a whistle.

I quickly pull a fresh orb of ley magic and chuck it to the ceiling. A moment later, two thousand banana peels tumble from the rafters to land right on Tory and Snory. The pair stumble about while trying to regain their footing.

Addie slips up to my side. "How did all those bananas get stuck to the ceiling? I didn't see them before."

"Me, either. So weird. Must be something about the new government food plan and waste disposal."

Yes, I pulled that last statement out of thin air. Thank you, amalgam!

Meanwhile, the mean girl stumbling fiesta continues.

"I hurt my tailbone," says Tory.

"I ripped my thong," whines Snory.

I focus on Miss Fran. "Did I win?"

The double doors at one side of the gymnasium swing open. Griff walks into the room.

"Miss Fran?" asks Griff. "May I have a word?"

Even though Griffin is the student, Miss Fran jogs over to chat him up. They whisper back and forth for a moment before Miss Fran waves in my direction.

"Calla, you're excused!"

I frown. This was really an enjoyable experience. Not sure I wish it to end early.

Plus, I specifically asked Griffin not to step in with teachers and stuff unless I asked him. What a pest.

Glaring at Griffin, I slowly make my way over to him and Miss Fran.

"What's up?" I ask.

"I'm here to give you a tour of the school," says Griff. "Including the basement."

"Oh, right." Now I can't be too upset at Griffin because checking out the basement is indeed the whole reason why I'm here. Even so, it's the principal of the thing.

Griff's shoulders slump. "Did I do something wrong?"

"I thought we'd discussed that I'd let you know if I needed some help."

"Oh!" Griffin bends his knees while tilting his head back. "Ugh, I can't believe I did it again. My bad. Do you want to finish gym class?"

The guy looks so genuinely upset, I can't stay angry. "We can go on the tour." I wave to the teacher. "Bye, Miss Fran. Thanks for letting me play in a dress."

Miss Fran grins. "Griffin is a new senior at the Headless Horsewoman High School. We're all so happy to have him here."

"M'Kay."

Griff and I step out of the gym and into the hallway beyond. "What was that?" I ask. "Everyone keeps saying the same thing about you. Even students."

Griffin sighs. "So odd, right? It's happened ever since I got kidnapped. It's some kind of side effect of being a possible changeling."

I bob my head and consider this. "Guess that makes sense." Not that I know for certain. Griffin is the only human I've ever met who's been to Faerie.

Griff reaches a metal door. "This way to the basement."

We march down some zigzag stairs that open onto a big concrete space. Lots of random stuff stacked against the walls, such as folding chairs and dented doors.

Kneeling down, I press my palms against the floor and check for ley lines. There's nothing. And whatever is in that vault, it's got to be the ultimate source of fae power. That's not here.

So disappointing.

I dust off my hands. This day had been pretty fun so far. English class was a blast. And flattening Tory and Snory? Incredibly enjoyable. But the whole reason I'm here is to complete the Ley Queen's quest. After a lot of running around, I thought for sure that I'd find some answers hidden in the basement.

Yet there's nothing here.

I need to regroup.

Maybe I can cast some amalgams who know about vault building from hundreds of years ago. Or I could conjure some of new wand creation books and see if they have any tips. I've been meaning to build out the library in the Castle of Badassdom anyway. Perhaps a kind of Quest Room could be useful.

"I need to cut today short, Griff."

His features slump with disappointment. "Really? Science is next on our schedule, just so you know. We're dissecting a frog."

"Not appealing." I dissect frogs all the time for Bilge. That's one class I could probably teach. "I've got to fly."

"What about if we—"

At this point, Griff is getting downright clingy. I summon another sphere of magic and toss it at my own face. With a burst of power, I turn invisible.

"Calla? Where did you go?" Griff steps around in a slow circle. "This is so cool."

I unfurl my wings and fly off. Is it a little mean of me to take off without saying goodbye? Maybe. But Griff totally enjoyed the magical disappearing act.

Plus, this is my diary and that means being totally honest. I spent my life alone. I wanted to attend school to be around other kids. Meeting Addie was fun. Taking down Tory and Story was also cool. However, dealing with a clingy Griff is just plain irritating.

I need a break.

While staying invisible, I fly my way out of school. The place remains a total labyrinth, so it takes me a little while to get it right. Along the way, I spy some girls standing in a circle and laughing. Two guys toss a crumpled-up ball of paper over everyone's heads while stepping down the hall. A teacher explains something called the French Revolution to her class. The students hang on her every word.

With every good human interaction I discover, an ache deepens in my soul. By the time I leave school, I want to find my parents so badly, it hurts. Maybe I even have siblings out there, too. And the Ley Queen's inscription talked about finding my family.

Please, let this quest lead me to them.

- Calla

DAY FORTY-ONE

*D*ear Diary,
Dare Adventure Day!

After yesterday's banana-fueled excitement, I thought I'd totally conk out. Didn't happen. I was up and down all night, worried about my big adventure in the Fens with Dare. There are dangerous orcs to be concerned about, sure. And we definitely need to find King Tristan and stop the blight that's killing Faerie. Again, having a diary means being honest. So I'll say this.

I have a bigger problem at this particular moment.

My badass pink leather body armor doesn't fit anymore. I can't zip it up past my stomach. The arms and legs are way too short. And I can't get the thing over my shoulders without doing some kind of backwards contortion.

Clothing spells are a particular type of magic. And they're one I don't know a lot about. For years, I conjured the same stuff—in all the same sizes—and it has always worked fine. Even after I left the ley prison, I could still squeeze into my pink mini-dress. Maybe it rode up a little on my butt. Still, that wasn't too big of a deal.

But I can't go to Dare with my body armor and ask him to repair things like he did with my dress. Mostly because I can't even squeeze into said body armor.

Also, there's a bigger idea at work here. I'm Calla the Outlaw who lives in her own Castle of Badasssdom. I can create a fortress in a fake sky, and yet I can't conjure my own clothes?

Not acceptable.

About 3am, I give up on trying to sleep and work on adapting my spell for body leathers. Turns out, the tricky part is that I have to be honest with myself about what I look like these days.

I spent so many years lamenting that I looked nine. Still, that was part of my deal. I was the little prankster pixie who caused trouble and had a wee little obsession with Prince Dare. Now my body is doing all sorts of strange stuff. And it's more than the clothes.

Time for some *super* honesty here.

Before when I thought of Dare, it was as if he'd been depicted on a great painting with lightning bolts fanning out around him. Thinking about my prince was like contemplating a character from a great epic song. Not that I ever hung around with bards enough to hear them plinkity-plink through their whole shtick, but that's the general idea.

Now thinking about Dare makes my insides get all twisty. An epic poem or song doesn't describe him anymore. I'm at a loss.

And at the same time, my body has decided it wants to take decidedly non-pixie shapes.

And-and I'm kicked out of Pixieland.

And-and-*and* I need to solve the Ley Queen's quest while saving all of Faerie.

Everything is a swirl of change and anxiety that winds down, tornado style, into a single question.

Why can't I fix my stupid body armor?

I cast and recast spells for hours. In the end, the arms and legs don't necessarily match. Zipping up the front means I can't breathe properly. And something pulls my panties into a literal twist. But it covers the important bits and I'm running out of time.

I'm off to meet up with Bilge and Dare.

Opening the ley door in my bedroom, I go straight into the basement of the Pixieland Citadel. The moment I step through, there's something I can't miss.

Bodies.

Delirious winter elves lay across the floor on cots. I count men, women and even a few children in the mix. Dare kneels beside one girl, taking her hand his his while gently brushing the back of his fingers across her forehead. Bilge stands nearby, his plump fists gripping a pair of large vials.

I close the ley door behind me. Soaking in the sight, shock skitters across my skin. "What happened?"

"The blight grows," says Bilge. "Half the citadel is full."

The girl opens her eyes a crack. "If I get better, can I go to your wedding?"

"Of course. You'll be my flower girl."

I catch Bilge's glare. I've known the hobgoblin long enough to realize what that face means. The wedding is still on and he doesn't want me worrying about it.

And Bilge has a point. *Orcs, Calla. Stay focused.*

Dare looks up from the sick child. "I asked Bilge to place some of the winter elves here so they'd be closer to the ley door. That way, I can check on them more easily."

I hug my elbows. "This is terrible."

"Finding Tristan is the best way to heal them," says Dare. "They aren't in any pain, thanks to Bilge."

"Here," says Bilge. "Drink these up." He hands me one vial, then the second goes to Dare.

I eye the swirling brown liquid. "What's this for again?"

"Orcs no smell you… and some other things," says Bilge.

"Good to know." I pull off the stopper and down the sludge quickly. I've been Bilge's potions tester since I was a kid. Over the years, my gag reflex has gotten destroyed.

Beside me, Dare does the same. After a gulp or two, his face flickers between shades of purple and green. To his credit, Dare finishes of the liquid before hopping from foot to foot while making *ack-ack* noises. Bilge and I exchange a sly look. I used to do the same thing when I was little. We called it my *potion dance*.

It takes a little bit for the liquid magic to kick in. A purple glow slowly rises on my skin. The same happens to Dare as well. The shine vanishes, which means the potions are in full effect.

We're off.

Kneeling down, I pull up the mat before the ley door. As always, a smattering of blue cords writhe inside the floor. More are colored gray with blight. The line for the Fens Citadel is knotted with what resembles flowers. I grip the cord, pull it up, and press the line against the door. The gray-blue magic seeps down the wood, showing a view of the Fens as they once were, with lots of trees, flowers and dancing elves.

I pull the door handle. Behind me, Bilge grabs Dare's arm.

"It will guard *it*," orders Bilge. No question what my friend means here. Bilge wants Dare to watch over me.

"Always," says Dare. The way the prince says that single word, it gets my insides squirming again. I set the thought aside and march past the threshold.

This next part involves lots of semi-embarrassing stuff with me and Dare.

Okay, really embarrassing.

- Calla

DAY FORTY-ONE AND A HALF

*D*ear Diary,
 Our adventure begins.

Dare and I step into the Fens Citadel. It looks just like its Pixieland counterpart, only this place is full-on red instead of pink. Old King Tristan colors. One fact hits me immediately.

Hoo-wee!

If I thought the *old man fart smell* was bad up on the Fens' surface? That's nothing compared to what's going on down here.

Three archways lead away from us. Dare shoots me a dry look. "Any ideas?"

It's good to see some of Dare's sass return. This adventure will be tough enough without severe depression hanging over our heads. You have to set things aside—even other elves with blight—and focus on the moment at hand.

Some people call it a short attention span.

I consider it a superpower of being me.

In that spirit, I blink excessively in Dare's direction. "What makes you think I should know?"

"My guess is you've been sneaking through catacombs like these for years."

"True. And I suggest taking the southern arch. That usually leads to the more heavily guarded chambers. You know, where they store the good stuff." I take a step toward the arch in question and pause. "One last thing."

I strike a dramatic pose under the doorway. It isn't easy to look tough

—I am sporting a rather uncomfortable wedgie by this point—but I'm pretty sure I nail it.

"Be on the alert for boobytraps," I warn. "This place was built by summer elves. You know how they can be."

"That I do. Thank you."

I head down the southern passage which branches off to still more hallways. The main corridor is lined with dust. Even so, there's no missing that one set of side passages have old footprints in them.

We follow that faded trail.

With each step deeper into the catacombs, more nervous energy streams through me. Someone—or more like a bunch of someones—marched through here while dragging something along.

Was it King Tristan?

The footsteps end in a square room lined with heavy stone doors and not much else.

"Do you see this?" I point to the floor. "All traces of footsteps have been carefully cleaned out."

"We're being led here. It's a trap."

I rub my palms together. "I do love a good boobytrap."

Behind Dare, a stone door falls forward, ready to squash the prince into a hottie pancake. I rush forward, kick Dare's legs out from under him, and push him out of danger.

Dare lands on his back with me on top of him. There is suddenly a lot of muscly guy under me. My mind blanks.

"Thank you for saving me," says Dare. His gaze turns all super intense again.

"No problem." I can feel his chest moving beneath mine.

"We should get up," I whisper.

An odd light shines in Dare's gray eyes. "You're the one on me."

"Right, right." For some reason, my gaze stays locked with Dare's. This goes on for a really long time before some kind of thought returns to my brain. "Right!" I slide off and stand up.

At this moment, one of my sleeves decides to fall off. Crap. I shove it up my arm in some lame attempt to fix it. Honestly, I'm not thinking too clearly. The Dare-muscle situation still has me very confused. In all my hero-poster imaginings of Dare, his muscles were always way across the room and shooting lightning bolts. It's very odd to have touched them. Sort of.

I keep playing around with the sleeve. Dare maintains his intense stare, and that makes my mind malfunction even more.

"My sleeve is off," I say lamely. "So I'm trying to fix it. That's what I'm trying to do. Fix. It. The sleeve."

Why can't I stop talking?

Dare moves closer. "It looks better now, in my opinion. May I?" He holds out his hand in a gesture that says, *I'll take that sleeve.*

"Sure." I hand it over.

Dare tears the part into leather strips. "Elf warriors choose colors for a particular battle." He ties one strip around his upper arm, then offers another to me "You?"

"Oh. You. Leather. I mean, yes."

With slow movements, Dare ties the strip around my upper arm. Considering how I am now sleeveless, his fingertips brush across my skin, leaving a trail of awareness behind.

The sensation clears even more thought from my head. As it turns out, that's good thing. The emptiness in my head somehow allows me space to figure out our boobytrap situation. Suddenly, I know exactly what happened.

"This room is a prank." I step back to the archway and wave Dare over. Sure, I could grab his hand or whatever. However, seems like a bad idea at this point. My mind seems to be functioning again. I'm in no mood for it to blank out once more.

Dare moves to step by my side. "What is it?"

"Watch this." I cup my hand by my mouth. "Boobytrap."

Another door whooshes open, this time it slams into a nearby stretch of wall. *Slam!* There's nothing beyond the door, though.

"Nice work," says Dare. My heart sparks with the praise. It's nice to have my brilliance appreciated.

I keep going. "Boobytrap. Boobytrap. Boobytrap." The doors swing, slide and slam all over the place. The last one actually opens to a passageway beyond.

The lines of Dares face harden with determination. "I'll go first."

I'd fight him on this, but I just had my boobytrap moment. He can be the hero of the next room.

Dare stalks into the shadowy hallway. It soon opens into a large chamber. As we step inside, enchanted torches flare to life. Four murals line the walls. Above them is written in large script, *the Fall of King Tristian*. The first image shows Reiver stabbing Tristan. You can't see the king's face, which is even worse. Nothing like stabbing someone in the back to prove that you're an ass.

I inch in closer for a better look at Reiver. He looks a lot like Dare, only with small, flinty eyes and scooped-out cheeks. The guy is tall and lean. It doesn't look like Reiver's eaten a full meal in his life. A long scar runs from his eye to his chin.

The second mural shows Halcyon stepping forward to protect his king. I can see why Lotti would like this guy. He's got way too much puffy blonde hair, every strand of which matches his golden armor. A long list of titles are written under his mural.

I step closer and read them aloud. "Halcyon, Explorer of Faerie, Knower of Everything, Master of Glamours, Lover of Elf Ladies, Player of Lutes..." I shake my head. "They missed Lover of Hair Products." I look to Dare. "Is that a spell or do you think Halcyon uses mousse?"

A ghost of a smile rounds Dare's mouth. "Calla."

"Right, right. We're finding King Tristan." By the way, I'm super happy that I can speak in full and coherent sentences again.

The third mural shows Reiver and Halcyon stabbing each other at the same time. The forth and final image shows both of Reiver and Halycon resting in a pool of blood. Dead. Dare pauses before this picture.

I slip up to his side. "Whatever else he did, Reiver was still your brother. This can't be easy."

"Reiver died when I was a toddler. Before that, my brother spent a lot of time on Earth, teaching humans how to raid each other."

Dare's stance firms up. It's as if he's bracing for a blow. I don't know my family. Even so, I always pictured them as loving and kind. I can't imagine getting stuck with a sibling lemon like Reiver.

A shiver runs up my back. Who knows? Maybe my real family is way worse than Reiver. Ack.

"The exit archway is over here," I say gently. Dare nods. Together we move into the largest space of them all. Candle-heavy chandeliers flare to life as we enter. Tapestries made of golden thread line the walls, all of them proclaiming the rule of Protector Lazare. A wide altar sits in the center of the space.

We step closer to the stone altar. As we move forward, our footsteps crunch on broken bits of something.

"That altar had a glass covering on it once," declares Dare.

"That's a standard move in cases like these," I add.

What else can you do when someone is stuck in an eternal sleep? If you just leave them in a tower bedroom or whatever, they get covered in dust and who knows what else? Take Sleeping Beauty, for instance. That chick woke up with a literal rat's nest in her hair.

Long story short, if you care about someone who's under a sleeping enchantment, then you set them up with a combination altar and glass case... and that's at a minimum. Clearly, that was done for Tristan. Which leaves only one explanation for what's happened here.

"Someone stole King Tristan's body," I declare.

"Agreed." Dare lifts his hands. A sphere of white power appears between his palms. "Now let's find out the identity of our mystery thief."

A new voice echoes into the chamber. "Intruders! Find them!"

Every nerve ending in my body goes on alert. I look to Dare. "Did you hear that?" I whisper.

"Orcs are coming." He narrows his eyes. "Are you ready? This isn't like the time we fought lightning toads."

"No way. This will be better." I summon a sphere of my own. "I have so many attack spells planned. Finally, I'll get a chance to use them."

I've had some amazing adventures with Dare, but never a scrape as serious as this one. Strap in, dear Diary, because we're in for a serious ride.

And a new page.

- Calla

DAY FORTY-ONE AND THREE-QUARTERS

*D*ear Diary,
I'm stuck in the fens Citadel with Dare. Using my exceptional stealth abilities, I peep my head to check the hallway beyond. The place is crawling with orcs.

Literally.

Crawling.

These are spider orcs, so they have an extra set of arms and super-sticky skin. This kind of orc even skitter across a ceiling while staying upside down. The rest of their bodies are standard orc stuff: I'm talking hefty form, slimy skin, and excessive piercings. They wear oily loincloths and carry clubs or short swords.

And like all orcs, there are only dudes running around.

Which raises a particular thought in yours truly.

I round on Dare. "I've got an idea for a prank."

"I take it finding the ley door isn't an option."

"Nope. The hallway is too full. And I enjoy a good fight, but not when I can get the job done with a prank."

"Go on."

"You know how I experiment with new spells."

"I do."

"Well, you must also know that there are no female orcs."

"Common knowledge."

Magic spontaneously creates orcs from nasty spots in Faerie. If you leave a stinky bog alone for too long, you'll get an infestation. Personally, I think the lack of females is what makes orcs so incredibly grumpy.

Back to our adventure.

"I've been working on a spell in my spare time where I can glamour up both a male and female orc."

"How will that help? Orcs can scent others of their kind. They'll never believe the glamour."

"Nuh-uh. They'll be so shocked that a female orcs exists, they'll never notice anything else. She-orcs are a favorite myth in their kind. It's like Bigfoot to humans."

"Bigfoot?"

"I haven't been on Earth for long, but I'm learning a lot."

Dare's mouth thins as he considers my plan. "I take it you'll be the female orc in this scenario."

"I've got insider knowledge."

Dare rubs his neck in a slow and contemplative rhythm. "It's too risky. You'll be attacked."

"False again. The others will leave me alone because *you'll* be the biggest, baddest orc of them all."

Dare lets out a low growl. No question what that means. I'm wearing him down.

"This will work and you know it," I declare.

Dare nods. "Let's do it."

I pull in fresh orbs of power and chuck one each at me and Dare. For my part, I transform into a female spider orc. I give myself a little pink dress because even we girly orcs need decent wardrobes. I also have scaly skin, big eyes, and tusks jutting out from my lower lip. My hair stays long, pink and fabulous.

Dare is a super spider orc, what with his extra height and not two, but three sets of arms. He also six spider eyes and pointed teeth. If I were an orc, I'd certainly avoid him.

With our disguises in place, we step into the outer hallway. Dare goes first; I hang back. The regular orcs pause and inspect the amazing glamour I just created. A few of the monsters inhale deeply.

Here it comes.

"Not an orc!" cries one.

"Kill!" adds another.

Now for my big entrance.

I strut out into the hallway. "Hey, boys! It is I, the very first shorc."

"Shorc?" asks Orc Dare.

"She-orc. Shorc. Work with me."

Al the orcs pause and gape. I saunter over to the chamber that holds the ley door. Six orcs stand within.

Sadly, these monsters have ripped the ley door straight off the wall. The thing now lays in pieces on the floor. All the ley lines have been torn up from the floor, as well. Say what you want, no one knows how to destroy stuff like an orc.

No question. We aren't escaping this way.

"Change of plans," I say to Orc Dare. "Let's walk out and across the surface."

"Grr," says Orc Dare.

Together, we lumber toward the exit archway. All these citadels are laid out the same way, so I know exactly where to find the spiral staircase to the surface. As I saunter toward my new destination, I look down my piggy snout at the nearby orcs. "What? Haven't you ever seen a shorc before?"

"Shorc," whispers the crowd.

"That's right. I'm a miracle of orc development."

Orc Dare and I march up the stairs and out onto the stinky Fens beyond. The citadel strikes up from the ground, like a single tooth on a rotten gum line. The rest of the landscape is nothing but orcs in every direction. All of them seem to be staring right at me.

Gulp.

I raise my hands. "Shorc here! That's a she-orc, people. I'm here with my personal bodyguard. Stand aside."

This works until one of the shorter orcs steps forward. Typical. In my experience, it's always the little monsters that give the most trouble.

"You are female orc?" asks Mini Orc.

"That I am."

"Prove it." Mini Orc waves between me and Orc Dare. "Kiss."

I stagger a half step backward. "Kiss?"

The entire orc army takes up the chant. "Kiss! Kiss! Kiss!"

Little by little, I force myself to face Orc Dare. "I guess we could do that. It's better than dying and whatnot. I think."

Orc Dare leans over and presses his lips to mine. Glamours only give the impression of a different form. When you touch, you can sense the true self beneath. All of which means that it's Dare's real mouth that moves so gently against my lips. The touch is both feather soft and intense, all at once. Magic moves within me. Every corner of my soul comes alive.

Mini Orc breaks up the moment. "You no shorc! You faeling!"

Once again, the mob takes up the cry. "Faeling! Faeling!"

Stepping away from Dare, I realize the truth. That kiss was so distracting, it somehow screwed up my glamour spell. Now I no longer resemble a shorc. I'm Calla once more. For his part, Dare is back to being his regular elfy self.

Eek.

Originally, our plan was to march past the army while they worshipped my shorc-ness. Now things have changed.

"Fly!" I call. Unfurling my wings, I take to the skies. Beside me, Dare does the same. A heartbeat later, we're soaring over the massive army.

Below us, the spider orcs get rowdy. Most howl in fury. Some chuck things at us. There are a few clubs and swords that head in our direction, all of them badly aimed. Mostly, the warriors toss handfuls of sludge or rocks in our direction.

Orcs really aren't all that clever. Getting out of confined spaces with them was truly the tricky part.

Once we're well past the army itself, I swoop down, grab a ley line, and form it into a door. Dare and I step through and leave the Fens behind.

We return to the Pixieland citadel and a very worried Bilge.

"It is back." Bilge twists his hands at his waist. "It must help with ingredients."

Normally, Bilge would never chat up ingredients in a situation like this. He'd demand to know how it went at the Fens. The fact that my favorite hobgoblin is asking about potions? The blight must have gotten very bad, very quickly.

"I'll help you, no worries."

"Have more of my people come in?" asks Dare.

"Yes, yes." Bilge waves off Dare before focusing on me. "I have a list of ingredients for it to make and it is—""

"On the blackboard," I finish. "I'll get to it right now."

So that's what I do.

While Dare checks on his people, I head to the potions room and get to work. As I wait for ingredients to boil or sift, I write the latest news in you, dear Diary.

After all, the Great Shorc Adventure is one of my best pranks ever. It deserves to be remembered.

- Calla

DAY FORTY-TWO

$\mathcal{D}$ear Diary,
I work all night on preparing ingredients. After I finish setting up each item, I mark it off on Bilge's blackboard. And since it's me, I also write little comments.

2 sacks of sifted fairy dust? Done.
8 eyes of newt? Gross, but done.
14 pounds of ground-up dragon scales? Done. And my arm is now a limp noodle.

Bilge waddles into the room. "It must go."

Oinky hides behind Bilge's ankle. I know that piggy pose. That's a stance I like to call *the guilty Oinky*. I'm being asked to leave, yet there's more to the story here.

I fold my arms over my chest. "What happened?"

"Poppa and Muti are fine," says Bilge in an over-bright voice. "It should go home."

Bilge is a terrible liar. The fact that he volunteers that Poppa and Muti are well? It means one thing. Bilge is hiding something. Waves of worry chill my soul.

"Where are my parents?"

Bilge rubs his face. "It should go home."

"Where, Bilge?"

"In the basement with the winter elves."

I unfurl my wings, ready to fly off. Bilge steps into my path. "It can't be seen."

"That's over. About a million orcs just saw me at the Fens."

Bilge steps aside. Taking to the air, I speed toward the basement. As I fly along, I'm vaguely aware of the many fairies crammed onto beds and the many more lined up along the floors in corduroy-style rows. Spell books are being used as pillows. Old rugs serve as blankets. About a dozen sprites flit through the air, delivering Bilge's potions. I recognize their faces.

All are friends of Poppa and Muti. Citadel workers, every last one. Most haven't been inside this tower for years. And when they did work here, these sprites helped brew potions and store scrolls, not care for patients. Things are bad if Bilge called them back into service.

It's a short flight to the basement. Even so, it's as if every inch I pass over moves at a glacial pace. At last, I reach the round chamber with its single ley door. A half dozen winter elves lay on frail wooden cots under thin blankets.

Poppa and Muti cuddle on a shared pillow on the floor. Since they are now at full height—which is about six inches tall—the two remind me of lifeless gray dolls. My eyes sting. How long have they been this way?

Pulling in ley power, I press an orb of magic into my chest and shrink to their size. Soaring down, I land between them. Kneeling, I stare at the familiar lines of their beloved faces.

As long as I can remember, my parents have always seemed frail and wrinkly. Yet now, Poppa and Muti's skin are covered in what look like gray bruises. Bands of worry tighten around my throat.

"Poppa, Muti. It's me, Calla." Neither of them move. Their chests rise and fall in an uneven rhythm.

A nurse sprite, Sophie, flits up beside me. Her smooth pink skin contrasts with her silver hair. "It's good you're here."

"When did they come in?"

"An hour ago."

My lower lip wobbles with held-in grief. "How are they doing?"

Her large brown eyes seem to overflow with sympathy. "They are stable. You don't need to worry so much."

Says her.

I tuck their threadbare blankets under their chins. "Aren't there nicer coverlets for them?"

"We're though all the fancy things," says Sophie. "We could cast new supplies, but that magic needs to be saved for the pain medicine."

Sophie flies off. I pull in sphere after sphere of power, trying every spell I could think of to help them. Nothing works. It's all I can do was sit beside them and not cry. To that end, I've taken out my diary to record everything.

Which brings me to the current moment.

While I scribble away, Dare has arrived through the ley door. Once again, he's casual-style prince today in dark pants and shirt. Dare checks on his own elves before standing a few yards away, his steady gaze fixed on me. There's no question why he's waiting.

Dare wishes to take me home.

And there are good reasons to leave.

I can't do anything more for Poppa and Muti at this point. Plus, I still need to find the source of all fae power for the Ley Queen. It's the only way to defeat Lazare and end this blight.

"Are you ready?" asks Dare in his deep and rumbly voice.

"I am."

For now, I close my diary, head home, and keep my parents in my heart. The next page is a picture of a sick elf from the citadel.

I simply can't bear to draw Poppa or Muti.

- Calla

Elf Blight

DAY FORTY-TWO AND A HALF

*D*ear Diary,

Leaving the Pixieland Citadel should be easy. Notice my use of the word *should* in that sentence.

That's not how things turn out.

I select ley lines for my Castle of Badassdom. Instead the door swings wide to reveal the sign for Glover's Hollow. It's nighttime and not raining, so I've got that going for me. Otherwise, one thing is clear. I'm off my game. I haven't screwed up the doors in the Pixieland Citadel since I was nine years old.

Dare follows me to Earth and the infamous Glover's Hollow sign. "I was hoping this would happen."

"Really?"

"Yes. I saw your castle. Now, I should like to explore the forest surrounding it as well." He offers me his arm. "Care for a walk, Milady?"

Every once in a while, Dare acts super formal and courtly with me. What a goofball. Still, I'm game. After all the pain of seeing Poppa and Muti, I could use a little break.

I wrap my hand around his forearm, the way I've seen ladies do at court. Even through his shirt, I can feel the ropes of muscle in his forearm.

Dare and I walk through the forest to reach my tree. Once we get there, a single fact is clear.

There are sneaker marks all over the soil, along with a distinctive logo on the tread.

The Hollow Company.

Kneeling down, I check the markings more closely. *Size 12 and two-thirds.* I haven't been around humans very long, but even I know that's not a standard thing. It must be a special size made especially for Griffin. And why not? He's the heir apparent and all that.

"Who's been lurking around your home?" asks Dare. And if he growls a little, I can't say that I mind.

I rise. "It's Griff. He must've been looking for me."

Dare narrows his eyes. "I do not like this human."

"Hey, he's no worse than Lotti."

Did I say that out loud? You bet, I did.

"She didn't keep her side of the bargain," says Dare. "We have not yet found King Tristan. I shall call our engagement off."

"But it's technically still on?"

"For now. And what about your human? You remain friends despite this odd behavior?" Dare gestures to the sneaker marks as sign of this strangeness in action.

"Sure. He's a little weird; I'll give you that. Going to Faerie made cuckoo things happen around him. Griff just wants to help me out."

Dare chuckles. "I may wish to aid the sunrise, but I realize my assistance is unnecessary. And I'm a fae."

I tap my chin dramatically. "Did you mean to say I'm as powerful as the sun?"

"I most definitely did." Dare leans in closer. "There's something I've been meaning to tell you."

My tongue decides that now is a great time to block access to my throat. *Stupid tongue.*

"Oh?"

"I loved pranking orcs with you today. "

A blush colors my face. *So embarrassing.*

"It's not that big of a deal," I say quickly. "We've fought together tons of times. Never an orc army, but grouchy dragonlings must count for something." That happened when I was twelve. In my opinion, it was one of our best prank battles of all time.

"Over the years, we've often fought side by side." Dare runs pointer finger along my jawline. Everywhere we connect, my skin soaks in the sensation of his touch. When Dare reaches my chin, he gingerly guides my gaze to meet his. "And every time it happens, it means the world to me."

A knot of excitement and terror decides tie itself around my chest. *Panic!*

I take a big step backward and force myself to speak. "Glad we cleared that up. I'll, uh, catch you later. Bye, Dare!"

Rushing forward, I whip open the ley door on my tree and step inside. The last thing I see is the intense stare on Dare's handsome face as I slam the door on him. Turning about, I find myself looking out across my mini realm of awesome. Somehow, I got so flustered I didn't open the ley door in my bedroom. Instead I'm at the main entrance.

For a moment, I soak in the sight of my churning dark clouds. The cascading bolts of yellow lightning. And the thin walkway from my main door to the pointy Castle of Badassdom. Normally, this view makes me smile.

Not this time. Instead, I can only feel a tingle along my jawline. Every spot Dare touched still carries the echo of something I don't even know how to name.

This isn't the first time I've obsessed over what I call a Dare Touching Incident or DTI. Yet this one is different somehow. Before, I was always thinking about that poster version of Dare. This new one is real, warm and somehow terrifying.

Things between us keep changing, and it's all beyond confusing.

- Calla

DAY FORTY-THREE

ear Diary,

Today I slept in.

Way in.

Then I returned to school. Sure, Griff and I checked the basement and all, but it just doesn't feel like enough. I stand in the parking lot, debating my next move, when Addie steps up.

"Hello, Calla!"

I give her a friendly wave. "Hey."

"Are you on your way to advanced math? That's what I have now. Last class of the day."

"Not exactly."

"Too bad you had to leave gym early. Having you around was a blast."

I bob my brows. "I'm always fun."

She giggles. "Everyone is still talking about the banana peel incident. No one will own up to it."

"Well, even more interesting things might have happened if Griffin hadn't arrived."

A glazed look takes over Addie's eyes. "Griffin is a new senior at the Headless Horsewoman High School. We're all so happy to have him here."

"Right."

And creepy.

Best to change the subject.

"If there were something under the school—I mean deep in the ground—how would you get to it?"

Addie's gaze clears right up. "Oh, I'd walk around the greenhouse. There are lots of pits in there."

That perks my interest right up. "Thanks, Addie. I think I'll check that out now."

She frowns. "You aren't going to class?"

I lean in and lower my voice. "It's like this."

"What?"

"The school thing? No."

Addie gasps. "You're skipping?"

My amalgam spell told me about this. Skipping is a big deal.

I have a number of choices now. Telling Addie the truth is an option. An image takes over my mind—me and Addie off on an adventure. Hope sparks in my heart. I might be about to make my first real friend here.

"Question for you," I begin.

"Sure thing."

"What do you think of… fairies?"

"Are some nearby?" Addie pales. "They are such evil little creatures. Is one of them about to knot up my hair? Get it off!"

Guess honest friendship is off the table.

"Nothing's in your hair."

Addie folds her arms over her chest. "Are you skipping or what?"

Which brings me to option number two: *ask Addie to stay silent.*

I scan the parking lot in what I consider to be a super conspiratorial way. "What if I was?"

"I'd have no choice but to report you. Skipping school is a big deal, Calla."

Then again, I could always cast a memory wipe.

One spell, coming up.

I pull up ley lines and twist them into a sphere. Instantly, I notice patches of grey on the cords. The blight is getting worse. All the more reason to check out the greenhouse. I toss the spell at Addie's chest. A moment later, that same glazed look returns to her eyes.

"I remember nothing," says Addie.

"Good news," I state. "You don't want to be late to class."

Addie marches off to math. As I watch her leave, a weight of sadness settles onto my shoulders. Not sure what I expected when it came to other kids, but this is a disappointment.

Ah, well.

I soon reach the greenhouse. It's a single story affair made of sheets of glass. There's no sense of magic around it whatsoever.

Bummer.

A line of topiaries catch my eye. I step inside to check things out. Sure enough, these are just like the ones I saw at the summer palace and masquerade party. They perfectly resemble humans and elves, only in this case, the leaves are anything but green. Each tree is covered in blight. The branches are brittle. Totally dead.

"Calla!" a familiar voices sounds nearby.

Griff.

I raise my hand. "Over here."

Griff rushes into the greenhouse, his face flushed with effort. "So glad I found you. I was so worried sick when I couldn't find you yesterday."

"I'm fine." I gesture toward the topiaries. "What do you know about these?"

"You can see them?" asks Griff.

"Sure."

"No one else can. They showed up right after I left Faerie, looking just like this. I figured Lazare was dumping his trash here."

"He might have been." Griff returned way before the blight got bad. This could just be dead trees, nothing else.

I hope.

"Are these trees what you're looking for?"

"No, sadly enough."

Griff lifts his chin. "If you're done for now, you should show me your lair." His voice takes a decidedly bossy edge. "After you ran off on me at the festival, it's the least you can do."

Anger corkscrews up my spine. I have to show him my home? I owe him things? What the WHAT?

"Here's the line." While glaring at Griff, I draw a pretend border in the air with my pointer finger. "You just went over it."

Griff's blue eyes widen. "I'm doing that thing again, aren't I?"

"Actually, it's multiple things." I count them off on my fingers. "One, you don't order yourself in my home. Two, I owe you nothing. And three, *you* ran off on *me* at the festival."

"Ugh. I did that, didn't I?"

"You did. And now you can go."

When Griff's next speaks, his voice cracks with grief. "I know I act strangely around you. This isn't the first time I've ruined a friendship. Once, I put someone on a pedestal. Her name is Olivia. I came on too strong and drove her away. It was such a loser move."

A long pause follows where Griff stares at the ground and sniffles. Some of my anger melts away. "Hey, it can happen to anyone."

Griff sighs. "I thought things were bad when I discovered that Olivia started dating someone else. But now, it's so much worse. I just found out that she's getting married. Can you believe it? Who gets married at eighteen?"

I force a smile. "Hard to imagine."

There's no point in avoiding the truth. Much as Dare says it's impossible, marrying Lotti could really happen. Then I'd be the not-a-loser wah-wah-waahing my way around random greenhouses, just like Griff.

"May I ask you a question?" Griff hugs his elbows. "It's a little personal, so you don't have to answer if you don't want to."

"Give it a try."

"You still have a palm mark from that guy, Prince Dare."

"Hard to miss."

"I get the feeling he's like your Olivia. Is that true?"

"That *is* too personal."

Griff shakes his head. "I shouldn't have asked that. Maybe we should talk about something else."

"That would be a good."

Griff gestures across the greenhouse. "Are you here to find the Headless Horsewoman's vault?"

"I was. It's not here."

Griff snaps his fingers. "There's another option. The Glover's Hollow Graveyard is nearby. If I were a Headless Horsewoman, I'd bury my vault there. I can help you search."

I glance through the glass walls. Outside the greenhouse, the sun now touches the horizon line. My stomach growls. All of a sudden, my library back at the Castle of Badassdom seems a much better place to be. I'm all about adventure, but meandering around a graveyard at night with Griff? Just no.

"What do you say?" asks Griff.

"I'll pass, thanks," I say. "Good night."

"Sure, whatever you want."

I'm tempted to tell Griff to leave me alone forever, but the human looks so bright eyed and hopeful, I just can't kick him to the curb right now.

But I will later.

- Calla

DAY FORTY-FOUR

*D*ear Diary,

I checked out the graveyard today. The place super cool and spooky with cockeyed headstones plus lots of creepy mausoleums.

Good Things About The Graveyard

One. I visit during daytime.

Two. Griff isn't around. Not directly anyway. Once or twice, I hear his sneakers squeaking nearby. I figure that as long as he isn't clinging too closely, he can do what he wants.

Something has been bugging me about point number two, other than the obvious thing that it's weird to have a well-meaning stalker. Namely, the whole situation makes me wonder something… Do I act around Dare in the same way that Griff seems around me? If so, I'd like to crawl under a rock and hide for a few millennia. Needy and weird is such a bad combination.

The Not-So-Good Graveyard Stuff

One. I don't find anything.

Two. Searching takes up my whole day.

Three. This is getting irritating.

Huh. I'm starting to wonder if this is all a big trick from the Ley Queen. Maybe some kind of punishment for escaping her prison?

When it comes to the fae, anything is possible.
- Calla

DAY FORTY-FIVE

$\mathcal{D}$ear Diary,

This morning, I wake up to the most delicious smell—it's my favorite apple pastries, freshly baked. Once I'm fully awake, I notice a steady knocking, followed by a familiar voice.

"Calla?"

That's Griff all right.

I force myself to stand up and pull my robe more tightly around me. After padding across the floor, I pull open the door a crack.

"Hey, Griff."

"I brought treats." He holds up a small box.

"Thanks." I jut my hand out, grab the container and whip the treats inside. "See you later, Griff."

"One second, Calla. Please?"

Now I could be a mean fairy and just slam the door in Griff's face. But that's rude. And I might never get free pastry delivery again. So I pause and say zero. Griff gets the idea, even though it isn't spoken. *Say your bit and buzz off.*

Griff sets his hand on his heart. "Please accept my apology."

"For what?"

"I try so hard around you and just screw everything up. It's like I told you before—I put you on a pedestal." He huffs out a long breath. "I've been thinking. Maybe seeing another part of town will be interesting. The Headless Horsewoman Festival takes place tomorrow."

A memory appears: my first visit to Glover's Hollow. Arnold the pasty guy told me about the Headless Horsewoman Festival. According to Arnold, his orchards play a big part in the fun. And I am sixteen, after all. A little enjoyment wouldn't be the worst thing in the world. Plus, Griff could be right. Maybe I do need a break.

"When is the festival?" I ask.

"Tomorrow afternoon."

I rub my neck and think things through. "How about we meet at Arnold's Orchards, say around one o'clock?"

Griff beams. "Perfect!"

"Later." I close the ley door. The thought of Arnold's Orchards has me excited. Holding the pastry box against my chest, I march over to my library, which I have now re-named the Quest Room. And it's definitely something to record for posterity.

What's In Calla's Super-Cool Quest Room

One. A tabletop model of Glover's Hollow. I even put little paper ghosts on toothpicks so it looks like they're hovering the graveyard. Detail is very important.

Two. My library corner. This area is complete with nice shelves and wooden bookends of Bilge and Oinky. The books focus on stuff that stores magic, like wands, rings and scepters. If you're looking for the ultimate source of fae power, it's got to be one of those.

Three. The Picture Web Wall. On one wall, I tape up key images and notes. Then I connect them with pushpins and string in order to show possible links. Basically, it turns one wall of my Quest Room into a huge pink spider's web. So there's that.

I plunk onto one of the cushy chairs in my library corner and tear open my box of goodies. While chomping down on the yumminess, I scan all the picture web wall.

Something's missing.

Sadly, I don't have forever to find it.

- Calla

DAY FORTY-SIX

*D*ear Diary,
I don't leave my Quest Room all night. Around 2 am, I add a mini toilet to the library nook. Saves time flying over to my bathing and cleanliness arena.

This place might be a tad overlarge.

Hour after hour, I search for answers. This means casting fresh amalgam spells, sending out summons for new books about wands, and reworking my picture web wall.

Worry weighs on my soul. The truth is somewhere in this chamber. I can sense it.; I just need a missing something-*something* to put it all together.

Before I know realize it, the time has almost arrives for me to meet up with Griff. I debate about bagging on him, but it's not like I'm making huge progress here. Who knows? A change of scenery might be exactly what I need.

After forcing myself to leave my hidey hole, I get myself ready in record time. At one o'clock, I wait by the sign for Arnold's Orchards while wearing a forced smile and my new pink dress.

No Griff.

Considering how this human is my junior stalker, I must admit one thing. I'm surprised he isn't here. To kill some time, I scope out Arnold's Orchards. The place consists of a small red farmhouse atop a rolling hill of green. At the base sits a small lake. Beyond the water, there stretches the neat lines of the apple orchard.

Everything is done up for the festival. Small rowboats circle the lake.

Humans stroll around the orchard, picking ripe apples from the heavily-laden trees. And the rolling green is filled with tents and tables, all selling different wares.

And the humans! Folks wear costumes of all kinds. Many dress up as the Headless Horsewoman and her lover, the Apple Elf.

Wait, Apple Elf?

Where do humans come up with this stuff?

Still, a small tent grabs my attention. In it, a group of humans put on a play about this unfortunate pair. The Headless Horsewoman is first on stage. She wears old fashioned riding gear and yes, she still has a head. Obviously, that must change over the course of the tale. She also rides a cut-out unicorn and has a marionette sprite for a friend.

Considering how this is the backyard of an orchard, these humans do a pretty good job of set design. In fact, the scene is so pretty, I'll stop writing for a minute and sketch out everything.

Art break!

- Calla

Headless Horsewoman

DAY FORTY-SIX AND A HALF

*D*ear Diary,

So that's how the play looks. Pretty fancy, eh? While the design is sweet, the actual play itself is not as awesome. Here's some dialogue.

"Oh, I am the loveliest lady in Glover's Hollow," says the soon-to-be Headless Horsewoman. "How I adore riding my horse."

Technically, it's a unicorn. *Whatever.*

The actress holds a pair of coconut shells, which she now uses to make clip-clop noises as she circles the stage. My mouth falls open in surprise.

The things humans do. Oy.

Pausing, the actress squints to gaze upon something in the distance. "Oh, my. Who can that be wandering under yon grove?"

A guy steps on stage. He wears a green suit, which is not a very elfy fashion choice. However, he has super-pointy ears, which leaves no question about his identity. "It is I, the Apple Elf. Come down from thy horse, fair maiden. Let us walk through the orchards together."

The lady steps forward; the pair kiss. Seeing that smooch makes me wince. Humans really shouldn't get romantically involved with fae. It never ends well.

"Bwah hah hah!" cries the guy. "Goodbye, silly mortal." Sporting an evil grin, the Apple Elf slink-walks offstage.

"Argh!" cries the lady. "I am so miserable without my love. I shall now chop off my own head."

This is a total stumper. How does that self head-chopping work when you have no magic? I know some decapitation spells, but I can't see how that would work for a human. The play doesn't seem as hung up on that point as I am, though. The actress keeps on going.

"Soon I'll be dead and headless." She throws up her arms. "Then I shall haunt Glover's Hollow *forever*!"

The way she drags out the word *forever*, it's clear the play is over. Everyone politely claps. The players come out for a lot of bowing, even after the applause is way over.

Humans. Sometimes, there are no words.

Griff taps my shoulder. "Hey, Calla! Sorry I'm late." He looks to the now-empty stage. "What did I miss?"

At this point, it's interesting to note that Griff—or as I usually consider him, the human bit of gum stuck to my fairy shoe—is now very tardy. That play took a while.

I ignore Griff's question. "What held you up?"

"My parents ordered a dozen new plants for our gardens without telling me. The delivery came this morning. I spent hours finding a place for each one. You can't just leave plants around without grounding them. They'll run away, you know."

I frown. "Run away?"

Griff rolls his eyes. "Silly me. I meant they'll die unless you get them into the earth quickly, that's all."

Not for the first time, I come to an important insight. *Griff is a strange ranger.*

"How about we take a rowboat around the lake?" asks Griff. "I'll pull the oars." He angles his arm in a way to show off his muscles. It works. The guy is ripped.

"I could always cast a spell to propel the boat."

"By why? Magic is precious resource."

"You're making that up."

"Absolutely. I just want to show off." He flexes his arms again.

Here is Griff, displaying his muscles. Inside, I feel zero. Meanwhile, I recently touched Dare's forearm and my soul practically zoomed off to outer space.

"All right," I declare. "You convinced me." Maybe Griff won't seem so gross if we hang out more.

As we walk over to the little dock, the Griff v Dare thing goes around my mind on a continual loop. *Why can't I like Griff?* He's smart and kind. I never spout off nonsense around him. There are no odd questions about whether we should be friends or not. And Griff isn't engaged to another person.

Stupid heart.

We slip onto a small boat. Griff hauls us about the little lake. With every pull on the oars, Griff maintains a steady stare in my direction. I don't even think the guy is blinking. Finally, I can't stand it any more.

"What?" I ask.

Griff pauses from hauling on the oars. "You're beautiful, Calla. You have to know that. Someone should tell you every day." His blue eyes go wide. "Worship you."

Whoa. This certainly went awkward and fast.

I twist my hands in my lap. "I'm not sure what to say."

"Then say nothing. Simply let me gaze upon you."

It hits me that I'm in boat with a stalker turned stare monster and with no easy way to escape.

That's when it happens.

A chill crawls up my neck. Someone is watching me. Twisting, I scan the water's edge. There he is.

Dare.

The winter prince stands at the dock. Once again, he's casually dressed, this time in black jeans, bolshy shoes, and a matching henley. The outfit highlights how Dare's broad shoulders taper to a slim waist. His gray eyes fix in my direction. A smile quirks his lips.

Jolts of awareness move through me. I grin so hard, my cheeks hurt.

Dare tosses a small orb of white magic in his right hand. To the nearby humans, it would look like nothing more than a white tennis ball. He chucks the sphere into the water.

From the impact point, a sheet of ice moves across the lake. Frozen water quickly surrounds our little boat. Crackling sounds as the ice breaks. Dare is dragging our little vessel back to shore.

Griff leans over the boat's edge. "What's happening?"

I shrug. "Looks like a freak winter storm."

"But it's October."

Our boat pulls up to the dock. Dare steps closer. "Hello, Calla."

"Hey, Dare."

Griff's stare flickers between me and Dare. "You." Griff points to the winter prince. "You're the one who marked her palm."

"That's a matter between friends." Dare offers me his hand. His hand looks as big as a dinner plate.

"Right." Griff glares at Dare. "Aren't you getting married?"

I take Dare's outstretched palm. Wherever we touch, a prickle of awareness flares over my skin. I step out of the boat.

"Shall we go for a stroll?" asks Dare.

"I can't believe this," snaps Griff. "Fine. Go off with him. How am I supposed to compete with an elf?"

A nearby human stops to glare at Griff. Sure enough, that guy is dressed up in elfy glory. "What's wrong with being an elf?" he asks.

"Everything," snarls Griff. He climbs out of the boat and stomps off into the crowd.

Now, I didn't say that I would dump Griffin for Dare. After all, I did make plans with Griff first. But seeing Griffin stomp off into the crowd like a ticked-off two year old? It really makes me wonder about the future of our friendship. Because the romantic thing? Not happening.

Griff and I step off toward the orchard. This next part is amazing, so I'll start a new page.

- Calla

DAY FORTY-SIX AND THREE-FORTHS

*D*ear Diary,

Humans mill under the apple trees, filling paper bags with fresh apples. Other parts of the orchard have already been harvested. It's deserted, so that's where Dare and I head off to now.

With every step, my heart pounds harder. Humans talk about how you can be deer who's trapped into staring at headlights. We fae say someone's been stunned by a will-o-the-wisp.

Whatever example you use, that's me right now.

Before I got chucked into the ley prison, all I wanted was for Dare to notice me. In fact, I felt certain it was only a matter of time before he did so. That said, on some deep and secret level, I knew a real relationship with Dare wasn't happening.

Now, things have changed.

For some reason, I'm growing taller and my feelings for Dare are deepening. All of a sudden, the prospect of merely walking around with the winter prince sends me into a freak out.

What's happening to me?

Dare pauses in a small clearing of trees. He lifts his arms with his palms facing upward. White power flows off his hands like so much cascading water. As the liquid magic hits the ground, it piles up higher, ending when it takes the form of a ley door. This particular structure has a curved top and large handle. The entire thing stands alone on the earth, every inch of it made from ice.

Dare grips the handle and pulls the door open. Beyond, I spy a wintry vista that's simply too lovely to be real.

It's a pocket realm.

I pause outside the threshold. "When did you build this place?"

"This morning. Your Castle of Badassdom inspired me."

Grinning, I step through the door and into a landscape made completely of ice. Pine trees tower overhead, their glass-like forms reflecting light from the winter sun. Ice birds arc and dive through the sky, their bodies clear and shimmering. The air is crisp with the clean smell that only winter can deliver.

We step into an open stretch of snowy ground. Like my hall of conquests, Dare has created statues. I pause before the first one. It shows young versions of me and Dare as we battle three dragonlings in order to rescue my shoe. That was fun. Dragons will hoard everything and that was my favorite pair of shoes at the time. No one got hurt and my footwear was returned with only a few chomp marks.

Next there's a massive statue of Princess Pampertoes in all her flying dog glory. There's even one of the Shorc adventure. Beams of clear sunlight dance through the ice sculptures, giving the place a reverent feel.

Each ice creations shows one fact, over and over. Dare and I are a team. We have been for years. Bit by bit, my panic eases. Whatever the future holds for me and Dare, we're friends, first and foremost.

We walk through the clearing and say little. At some point, we both decide to return to the task of finding King Tristan, booting Lazare, and ending the blight.

Dare walks me back to my home tree. We say our goodbyes—it's far less awkward this time—and I head straight for my Quest Room again. As I settle in to my library chair, I come to an important decision.

I must cut Griff loose. I don't want to be the Apple Elf to his Headless Horsewoman.

I've got enough to worry about as it is.

- Calla

DAY FORTY-SEVEN

*D*ear Diary,
More hours get spent in my Quest Room.

Yet I make less progress on finding the ultimate source of fae power.

All the while, Griff keeps knocking on my door and offering apple treats. He's back to saying he's sorry for being such a loser. It's super distracting.

Time to cut him loose.

Sadly, I know what it's like to be really into someone who—let's face it—is still technically engaged to someone else. Even so, the sooner I set Griffin loose, the faster he'll find someone who really cares for him.

Maybe.

Possibly.

Some girls like clingy, right? Griffin will be fine.

I wait until after dinner time to fly my invisible self over to Griffin's house. It's just as I remember—a massive mansion with lots of stucco and columns. After making myself viewable again, I ring the front doorbell.

No one answers.

Voices echo from around the back of the house. Maybe Griff is out there. I step around to find a grid of formal gardens. The voices grow louder. As I get closer, I see who is talking.

The trees.

Or more accurately, the topiaries.

I step closer. "Hello?"

Silence.

I remember the topiaries from Lazare's palace. They'd seemed to speak. Later, I saw some in the greenhouse by the high school. They were totally dead, so they didn't say a word. These seem pretty green and lively, though. Still, if they're here on Earth, it's likely they're inanimate objects that got charmed into having a magical life. It's like what happened in the story of the sorcerer's apprentice. Only instead of charmed-up mops, this situation is all about intricate trees.

I inch closer. "I'm Calla and I'm a pixie. I won't hurt you."

Just like back at Lazare's palace, these trees are shaped to look like humans. One is set apart from the group. I approach slowly.

"I heard what happened," I say in a soothing voice. "Griffin was taken to Faerie. Most times, when humans visit the fae, they never return. When Griff came back, he dragged some magic along with him. That's how you got here. It must be very upsetting to suddenly have magical consciousness."

I slowly circle the topiary until I can look at it straight on. What I see shocks me.

I know this face.

It's Griffin.

"Why would you look like..." I can't speak the name out loud. It's simply too unbelievable.

"Ruuuuuun," says Green Griffin. His voice is reedy and high, reminding me of tall trees rustling in the wind.

"Not a chance. I'm staying right here until I figure this out. Did someone charm you to look like Griffin?"

"Nooooo."

So this isn't an inanimate tree that got charmed into having a magical life. That leaves another option. "Are you fae?"

"Huuuuman."

I take a half-step backwards. Every inch of my body goes on alert. All those threads I'd been criss-crossing on the wall of my Quest Room... for days, they've been nothing but pink decoration. Now one of the patterns becomes clear.

"You're the real Griffin, aren't you?"

"Yeeees."

"So the guy I've been talking to is a actually fae changeling, just like that poet from English class. Changeling Griff came here to replace you. Meanwhile you were supposed to stay in Faerie and become a slave." I shake my head. "Only you aren't in Faerie. Someone turned you into an enchanted topiary and left you here. Why would anybody do that?"

"Ruuuuuun."

At last, I hear what Green Griffin is talking about. The real Griffin—

or what I actually suspect to now be the elf changeling version of the guy —is coming this way.

"I wanted my order yesterday," snarls Changeling Griffin. No doubt, he's talking on one of those hand-held human devices. "I do not tolerate failure. Your business will be destroyed before the sun sets tomorrow."

This isn't the sweet guy who sticks to me like a human barnacle. He's a mean dude.

At this point, I don't need Green Griffin to warn me again. I cast a quick invisibility spell, unfurl my wings and take to the skies.

If the Griffin I've known is really an elf, then there is one way to be sure. I fly over to Glover's Hollow and return to the spot where I'd first opened a pit in the asphalt. Soon I stand before the brick wall that has stopped me before. Now, an intricate red door sits in the brickwork. Three words are written upon it in glowing yellow letters.

Open At Midnight

My breath catches. This isn't what I saw before. There wasn't a door at all. Kneeling down, I touch the earth. Sure enough, the pulse of ley lines moves beneath my fingertips. That was blocked before as well.

Memories appear. Back when I visited the Ley Queen, she warned me that I had to do this quest on my own. No fae could come along to help. If Griffin is really an elf changeling, then his very presence would prevent me from finding what I needed.

A sinking feeling moves down my rib cage. That would mean changeling Griffin has known all along what I wanted. He hasn't been following me around because he's lovesick.

Changeling Griff has been blocking me from finishing my quest to find the ultimate source of fae power.

What an ass.

Bile crawls up my throat. This can't be right. I like Griffin. Trust him. There simply must be another explanation.

I fly off to the graveyard. The moment I land, one thing is clear. Every mausoleum is marked with a red door that says the same thing.

Open At Midnight.

Now, I'm just on a mission.

Next I visit the high school basement of the high school. Another door sits on the wall there with the very same words upon it.

There's no avoiding the truth.

The guy I know as a human named Griff is actually a fae.

And not just any fairy, but a totally evil dickhead who's been actively trying to ruin my life. And more than my existence is on the line, too. Because of Changeling Griff, the blight is getting worse. Poppa, Muti, and many more fae suffer more by the hour. No doubt about it.

Changeling Griff is going down.

My hands ball into fists. I unfurl my wings, ready to take to the skies, track Changeling Griff down, and pound him. I rise a few yards from the earth before I realize one fact.

That would just be playing into the evil fae's plans.

This has all been about keeping me from whatever is behind those red doors.

Focus, Calla. Changeling Griff later. Door now.

I plunk down before the greenhouse. If I'm right, these doors only appear if I'm around and alone… and they all lead to the same place. Only fifteen minutes remain until midnight, but that's enough time to summon Dare using the connection on our palms. I speak into my palm. The light glows white.

No reply.

Not even a pulse.

Zero.

Not that I blame him. Most likely, Dare is dealing with more cases of winter elf blight. Of course, I can pass through this door at midnight, but I'd still like to talk to my best friend first.

All of a sudden, fifteen minutes stretches before me like a never ending timeline. Waiting by myself seems like a horrible idea.

So I consider opening a ley door to Bilge. But that hobgoblin has more than enough to do with helping everyone who's been struck by the blight. And what could he get done in fifteen minutes anyway?

No, my best option is to sit here, write in my diary and *try* to be patient.

- Calla

DAY FORTY-EIGHT

*D*ear Diary,
            Almost 12 am.

Moonlight reflects off the glass panes of the greenhouse. The starry sky arches overhead. Moments tick by, each one bringing me closer to midnight. Silence presses in around me.

Midnight strikes.

The red door swings open.

Past the threshold, there is only darkness. Rustling sounds. A pair of luminous pink eyes stare up at me from the shadows. Something about the size and shape brings back a memory.

I step closer.

As my vision adjusts to the dim light, I find a baby pink llama staring up at me. This is the same costume I wore at the masquerade.

What a stumper.

This doesn't look like ultimate source of all fae power. I blink, wondering if there's some kind of magical cloaking spell at work here.

Nope.

I'm still face to face with a llama.

And not just any animal, King Tristan's childhood pet... Who for some reason is hiding in a magical underground vault.

For a full minute, all I can do is stand on the threshold and stare. The baby llama prances around in a circle. Without saying a word, it tells me that it has all the answers. The creature takes off into the shadowy hallway.

I follow.

With every step, my mind races, trying to figure out what's really going on. Maybe this is some kind of underground menagerie of magical animals? Perhaps they're super-powerful llama monsters who shape-shift and control everything while still looking cute, small and harmless?

I could get into that.

I follow the little llama deeper into the narrow stone hallway. The passage opens into a chamber. For days, I've been thinking this is a vault.

It's not.

The stone passageway ends in a pocket realm. Instead of the Castle of Badassdom, this magical space is a nighttime forest. Willow trees encircle a large pond. Purple fireflies dance through the air. The grass lies thick beneath my feet. A gentle breeze rustles my hair.

Excitement speeds through my limbs. Something in here is the ultimate source of all fae magic. I just need to find it.

The llama nips at the hem of my dress, dragging me forward. I get the idea. And since this is my favorite dress, I make sure to follow the llama more closely.

The little pink creature pauses before a bed of fresh pink flowers. And atop that pallet lies a figure I never thought I'd find in the this vault.

King Tristan.

The baby llama trots over to the sleeping king's side. The animal nuzzles Tristan's hand before laying down before the nest of flowers. Clearly, this is the place where the magical llama spends most of his time.

With hesitant steps, I move closer to King Tristan. He wears red silk robes. Long white hair hangs to his shoulders. A perfectly trimmed mustache and beard frames his long face. His chest rises and falls in a steady rhythm.

The sight is so unexpected, my mind blanks.

Tristan isn't the source of all fae power, is he?

There's no doubt he was a powerful king. But if the guy was the ultimate in fae power, Tristan would never have gotten himself sent to eternal sleep by Dare's stinker of a brother.

That's when I notice them.

All the flowers that make up Tristan's bed are apple blossoms. Every blooms appear perfectly fresh and alive.

And each one has exactly seven petals.

These aren't just any apple blossoms, they're the very same ones from Arnold's Orchards.

Memories appear and realign. There's the story of the Apple Elf and the Headless Horsewoman... the statue in the Glover's Hollow town square that resembles the Ley Queen… and the way I wield ley power with ease.

The baby llama rises to cuddle against my side. A chill runs up my back as the answer to the quest appears to me in a flash.

I now know exactly what is the source for all fae power.

All that remains is telling the Ley Queen.

Well, and trying to cast a few spells and wake up King Tristan. It's a long shot, but I'm a thorough gal.

So I cast some of my own special creations for the occasion. There's the Owl of Alertness, who lands on the king's face, hoots, and transfers some of the bird's inner energy. Not a good choice. The owl scratches Tristan's nose. That will heal quickly, for sure.

Hopefully.

Possibly.

Actually, I have no idea. King Tristan could spend all eternity with claw marks on his nostrils.

I move on to other spells, all of which have particular names because I made them up and that's how I roll. There's the Blue Mist of Vigilance, Sparkly Shower of Magical Action, and Enchanted Rooster Call Of, *Wake Up Already.*

Nothing works. I knew it was a long shot. Still, the Owl of Alertness was really cute.

I motion to the baby llama. "Want to leave with me?"

The animal returns to its spot at the king's bed of flowers. Which makes sense. They've been together since Tristan was a child. And honestly? This pocket realm is a pretty sweet place. It's the type of fantasy built to keep n enchanted someone very comfortable without a glass covering or anything. If I were a llama, I'd hang out here. Especially if magic meant that I didn't need stuff like water or food.

After waving goodbye to the baby llama and its fully-grown friend, I take off through the exit passageway.

Thus ends my adventure with the Ley Queen's so-called quest to find the ultimate source of fae power.

What happens next is even more surprising than meeting a baby llama in an underground forest. In fact, this is one story that definitely requires a separate section.

- Calla

DAY FORTY-EIGHT AND A HALF

*D*ear Diary,

The moment I step through the red door, the appearance of the fae door vanishes. The greenhouse becomes merely a glass structure again.

Crickets chirp. The heavy smell of wet grass hangs in the air. The moon hides behind a dark cloud. It's all here, yet none of it seems real.

Did I truly just walk though a fae door and find King Tristan? That's some freaky stuff. It's also what Dare's has been after for ages.

On reflex, I check my palm once again. The white magical line still glows on my skin. There's no pulse that shows Dare has received my message. A fresh sense of worry winds through me.

I shake it off. Dare is a big guy. A really large dude, as a matter of fact. The Ley Queen was very clear that I must finish this quest without fae help in general, and Dare's in particular.

I'm going it alone. For Poppa and Muti.

Straightening my shoulders, I get to work. Kneeling down, I grab a fresh ley line from the earth. Pulling the magical cord up, I wind it into a ley door. As I form the shape in mid-air, I imagine the portal opening right into the Ley Queen's palace. Within seconds, a glowing blue door stands before me.

I pull on the handle. The door opens to reveal my ex best friend, the infamous Spaghetti Man.

"Hello, Calla." He steps back and motions for me to enter. "Come inside."

I march into the Ley Queen's palace. The magical door slams shut behind me. "Take me to her, please." There's no question who I'm talking about here. The Ley Queen.

"She's away from the palace now," explains Spaghetti Man. "We expect her to return in the morning. I've your old room prepared for you."

This raises some big questions for yours truly. Namely, how much do I want to hang out in an all-blue room?

How I, Calla, Should Spend My Precious Time Right Now

One. Confronting Changeling-Griffin. This guy is a nasty piece of work, pure and simple. I need to let him know that it's not okay to d0... whatever it is that he's been up to.

Two. Check on Poppa and Muti. What is up with them? Do they need more medicine? No doubt, they could use a fresh pillow by now.

Three. Find out what's up with the rest of Faerie. I should connect with Bilge and get news on the blight.

Four. Discover what's happening with Dare. He's still not answering my summons.

Five. Wake up King Tristan. Sure, I tried some spells in the vault. And not only did the king end up with claw marks on his nose, but now there's also a thin layer of blue dust and pink sparkles all over him. Definitely need a new direction there.

Six. Face the Ley Queen. Of all these, this one's the most life shattering. All of which is why I'm actively ignoring it. That human stuff about adoring diamonds is total bunk.

Denial. Now *that's* a girl's best friend.

"See you later. I'll just come back in the morning." Turning around, I find my ley door has vanished. *Dang.*

"I am instructed to say that if you try to leave, then you shall experience the spell of binding again."

"Good to know." I give Spaghetti Man my sweetest smile, because it's always good to grin at people before you totally ignore their advice.

Here's the deal. The Ley Queen can take her spell of binding and kiss my little pink butt. Kneeling down, I pull up fresh ley cord.

This is me, leaving.

That's when bands of owie-ow-ow tighten around my rib cage. I freeze, trying to pull in a breath. Pain radiates through my torso. *Woo-eee!* I forgot how much this hurts.

I drop the ley cord like it's a poisonous snake.

Who happens to be on fire.

All while excreting acid.

The moment the ley line is released, my chest loosens up. I pull in deep breaths once more. Spaghetti Man steps up beside me.

"That would be the spell of binding." Spaghetti Man follows that up with a sweet grin. Or as sweet of a smile as you can make when your face is basically a pile of string art.

"I got that."

"Shall I show you to your room?"

"No choice, huh?"

"Correct."

"In that case, it sounds like a plan."

Spaghetti Man leads me through the Ley Queen's Palace. It looks the same as last time—a lot of bright blue stone with matching tapestries and stuff. My room remains unchanged as well. Spaghetti Man drops me off and steps away.

I give him all of five minutes before I push open the door a crack.

Sure enough, Spaghetti Man is outside.

"Leave the room and you'll regret it." He adds a smile again and you know what? I was totally right. Grinning while you say mean things does soften the blow, even if you have a super odd face.

"Just checking."

"I shall have some elf wafers sent to your chambers," says Spaghetti Man. "You must be hungry."

I smack my lips, thinking about how all the saliva in my mouth gets sucked off into oblivion the moment those super-dry wafers hit my tongue. Still, it's the thought that counts. "That would be nice, thanks."

And I shut the door again.

Which beings me to the present moment. I now sit on the bed, my coverlet dotted with crumbs from a filling meal of elf wafers. An empty jug of water waits on a nearby side table. I've written down my latest adventures and have yet to hear from Dare.

Nothing left to do but try to sleep. Honestly? I'll probably spend lots of quality time sprawled out atop my very blue comforter while staring at the ceiling.

At least I can breathe.

- Calla

DAY FORTY-NINE

*D*ear Diary,

While I wait for the Ley Queen, I eat my weight in elf crackers.

Twice.

And I've spun through everything I've learned lately. No new insights appear. If anything, I'm only making myself super-anxious while over eating the equivalent of saw dust.

Finally, the Spaghetti Man knocks on my door once again. "Come along, Calla."

At last.

Spaghetti Man guides me through the labyrinth of hallways that make up the castle. With each step forward, my pulse speeds faster. Yesterday, I'd placed confronting the Ley Queen dead last on my list of stuff to do.

Now my denial skills are failing.

A dream-like haze clouds my mind. Everything in the Ley Queen's castle seems merge together into a great blue smudge.

Spaghetti Man leads me back to another work room. Like the one I visited before, it's a blocky chamber made of blue stone. The floor is mostly open. Inside the gap, magical blue lines criss-cross within the open pit. The Ley Queen stands still as a statue, her gaze locked onto the churning mass of threads. Every so often, she raises her hand. A gray thread zooms up from the pit to her palm. She clenches her fist and the line vanishes.

The Ley Queen's movements are hypnotic. Every flicker of her fingers captures my attention. I don't notice Spaghetti Man leaving a gentle noise echoes through the room.

Click.

The door shuts behind me.

We're alone.

A ball of panic tightens my throat. *This is it. I'm here.* I straighten my back and say the two words that sum up everything I've learned.

"Hello, Mother."

A long pause follows. The air turns heavy with anticipation. I maybe pee a little in my panties. Good thing there's a spell for that.

Inch by inch, the Ley Queen raises her line of vision. Her blue eyes lock with mine.

The moment freezes inside my soul. All my life, I thought I was a faeling who'd been rescued by the Ley Queen. It explained my power with ley lines. But that never made complete sense because I'm super charged with power. Traditionally, faelings can barely scrounge up enough fairy dust to fill a thimble.

I'd spent so many hours imagining my human parents that I never considered being related to anyone in Faerie.

The silence stretches on. What will happen? Am I right?

While bowing her head, the Ley Queen intones a single word. "Daughter."

And that's it. The confirmation I'd been waiting for. And also dreading. And also-*also* super-confused by.

I really miss the denial stage.

"What did you discover?" she asks.

My legs go watery beneath me. "I found my father. I discovered King Tristan."

The Ley Queen's face turns annoyingly unreadable. "And what makes you call him that?"

"Dare and I found the place where the sleeping king had been placed. The Fens Citadel. Someone stole Tristan from there and moved him over to Earth. And not just any place in the human world, but a pocket realm that's a lovely nighttime forest just like the summer lands."

"That doesn't make Tristan your father."

She's not making this easy on me. Thanks, Mom.

"I heard about the legend of the Headless Huntress and the Apple Elf. That's you and Tristan. Your love was a secret. You met on Earth at what's now Arnold's Orchards. It's why you placed apple blossoms around Tristan's resting place in the pocket realm."

The Ley Queen nods slowly. Her eyes line with tears as she speaks.

"Tristan has no wife. Not officially anyway. There's no declared heir. We never saw it as a risk. I suppose love was all we focused on."

This is sweet to know, by the way. I don't think I've ever heard the word *love* spoken so genuinely by an elf.

The Ley Queen sighs. "When Reiver attacked Tristan, it gave Lazare the chance to take the throne. That's all he wanted."

This news spins through my head. More strands on my web wall connect and align. "I see it now," I say. "That's why you hid me with Poppa and Muti. It's the reason you told Bilge never to let me learn ley magic. You wanted to protect me."

The Ley Queen nods once more, and the movement is both regal and heartbreaking, all at once. "You are the only of your kind. I have never taken a lover. Only your body combines royal summer fae power with the unique properties of ley magic."

"I don't understand. If I'm so powerful, why would you think Poppa and Muti could protect me better than you?"

"Sometimes a solid and simple cloak hides the best," answers the Ley Queen. "When I lost Tristan, it erased the very star that guided my life. It was all I could do to wake up and check the ley lines that weave our worlds together. I didn't trust that I could protect you properly as well. So I hid you instead."

More strands of the story align in my mind. "You also used magic to hide me, didn't you?"

"Meaning?"

"You placed a ley spell on me to hide my appearance. When I escaped your prison, the spell got torn away. That's why it felt like my skin was peeling. Ever since I left, the spell has been broken. I'm now growing into my true form." My eyes widen. "I'm an elf."

A sad smile rounds my mother's lips. "You remind me so much of Tristan now. The way you carry yourself. How your presence bursts into a room. Of course, your mischievous side was always from him."

My mouth falls open with shock. "Tristan is a prankster?"

"When you got to know him." A wistful look shines in her eyes. "Do you know why I sent you on this quest?"

"You wanted me to find the source of all fae power."

"And what is that?"

My voice cracks as I say the next word. "Love."

The Ley Queen steps up and envelops me in her arms. "That's right."

This hug.

That word.

Love.

It means everything to me that being a good person is what my birth other sees as the greatest force open to any fae. True, she had me go on a weird quest to discover that fact, but she's fae. Logic isn't our strong suit. Also, she can see the future, so there's that.

I lean into her shoulder. "Everyone says Tristan died because he was too kind."

"Tristan is a pure soul. It's the way he stole my heart. The man held nothing but goodness in every corner of his being."

I soak in this moment greedily. My father is a good fae. And this woman holding me right now? She is my mother and has always loved me. Sure, she sent me to other people to raise me, but she did that for my own protection. Plus, if you're choosing parents, you could do much worse than Poppa and Muti.

"Know this," says the Ley Queen. "There isn't a day that passed where I did not think of you, or wonder if I did the right thing."

As she speaks, the Ley Queen keeps her arms around me as she gently sways from foot to foot. I'm being rocked for the first time. My heart wants to soak up this embrace forever, but there's still too much I need to know. It's hard to get questions answered when you're snuggling into someone's shoulder. I break the hug and step back.

"I have about a million questions. We need to wake up Tristan. He stopped the blight before. Once the true king is awake, he can heal everyone again."

Turning, the Ley Queen focuses on the churning blue lines in the floor. She stops being my parent. Instead, her features transform into a smooth and unreadable mask.

Goodbye, Mother.

Hello, Ley Queen.

This is a big change, and it's more than a little sad. I just found my mother, and I'm not ready to let go of that yet. All of which is why I'm setting side the next page so I can draw a picture of how the Ley Queen looked during this precious conversation. If I get the expression right, I'll record the caring woman who hid her own baby for only one reason: protection.

Thank you, Mother.

- Calla

The Ley Queen

DAY FORTY-NINE AND A HALF

*D*ear Diary,
    When we last left my life, I'd just confirmed the identity of my birth parents. Not only that, but I'd also tracked down my birth mother and got a hug.

All too soon, the Ley Queen is back to working her blue lines and acting super mysterious. It's tempting to ask one of the two dozen questions whizzing around my brain, but I think she needs a minute.

Maybe I do, too.

"There is one problem with seeing the future," the Ley Queen says at last. "You must choose the thread of that holds the most weight, not the one that is closest or easiest. Do you know what I mean?"

"I can guess. By saying, *the thread that holds weight,* you mean that you choose a future path that's strong, even if it is tough. In other words, I'll soon have to do some stuff I hate."

"Correct."

"Whatever this unpleasantness is, does it all end with the blight over and Tristan free?"

"Possibly. Eventually."

That answer isn't exactly making me jump for joy. Still, this is the Ley Queen doing the talking here. If anyone knows my next step, it's her.

"There's a reason I was not here when you arrived," says the Ley Queen. Reaching into the folks of her dress, she pulls out a small golden envelope. "I was looking into a certain matter that determines the next thread you must follow."

I scope out the envelope. It's gold. That's Lazare's fave color. Which means one thing. This won't be a happy fun message. I take the envelope, tear it open, and read.

You are cordially invited!
Please join us for the wedding of
Princess Lotti Manare Solaris Beauchamp La Silva, first born daughter of
Protector Lazare
and
Prince Darius of the Winter Realm.
Sunset on the night of the summer star.
The new summer palace.

I have to read the thing three times before coming to a serious conclusion.

"Dare isn't really marrying Lotti." I nibble my lower lip. "I think."

"The eve of the summer star falls in two days' time," declares Mother.

On a side note, it's really strange to write the word Mother (with a capital M and everything) in actual sentences here. For most of my life, people had names and roles that were basically written in stone. Muti is Muti. The Ley Queen is an aloof chick who handed me off years ago. Maybe I'll call her Queen Mother? That's weird too. Guess she's staying the Ley Queen for now.

But I digress.

"There is another matter I wished to discuss," adds She Who Needs A Name. "I reviewed the guest list. You recently saved a human from becoming a slave changeling to Lazare. That same boy is attending the wedding. Griffin Hollow."

"He's not human; he's an elf changeling." I hand the message back to the Ley Queen. "And he's next on my list of *stuff to take care of*. It's time Changeling Griffin and I had a heart to heart."

A look of worry cinches the Ley Queen's face. "That is the path you must take. It is the strongest thread."

"I've talked to Changeling Griffin many times. I'm not worried."

"Do not be so certain. Ley magic is dynamic and unpredictable. For example, the ley prison has already adapted to close your last means of escape."

"You don't plan to lock me up again, do you?"

"Know this. Once you leave my castle, we can not see or speak to each other until I determine you have reached the end. That is how the thread unwinds."

I raise my pointer finger. "I can't help but notice that you didn't say anything about me and the ley prison thing."

The Ley Queen returns her focus to the shifting cords below. I guess that's Mother-talk for, *figure it out on your own.*

"Before I go, I really do need some answers. Did Tristan ever tell you how he stopped the blight?"

No response.

"Do you have any spells that can release my summer magic?"

Still nothing.

"Is Dare all right?"

By this point, all the silence is getting irritating. I frown. "Can you tell me anything at all?"

"Yes," replies the Ley Queen. "You must leave. Now."

I can't help but wonder—*would a human mother kick me out now?* Probably not.

That said, a human wouldn't see the future, so that's a definite factor here. Also, my Fae Mommy Dearest is a big fan of corporal punishment. So not only am I getting unceremoniously booted, but there could also be some super-uncomfortable chest-squeezy action if I stay behind.

Even so, would I trade the ability to see the future for a more typical mother? No idea. And there's no time to wonder about that kind of stuff anyway.

I've got to go.

After pulling up some of my own ley lines, I fashion a door and exit out onto my classic spot on Earth—the sign for Glover's Hollow. Taking to the skies, I fly off in search of Changeling Griffin.

Dang, but this next part turns into a total *thing.*

- Calla

DAY FORTY-NINE AND THREE-FORTHS

*D*ear Diary,
Thus begins what I officially call the... Find Griffin Fiesta.

To start my search, I speed my sweet self over to Headless Horsewoman High. It's school hours, so Griff should be around.

He isn't.

I ask a few students where to find Griff. All I get is the repeated response.

"Griffin is a new senior at the Headless Horsewoman High School. We're all so happy to have him here."

Before, I totally bought Griff's story. What a bunch of bull. Visiting Faerie made his human life chock full of weirdness.

Right.

Now I see the truth. Changeling Griff was casting spells on all these humans.

Was he even going to school at all? One way to find out.

Taking to the skies, I zoom over to Griff's mansion. Along the way, I pull in fresh ley magic. By the time I reach my destination, I grasp a sphere of power in each hand. No way am I facing this guy without some magical ammo.

I swoop past the gardens. Even since my last visit, a dozen new topiaries have been added. I shiver. What has Changeling Griff really been up to?

As I close in on the mansion, I spy my target. Changeling Griff waits inside his living room. He lounges on a leather couch and watches one of the human ball games he showed me before.

Was it only weeks ago that I curled onto that same couch? At the time, my biggest shock was all the crazy things that thirsty humans would do with urine. Now, I'm confronting an elf in disguise.

I toss one of my spheres of power at the window, making the glass pane disappear. In such situations, it's important to make a big entrance. Therefore, I land on the living room floor, blocking Changeling Griff's view of his screen. At the same time, I pull in a fresh sphere of power into my hand. I'm staying prepared.

Changeling Griff lifts a little black thingy. Pushing it, he turns off the screen before him. If he seems shocked that I just erased his living room window and landed on his carpet, the guy doesn't show it.

I toss up and catch the spheres of power in each of my hands. "You're an elf changeling who took the human Griffin's place. *That's* why you said you forgot what it's like to be in a car for the first time. You has that experience yourself when you first came to Earth from Faerie."

"So?" He shrugs. "Swapping with humans—it's what our people do. Not that you're really one of us, faeling. Count yourself lucky I was forced to befriend you at all."

My thoughts whir through his words.

You're not really one of us, faeling.
Count yourself lucky I was forced to befriend you at all.

Someone else had said that exact same thing to me. And that person would be Lotti the Snotty Potty. She snapped that phrase in my face back at the masquerade. It's unusual wording, too. Maybe Lotti and Changeling Griff hang out in the same circles.

I nod to myself, deciding I'm on the right track. Most likely, Lotti and Changeling Griff belong to the summer court. Next there's the whole *forced to befriend you* line. Only one summer elf is powerful enough to order around a summer noble. And that particular elf happens to hate my guts.

Lazare.

My eyes widen. Lines of fact realign and connect. Realizations appear. All of a sudden, I know the identity of this mystery elf.

"You're Halcyon."

"That can't be," says Guy Who Is Totally Halcyon. "Dare's brother murdered the Captain of King Tristan's guard."

I recall the murals on the walls of King Tristan's first resting place in the Fens. There was nothing about the great things Tristan did as king, such as they way he ended the last blight. Nope. Instead, way too much effort went into showing how Halcyon had bravely fought to protect King Tristan.

That's what humans call, *spinning the truth.*

More strings of memory appear. Together, they loop into a bigger picture. I point right at Halcyon's nose. "All three of you attacked Tristan. You, Lazare and Reiver."

Halcyon breaks out into fits of laugher. With every guffaw, more of his glamour spell falls away. Short red hair gets replaced by long blond locks. A slim and wiry frame gets an extra six inches of height. Jeans and T-shirt are swapped out for golden armor. The matching golden helm sits beside him on the couch.

That's Halycon, all right.

Turns out, the murals in Tristan's first crypt got one thing spot on. Halcyon has mega hair.

"I'm surprised you guessed it," says Halycon casually. "For someone so weak in character, Tristan was surprisingly strong in magic."

Bolts of defensive energy moves through my soul. This is my father he's talking about. "Tristan was a good king. Being kind hearted doesn't make you weak."

"Says the faeling." Halcyon rolls his eyes. "Tristan was good enough to fight us off, I'll grant you that. When the battle turned hopeless, Tristan put himself in an eternal sleep. Protector Lazare came up with the cover story. If both Lazare and I had lived, then it might have looked suspicious. The winter elves buried Reiver. I officially died as well. In reality, Lazare sent me off to be a changeling here."

I hate to admit this, but that's a good plan. Humans at ley points are more accustomed to devious acts from fae. Arnold said that to me many times. And it makes sense to turn the human Griffin into a topiary and keep him here. It makes for a cleaner disguise.

"I'm a Master of Glamour," continues Halcyon. "And yet, I'm trapped in this backwater. What a disgrace! For years, I had to attend the same human school. There are only so many soccer trophies one can win."

I nod. *That was an excessive trophy wall.*

"So you cut school and cast spells on all the humans," I state, "That's why they say the same things about you. You've been a senior there for decades."

"Yet that wasn't the worst indignity I had to suffer. Word came from Lazare that a certain annoying pixie would come through to my hiding spot. I was asked to spy on you. A faeling, no less! I'm the betrothed of none other than Princess Lotti. I am not some sad babysitter for a pathetic court jester."

"Boo hoo."

"Still, even more suffering was to come my way. The Ley Queen sent you on some false and meaningless little quest. Lazare ordered me to foil your silly attempts to find the ultimate source of fae magic. After a minor detection spells, I knew how to do it."

"Bully for you."

Halcyon grips his hands under his chin. When he speaks, it's in a ridiculously high-pitched voice. "Oh, Calla. You're so lovely! Can I follow you around and ruin your chances to find some non-existent super wand of power?"

At this point, I'd love to tell Halcyon that I totally succeeded in the Ley Queen's quest… and it wasn't for a super wand.

Tempting, but no.

"It was all another waste of time," snaps Halcyon. "Greatest source of power for all fae? Bah! no such thing exists. If you should have succeeded —meaning you'd gotten the Ley Queen whatever she wants—then she would have turned on you, same as I have."

Again, Halcyon totally miscalculated what the Ley Queen is up to… just like he missed the true source of Tristan's full strength.

Another phrase from Halcyon rings through my head.

I'm consort to Princess Lotti.

As in, that's the same chick who is getting married tomorrow. Halcyon is a Master of Glamour. Even more lines connect. Plans clarify. My heart sinks.

"Where is Dare?" I ask.

Halcyon grins. "Why, he's about to cement Protector Lazare's hold over the Winter realms via a very fortuitous marriage. Somehow, I doubt he'll live long after the nuptials are over, though. Such a shame."

"WHERE IS DARE?"

A shimmer of yellow fairy dust surrounds Halcyon. One moment, he's a dude who's way overdressed and hanging on a human couch. The next, he's Dare.

"Why, I'm marrying Lotti tomorrow." In one swift movement, Halcyon returns to his blond elf form and pulls three wands from beneath his armor.

This escalated quickly.

Chucking my spheres of power at Halcyon-Dare's face, I cast a straight up burn spell. Not the most creative way to kill, but it's pretty effective. Not on Halcyon. His armor is enchanted an absorbs the spell.

I cast another spell. This time, I choose a shield of protection.

It's not enough.

Wave after wave of power slams into me. Every muscle in my body hardens. My skin becomes rough with bark. Locks of my hair wind into small leaves.

I turn into a potted topiary.

Whistling, Lazare picks me up by my ceramic base and then sets me outside with the rest of his captured souls. He takes out yet another wand, opens a ley door, and is gone.

Turns out, we topiaries can talk and even move a little. "Hey, Griffin?" I ask.

That reedy voice echoes across the gardens. "Yessss?"

"Sorry you got turned into a tree. I'll figure out a way out of this."

"Pa… Pa… Parentssss."

That word took a lot of effort to spit out. Must be a side effect of being both enchanted and not magical.

"Your parents aren't here?" I ask.

"Nooooooo."

Poor human Griffin. And poor me, stuck on a porch while Lazare is doing *who knows what* to Dare.

Another memory appears. I'm back at the masquerade ball. A topiary asks me for help. The face looks familiar, and now I know why. It's Griffin's father—the same guy from the paining in the mansion, only with glasses.

"Don't worry," I state. "I know where your parents are. Once I get out of this, I'll save them too. Just know that I've got a long list of people to rescue here, and they aren't at the top. Nothing personal. Just magical people who can help me kick ass go first."

"You'll diiiiiiiiiiie."

Okay, so that sucked. I'm trapped as a tree, offer to do a good deed, and get told I'll end up dead. Nice.

Standing around as a topiary isn't exactly helping, so I decide to do something that always aids me. That would be writing in you, dear Diary. It takes some doing, yet eventually, I'm able to pull out my journal. After Halcyon's spell, the book is now filled with pages of smooth green leaves. I can scratch my thoughts by using a twig of a pencil.

As I scribble away, another image appears in my mind. It's the Ley Queen, saying how my life was about to take a decidedly downward turn.

Getting trapped as a tree while Fake Dare becomes married to Lotti… and all the while, the real Dare is missing?

That would count as downward. Good call, Mom.

- Calla

DAY FIFTY

$\mathcal{D}$ear Diary,

Being a topiary sucks, but there is one benefit.

Roots.

And if I can move my leafy bits to write on this page, why not shift my roots around? That's the idea, anyway. If I concentrate enough, I may be able to get my root-toes to break through the ceramic pot below me, grab onto a ley line and kick some butt.

With any luck, I'll be able to do this before Fake Dare marries Lotti tomorrow.

That's the plan anyway.

Better stop writing and focus on my feet.

- Calla

DAY FIFTY AND A HALF. MAYBE.

ear Diary,

Yay! I grabbed onto a ley line!

Boo! I got sucked right back into the ley prison.

My mother hinted this would happen. Still, it's one thing to consider you might return to magical incarceration. It's another to actually float around in an eternal swath of blue space.

Last time I arrived in prison, I balled my eyes out.

This time, I'm ticked off.

The Ley Queen said she closed the loophole that allowed me to leave before. But I'm her daughter. That means it's basically my job to screw with her schemes.

I will escape.

No question about it.

Okay, that's just a lot of tough girl talk. I have no idea how to get out of here.

I'm so screwed.

- Calla

DAY WHO KNOWS

*D*ear Diary,

I've been floating around for who knows how long. At least with the topiary situation, I had a friend. Sure, the guy was a whiny downer, but he was still someone to talk to. Now my only buddy is you, dear Diary. These pages are back to being regular paper, but that's about the only thing that's going well right now.

Last time, I escaped by reaching out for ley magic. So I try that again.

And again.

And—you guessed it—again.

Nothing happens.

The Ley Queen's words ricochet through my head.

Ley magic is dynamic. The prison already adapted to close your last means of escape.

Mother wasn't kidding.

Blue mists swirl around me. The colored tendrils seem to take the shape of the many pained faces in the Pixieland Citadel. How much longer can they stay alive? What's happening right now to Poppa, Muti and Dare?

My mind clouds over with panic. All of a sudden, it's as if I can't pull in enough air.

I curl into a ball and wrap my arms around my knees. This is too much for any one person to face, let alone me. Halcyon was right about one thing. I'm a prankster. A fool. Someone that makes the real rulers laugh.

Perhaps that's what the Ley Queen meant when she said the prison has already adapted. She might have been giving me a heads up—*hey daughter, you'll be spending a lifetime in prison!*

I've made many vows on the pages of this diary. Looking back, I know the truth. I didn't really mean any of them. This next one is different.

I may not succeed, yet no matter what, I will always fight to escape. Every moment, each thought, and all my powers... nothing will be held back.

Memories appear. I picture my six-year-old self running over a healthy Fens. All around me, the landscape glimmers with emerald grass, diamond sunlight and and a sapphire sky. There are no signs of blight or gray to be seen. Poppa and Muti flutter around me as I climb up a strong-limbed tree.

A fresh pang of grief runs through my heart. Those lovely lands are part of my soul, too. I cherish my home in Pixieland. It's never been that I belonged to the summer realm.

No, *it's* always belonged to *me.*

A flash of red light erupts from my palms.

Magic.

Summer power.

I gasp. Lazare locked up my summer power, but he wasn't the true ruler of that realm. And Lazare had no idea who he was dealing with.

I'm Tristan's daughter.

Uncurling my body, I size up the blue emptiness around me. This prison is for ley magic. It expects me to use more of the same to escape. And it also suspects that I've had all my other magic sealed away.

In other words, I can play a prank on the ley prison itself.

Picturing the summer realm helped me access my power before. Now, I force my mind to flicker through every beloved memory of summer lands.

I see yellow leaves falling in Buttercup Forest... hear the gurgling waters of the Rushy Glen... feel the roaring wind on the Airy mountain. And finally, I focus on the image of my father's sleeping face: ageless, handsome, and framed by a short silver beard.

It's that final mental picture that sends power rocketing through my soul. An orb of crimson energy appears between my palms. The sphere churns with inner threads of light and power.

Normally, I ask the magic to take a particular shape.

This time, I lean into the power itself. All I ask is that it sets me free.

The orb whizzes through the air, creating great tails of red brightness behind it. Sparkles of crimson light cascade from the orb.

It explodes.

When the crimson haze vanishes, there isn't an exit.

Instead, it's a woman.

I've seen her before. She appeared to me last time I'd been in the ley prison. Once again, I see an elf lady wearing a blue gown with a crimson blindfold. Tall yellow flowers float around her like sentinels. It's a classic look for elf royalty, except there's definitely something weird going on with her hair. It's like there's a claw on her scalp or something. Who does that?

Then again, I am in no position to critique. This chick may be getting me out of prison.

"Hello?" I ask.

She does not reply.

So I ask the same question about one hundred and fifty more times.

Still nothing.

As I plot my next move, something inside me calls makes my fingers itch. I wish to draw her portrait.

Which is a dumb thought.

Or maybe not.

How many times did I have a sneaking suspicion about griffin, only to dismiss the direction from my inner compass? I'd been told for so long that I was strange and different, I started to equate that with *bad*.

I didn't trust me.

And look what happened. I wasted so much time and allowed a puffy haired elf to derail my quest.

That ends now.

In this moment, I choose to trust my soul's voice instead of listening to the dark words of others.

Right now, my soul wants to record this stranger in pencil.

Here goes.

- Calla

Blue Stranger

DAY WHERE STUFF TAKES A STRANGE TURN

*D*ear Diary,

How excited am I about that picture?

Incredibly.

Stupendously.

I'm talking a *mistakenly fart while laughing* kind of happy.

Why? Because that drawing is what did it. By flipping back and forth between my other drawings and this most recent creation, one thing becomes clear. My new visitor looks a lot like the Ley Queen.

Only she's not my mother.

Nope.

She's me.

Or rather, a future version of myself.

This requires some finesse. How do you approach an older version of you? I could list out possible paths of my life and tailor my conversation accordingly. Sadly, I don't have that kind of time, so I just blab the first thing that comes into my head.

"Hello," I begin.

She float before me in her blue robes, the long veils swaying in an invisible wind. The only exception to her blue-ness remains her blindfold, which is colored red.

And she's still not talking, either.

"I'm Calla," I say.

The lady lifts her chin. *That* got her attention. We're not having a two-way conversation yet, but I'm starting to get the feeling I can break her.

"You're me, aren't you?" I ask.

She nods.

Progress!

"Here's the deal. I don't know how I did it, but I dragged your blue butt from the future to now."

"And when exactly is now?"

Future-Me speaks with the deep tone that only comes from being a super-senior fae. In fact, her voice reminds me a little of Poppa and Muti, and my parents are forty thousand years old.

"It's like this," I reply. "Exactly now is that Fake Dare is about to get married to Lotti the Snotty Potty."

A small smile quirks her lips. "Ah, I'd forgotten that nickname. We're rather clever, aren't we?"

It's mostly me doing the naming, but I'm not going to pick on Future Me right now. I need her help.

"Question. Do you mind pulling off the blindfold?"

"It's part of the spell you cast."

I round my mouth into an o-shape. "Which is why the blindfold is red."

"Correct." Future Me brushes her fingertips across the crimson fabric. "Once this comes off, I must leave soon afterwards."

"So it stays on for the time being. Got it."

"What do you require?"

"Are you serious? Fake Dare is about to get married to Lotti. Real Dare is in trouble somewhere. I need to stop the first and rescue the second. Only not necessarily in that order."

"I am not your *only* future, you know. Many possibilities exist for us. Over the millennia, I have learned the vagaries of ley lines. Such wonders await you, if you dedicate yourself to the effort."

Huh. I don't want to pooh-pooh her personal advertisement for dedicating my life to ley line research, but *pooh* to the *pooh*. I've got other stuff to fix first.

"Did I mention that Poppa and Muti are also sick with the blight? That's another thing I need to get on. So if you can send me back to…" I scrunch up my mouth, thinking through the possibilities. "Maybe land me on Earth about a month before the wedding, that would be great."

At this point, I'm fairly proud of my bad self. With thirty days of extra time, I can do some serious damage.

"I will send you back an hour before Dare and Lotti exchange vows."

"Actually, Fake Dare," I correct.

She pulls down her blindfold at last. And older me is lovely in the ethereal way of very wise fae. She sniffs, and the motion is a little elfier-than-thou. That's unexpected. I'm a prankster, not a snob.

"The real Dare is far more trouble than he is worth," explains Future Me. My own violet eyes glare with rage. It's unnerving.

"M'Kay."

"Save the winter prince now if you must, but then run for your life. No matter what he says or does, he will only ever see you as a friend and sister. Protect your heart while you can."

Here's the part where I should keep my mouth shut. I really should.

But I don't.

"How did I ever drag you back here with that massive chip on your shoulder? I must be more powerful than I thought."

Future Me vanishes.

Oops.

I wait a few minutes, hoping that she'll return and send me back to an hour before the wedding. It doesn't happen.

Maybe it never was going to in the first place. I seem to have turned into kind of a mean meanie after forty thousand years.

So I'm taking this break to write everything down. Once I'm finished, I'll start picturing summer realm vistas non-stop. Future Me is coming back here again, whether she likes it or not.

I just learned this lesson and I'm way younger than her. Future Me should know better.

You can't run away from yourself.

- Calla

DAY FIFTY-ONE

*D*ear Diary,

While pulling in fresh power, I chuck sphere after sphere of red magic into my blue prison.

I toss one, two, three...

Soon I hit fourteen.

Then I'm up to forty.

What can I say? I'm motivated.

Once I hit number sixty-three, a familiar sensation overtakes me—it's the not-so-pleasant sensation of being skinned alive. I scream my head off. My limbs get dragged in every direction at once.

The *yay* here? Getting out of prison.

And the *boo*? I really like my skin where it is.

Every second feels like forever as I'm torn from blue space and dropped off onto a cool and dry surface. It's like my eyes are stuck shut from squeezing them so hard. My throat is raw from yelling so hard.

Little by little, I open my eyes, finding myself in the basement of the Pixieland Citadel. Poppa and Muti rest nearby, their bodies thin and covered in angry red welts. One winter elf lies curled up on a nearby cot.

What happened to everyone else? How long have I been gone?

Bilge hobbles into the chamber, followed by Oinky. "It is here!"

I kneel beside Poppa and Muti. Can these be my parents? They resemble skeletons now, all bone and blight. "How much longer do they have?"

"Not very long. I'm so sorry." Bilge shuffles his feet. "We got new wands from the Queen Saita. Nothing works."

A chill crawls up my back. "What did you say?"

"They don't have long."

"No, the other thing."

"Queen Saita sent wands?"

"That's it." I pace a line between my parents and the remaining winter elf. "Wands store magic."

"It is right."

An electric current of excitement runs through me. "But they can magnify magic, too."

"Correct."

I exhale, pause, and kneel beside Poppa and Muti once more. The Ley Queen spoke about threads of the future. For the first time, I can see a new set of those strands coming together.

I gently set my pinky against Muti's tiny hand. She weakly clutches my skin. When I speak, my voice is all things quiet and determined.

"All my life, I've worked from the sidelines… pulling pranks… trying to influence those in power. I just escaped from the ley prison again. And I did it by trusting to my soul. Now, I need to do something else."

Bilge's tiny eyes widen. "And what will it do?"

"Step out from the shadows, grab my power, and fight with everything in me. Everything that I've learned collapses in to a single fact. The center of this blight—and of all my pain—is Lazare. I'm the rightful ruler of the Summer Realm. King Tristan is my father."

Bilge steps backward. Oinky shuffles away as well. "I always had suspicions." All the color fades from Bilge's face. "Now what will my Calla do?"

"Take what's mine," I reply. "And that's the Scepter of Summer. Everyone wonders how King Tristan healed the blight after he took power. And guess what came with the throne? That scepter. Once I can wield it, I bet I can wipe out this blight."

Bilge shakes his head. "It needs to find Protector Lazare first."

"He'll be at his daughter's wedding, won't he?"

"It shouldn't go to that wedding."

My brows lift. "Which means the *I do's* haven't happened yet. Future-Me did promise to drop me off an hour before the wedding. Looks like she kept her word. After a lot of magical encouragement, mind you."

"It makes no sense. Future Me?"

"Oh, I know exactly what I'm up to."

Marching across the room, I pause by the citadel door. Pulling up the mat, I find the familiar nest of ley lines for the Summer Citadel.

As I grasp them tightly, I know one thing.
This is it, one way or another.
- Calla

DAY FIFTY-ONE AND A WEDDING

Dear Diary,

Minutes later, I step through the Pixieland ley door and into the Summer Citadel. The place is as deserted and dusty as ever. Cobwebs handle from the ceiling, reminding me of so many hanging vines. If this were a minstrel's song, I'd race through the deserted tower and leap out into the Buttercup Forest. In my real life, I snort in a cobweb and have a mini-coughing fit.

In no time, I'm back at it. I slip out of the citadel, through the Buttercup forest and steal up to the summer palace. Once I reach the gardens, I freeze.

I'd seen a new topiaries outside Griff's house. That's nothing compared to what's happening behind the new summer palace.

Someone's been a busy boy.

Neat rows of green trees—all shaped into the form of elves and humans—stretch out in every direction. As I approach, leafy fingers brush against the bare skin on my arms. Many of them are pockmarked with gray splotches. Hoarse voices carry on the wind.

"Heeeeeeelp."

"Bliiiiiight."

And my favorite: *"Ruuuuuuuuun!"*

Part of me would love to stop here and give a rousing speech about how I'll rescue them all, but there isn't time. The sooner I get to the palace, the faster I can free them and end the blight.

With any luck, that is.

I rush around the topiaries until I'm right behind the new summer palace, which—*shocker!*—looks just like the old one. Lazare has zero imagination. This time, I'm thankful the guy is a knucklehead. It means the building's layout has stayed the same.

Moving with maximum stealth—I'm rather talented in the art of sneaky—I hide behind a line of trees near the main gathering chamber. It's more than a little strange. This is the same place I stood when I blew up Lazare's palace, back when Dare got engaged to Lotti. Now, the structure is magically rebuilt and Fake Dare is getting married inside.

Through a window, I spy Lotti and Fake Dare. A bunch of thoughts fly through my head at once. Here are the top five.

My Top Five Thoughts At Witnessing My Worst Nightmare

Five. Lotti looks great. Which makes me hate her even more.

Four. Fake Dare appears completely authentic. What have they done with the real one?

Three. Lazare stands nearby, the Scepter of Summer held firmly in his fist. On reflex, my own fingers curl into grabby hands. I totally want to snag that thing and pummel the folks involved in items five to three.

Two. The gathering chamber is packed with summer and winter elves. Everyone wears flowing robes with embroidered patterns, along with long braided hair and modified tiaras. Big takeaway? Once I change my outfit, I'll be the only one in pink body leathers. *Clutch.*

And now for the biggest, most overwhelming of all...

One. My very own mother, the Ley Queen, is conducting the cere-mony. Yow! We may need family therapy after this. Seems like this is something mothers mention to their offspring, especially after placing those daughters through an overly elaborate quest to figure out you're related in the first place.

Not that I'm bitter.

Moving on.

I turn away from the window. Pulling in a fresh orb of ley power, I toss it at myself. A shimmer surrounds my body as my outfit changes into pink battle leathers. I've had some time to internalize the fact that I'm a foot taller with curves. This time, the fit is pretty good.

Next I pull up a ley line. This time, the door won't connect me to Earth, but to a spot a hundred yards away. I pull on the handle and march through.

Voila.

I step out into a small chamber that connects to the main room.

This is one of the tiny spaces that I pranced through on the night of the masquerade. Now, I walk through with an entirely different purpose.

Kicking butt.

I pause on the threshold to the gathering chamber. Meanwhile, my mother the traitor raises her voice.

"Does anyone here know of any reason why this man and woman should not be bound in magical matrimony?"

Now, I've been trapped in a ley prison (twice.) Attacked by orcs and evil blond elves named Halcyon. Forced into completing a quest for my sneaky mother. Watched my parents and others get sick without being able to help them one iota.

And in this moment, it all feels totally worth it as I march forward and yell two words at the top of my lungs: "I do!"

Lotti pales. Lazare glares. Fake Dare looks stunned. Mother keeps her eternal and unreadable face on. Everyone in the audience gasps and stares.

I'm the center of attention once more. All is right in the universe.

"Why would you object?" asks the Ley Queen smoothly.

"Because this guy—" here I point to Fake Dare "—is actually Halcyon."

More gasps sound. More attention for me. This plan is humming along nicely.

"Halcyon survived the attack on Tristan." I point at the creep in question. "Now, Halcyon glamoured himself up to look like Dare and is marrying Lotti under false pretenses! Later on, Halcyon plans to murder the real Dare. When that's done, the summer realm can take over winter." I pause at the top of the aisle, only a yard away from the happy couple. "This is an invasion without armies!"

Queen Saita steps into the main aisle. Dare's mother hadn't been standing with the happy couple, so I didn't notice her before. Saita looks as she always does: pale with long black hair and eyes so dark they seem black instead of brown. She wears a white dress covered in small clear beads.

"Oh, Calla." She shakes her head.

I exhale. Saita is many things, but a dumbass isn't one of them. Along the way, she had to notice the change in Dare after Halcyon glamoured himself up to take her son's place. You can cast a spell to match someone's appearance easily. But to know their history and really pretend to be them? Not so simple.

And just the way Fake Dare stands at the altar, it's obvious Halcyon hasn't done his research. The false Dare nervously scans the room. Total bull. The real Dare has two expressions: intense and more intense. Anxious glances just aren't something he does.

I look to Saita like she's my lifeboat in this storm of lying liars. "Come on!" I gesture to Fake Dare. "You know that's not your son. If this were the real Dare—and I were truly breaking up a wedding he gave a crap about—then he'd have flattened me against the wall by now."

Fake Dare lifts his chin. "What a rude little creature."

I point right at Fake Dare's nose. "And that's another example of you being not-Dare. The real guy talks half the time in grunts, especially when he's ticked off. You didn't do your homework, glamour boy."

Saita sets her hand on my shoulder. "Calm yourself."

"No, I'm staying angry." I counter. "And I'm taking charge."

Speaking of taking stuff, I eye Lazare's scepter greedily. What's the best way to separate that mega douche from my super-wand? There are so many spells to choose from.

"I can't allow that to happen," says Saita.

All this time, everyone in the gathering chamber has been watching the Calla Show with rapt attention. When Saita says the words, *I can't allow that*, another loud gasp echoes through the air. I'd say something snarky, but I'm too shocked.

"You're not with me here?" I ask.

"The Ley Queen told us how you escaped her prison. It's clearly made you unbalanced. I'm here to celebrate the wedding of my son to his one true love. You must leave now and quietly."

I hitch my thumb toward Fake Dare. "You think *that* is your son?"

"Of course, he is." Saita stares at me with her big elfy eyes. In this moment, she's the perfect image of sympathy and sweetness. I've seen her use this particular look before. Mostly, she saves it for unwanted dignitaries. Dare and I call it her *dumpster tour stare*.

"Yeah, kay." Some guests stare at me funny. "That's a combination of yeah and okay." I like to keep my crowd involved.

I take a few steps down the main aisle. This time, I head away from Fake Dare and Lotti the Snotty Potty. With my back turned, I summon a massive orb of ley power.

Although there are fancier spells I could cast now, I decide to go with a classic summoning spell with level nine power. That ought to get me what I want. It won't be as much of a crowd pleaser as my Electric Eagle or Lasso of Death spells, but I'm here to get my scepter, not earn a standing ovation.

Spinning about, I set my orb of power loose. The blue sphere hurtles across the room and slams into Lazare's grip. The Scepter of Summer instantly breaks free from the fake Protector's hands and goes flying across the chamber. A second later, it lands right in my ready little palms. Lazare crumples to his knees, his shoulders slumping in defeat.

I raise the scepter high. After all, I do look fabulous in my pink leathers and I didn't use a fancier spell. This moment deserves a wee bit of drama.

Grasping the scepter, I sense the energy churning inside the golden rod. This is exactly like other magic I've wielded. No question what to do next.

Take down Fake Dare.

This is it. My moment. I know my true history. The legacy of my father lies in my hands. I point the thing straight at Fake Dare.

"Come out and play, Halycon!"

A line of yellow energy blasts from the top of the scepter and lands straight into Fake Dare's stomach. The imposter crouches over, moaning in agony. I'd feel sorry for his pain, but *nah*. Halcyon deserves what he gets.

The scene takes on a sunny glow. *It's happening!* Across from Fake Dare, Momma Ley Queen even cracks a smile. Hooray for me.

Seconds tick by. Fake Dare doesn't transform into Halcyon. I give the scepter a little shake. Maybe the thing hasn't been used in a while or something. Still Fake Dare stays annoyingly in non-Halcyon form.

Nasty, high-pitched laughter fills the air.

Sadly, it's coming from Lazare's direction. Little by little, the Protector rises to his full height again. Tears of joy stream down his cheeks. "You're not the only one who can play a prank or two."

I stare at the scepter in my hands. *Oh, no.* It's a fake. I should have suspected that Lazare might do something like this.

More guffaws fill the air. This time, it's Fake Dare, and he laughs with a kind of high pitched snake-hiss.

Well, if the scepter doesn't work, it's not like I'm out of magic.

I summon a fresh orb of ley magic to my palms. Doing this doesn't take long, but Lazare already has pulled the real scepter from the folds of his robe. He points the magical weapon straight in my direction. A blinding arc of yellow lighting slams into me, making every muscle in my body useless. I tumble onto the ground.

It doesn't escape my notice that while I only *believed* that I made Lazare fall over, the protector really did that to me. I make a mental note that, if I ever get the chance, he's got way more humiliation coming.

"Guards!" cries Lazare. "Throw her into the dungeons."

Rough hands grab my arms and drag me down the center aisle. My head lolls bonelessly from side to side as I'm hauled down into the bowels of the palace and chucked into a huge, dank prison.

My ability to move returns. With it, I can write this entry.

And maybe feel sorry for myself a little.

Grabbing that scepter was my best and only plan.

Now what?

- Calla

DAY FIFTY-ONE AND A DUNGEON

$\mathcal{D}$ear Diary,

For some reason, my life has become a lot of sitting around in dungeons. There was floating in the ley prison thanks to the Ley Queen. Being trapped in a bedroom-shaped chamber, also thanks to She Who Needs A Name. This is my first classic dungeon experience.

It's not pleasant.

Why Lazare's Dungeons Are Disgusting

One. Oinky manages his sty much better than this. Haven't you heard of plumbing, Lazare?

Two. I get it. This is a dungeon for fae. Magic gets blocked with ward stones. But would it be too much trouble to use stones that give off a nice scent, perhaps to offset item number one? Just throwing it out there.

Three. A threadbare blanket is not the same as a bed. I get that this isn't a fancy hotel or something, but have you seen this floor?

Four. You can open a window. Or have a window.

Five. Where are the other inmates? I just got tossed into a massive—and supremely gross—chamber with nothing but a blanket.

Update: I overhear the guards talking. Most prisoners get turned into topiaries. Lazare wouldn't do that to me again for obvious reasons. After all, I just escaped topiary-hood on Earth.

A low moan sounds from the far side of the room.

I suck in a shaky breath, which is an unpleasant experience in the extreme. The stench in here is something else. Still, it doesn't change the truth.

Another prisoner waits nearby. The body lies slumped in the shadows. I step closer.

"Hello?"

Rough breathing echoes through the vast and empty jail cell. My stomach lurches. I close in on the figure.

Oh, no.

It's Dare.

The real Dare.

I kneel beside him. As my eyes adjust to the dim light, I can make out his features. He appears gaunt and colorless. Streaks of gray blight mark his skin.

I take his hand in mine. His touch is cold as snow. "Dare, it's me."

He forces his eyes to open a sliver. "Calla."

"I'll save you, Dare."

His shakes his head. It's the barest of movements, but there's no missing it. "Escape."

"I won't leave you. I have a plan."

His brows lift. Again, it's a slight movement but unmistakable. It's Dare's way of saying, *go on.*

I pull on my ear, not sure how much to share at this point. After all, Dare is locked up in a jail and covered in blight. Maybe he can't handle it. I bob my head, considering.

Nah. This is Dare. The guy's tough.

"It's like this," I declare. "I'm not a faeling. My mother is the Ley Queen and my father is King Tristan."

Dare's brows lift even further. "Whoa."

"Crazy, right? The whole situation is almost beyond belief."

"No." Dare leans forward, the look in his bloodshot eyes turning intense. "You are extraordinary, Calla." He heaves in a rough breath. "It makes perfect sense."

My chest warms with affection and pride. Dare thinks I'm extraordinary. Go me.

"Here's what we'll do," I state. "We'll get out of this prison. After that, I'll grab the Scepter of Summer. With that in hand, I'll just wipe out our enemies and cure the blight." I frown. "Saying that out loud, it does seem a little vague. I mean, I don't know how I'll use the scepter or anything."

Dare chuckles. "Remember when you found the Winter Stone?"

I smile. "I'd forgotten about that."

"You'll figure that scepter out."

The stone was a white and magical rock, but no one knew how to use it. I monkeyed with it for two minutes and figured out it was a bomb. Then I chucked it at the stone golem who was trying to stomp on me and Dare. Fun.

"I can get you out of here," says Dare. "But once I do, you must leave me behind."

I roll my eyes. "Like I'd ever let that happen."

"Calla." Dare's voice takes on a warning-tone.

"Dare." I roll my eyes.

The prince exhales a sigh of defeat, but there's no real regret in it. Dare tells me his idea for escape. It's a good one, but it's something we can't launch into until the reception is well underway.

While we wait, Dare naps and I write in my diary.

If this is my last entry, then you know what happened. Dare and I went down fighting.

- Calla

DAY FIFTY-ONE AND SOME WINE

*D*ear Diary,
      An hour passes.

Two.

I spend quality time sizing up our guards, who I've decided to call Blond and Blonder. The pair hang by the exit door and look stunning in their golden armor. Their other qualifications for duty are rather sketchy.

A knock sounds. Blond pulls aside the view-slit on the metal door. "Who approaches the dungeons of Lazare?"

"It is I, Queen Saita."

Blond frowns. "Prince Dare's Mum?"

"That is correct," she says smoothly. "I thought you might appreciate some libation."

Blond and Blonder stare at each other before shaking their heads. "You're really hot and all," says Blond. "But it's against the rules to hook up with winter elves. Sorry."

Dare and I share a dry look. Like Saita would want a romantic liaison with either of these two.

"I am here to bring you honey wine in celebration of my son's wedding."

Blonder elbows Blond. "She's bringing us something to drink, dummy."

Blond pulls open the door. "Thank you, your Majesty."

Saita hands over a large jug. "Enjoy. I must now return to the celebration." The queen stares off into the depth of the prison. A look of pure rage flashes in Saita's eyes. And that's when I know it.

Saita has been on our side all along.

Or, more likely, the queen has been on Dare's side. Saita probably knew Lazare had a fake scepter, so she *pretended* to believe in Fake Dare and did a great job of *actually* stabbing me in the back. Now Saita's handing over what's probably some very drugged-up wine.

Smart lady.

"See?" whispers Dare. For hours, he's been telling me that his mother would show up and help us escape. After what happened at the wedding, I had my doubts.

Now, I'm all Team Saita.

"I've a second jug for you," says Saita. She moves to hand it to Blonder. With practiced care, she drops the container at the last second. Both guards lunge to catch the wine before it hits the floor.

Saita pretends to crouch in order to catch the wine. In reality, she uses the moment to toss a key across the rough stone floor. It slides directly into our cell.

How cool is that trick? It doesn't even use magic, either. Just leverages the inherent greed and stupidity of all elves. There is so much I could learn from this woman.

I'm not the only one who's excited, either. Blonder catches the jug before it breaks. He and Blond chat away about where to find glasses while Saita slips off.

Racing across the cell floor, I pick up the key and scurry back to the shadows. Meanwhile, Blond and Blonder are unable to find cups, so they start drinking directly from the jugs.

Enjoy it while you can, guys.

Whatever magic Saita put in that wine, it's strong stuff. Within a matter of minutes, both guards are conked out on the floor and snoring up a storm.

Slipping the key on the lock, I open the cell door. Dare and I sneak out of the prisons. Once we're beyond the reach of the ward stones, I can cast spells once more.

Whew.

Pulling in a fresh sphere of ley magic, I toss it at Dare. This is a glamour spell, so Dare now looks like a summer elf guard. He's all blond hair and golden armor. Even so, there's no missing the bloodshot look of his eyes and the faint echoes of blight on his skin.

"Do I look summery?" Dare asks, his voice hoarse.

"You do." I grip his hand again. The blight isn't contagious—it comes from the ley magic—but it wouldn't matter if it did. I'd still want to give Dare whatever comfort my touch might provide. It's tempting to try and cast more healing spells, but I already know how that will work out.

As in, not at all.

Plus, Saita's wine provides another chance for me to get the Scepter of Summer. That's the best way to save Dare and everyone else.

An unwanted imagine appears in my mind. Dare's immobile body rests inside a coffin. My eyes sting. That can't happen.

Focus, Calla.

Dare and I slowly climb the stairs to the palace's main floor. We run across a few summer elves along the way. I make a point to cower beside my so-called guard. No one gives it much thought. They probably figure I'm being moved to a new prison or whatever.

We pause outside the feasting hall. Lurking behind a stout column, Dare and I hide from the crowd while still scoping out the chamber within. I inspect the space with care. It's a long and rectangular room that's entirely decorated in gold. A wide U-shaped table encircles much of the floor. On the short side of the 'U,' there sits Fake Dare, Lotti, Saita, and Lazare. I scan the table carefully.

It's pretty wide.

I grin. That will work well.

Turning, I whisper to Dare. "I'll need a distraction in a minute. Got any ideas?"

Dare nods slowly. "Always."

I rub my palms together. "Heh, heh." I then slip off, careful to stick to back hallways and skirt behind long tapestries. In short order, I stand outside an archway that opens to the short side of that table's U-shape.

And I wait.

Lazare stands. "And now, we shall share in jelly cake."

A group of six servants march out. A large platter lies balanced between their shoulders. On that surface sits the largest and jiggliest cake I've ever seen. A hundred candles flicker atop the golden confection.

Going on tiptoe, I scope out each of the carriers. One has a loop of rope around his ankle.

That would be Dare's doing.

Nice.

The crowd *oohs* and *ahhs* as the servants step forward. Dare's cord goes taught. The front carrier falls flat on his face. After wobbling for a moment, the fiery cake tumbles. Clangs sound as the platter hits the floor. Everyone gasps.

I spring into action. While everyone's focus stays on the mostly-ruined dessert, I slip under the table. As I'd hoped, there's enough room for me to crawl about while staying safely hidden.

Beyond the tablecloth, I hear the feasting hall calm down. Some cake is salvaged. The wedding attendees are happy. Time to spring into action. I crawl forward, cataloging the footwear as I go. Some folks have shoes with curly toes. Summer elves.

Getting closer.

Up ahead, I spy a set of curly shoes made entirely of golden fabric. Lazare. He sits next to someone with shapely legs and black heels. Saita.

And they're playing footsie.

I freeze. Saita helped Dare escape. Is this somehow part of the plan? One can only hope.

Shaking my head, I refocus. Best to get my scepter, not think about Saita. Before, Lazare held a fake version of the precious object somewhere in his robes. The real one simply must be hidden under that golden fabric as well.

Hopefully.

I crawl up closer, scanning Lazare's golden robes for any sign of the scepter. My breath catches. He's got the scepter under his robes all right, but propped up against the edge of the chair.

Sweet.

With maximum sneakiness, I inch nearer. That's when the footsie fiesta gets worse.

Eew. Just eew.

Now I knew all winter elves had claws on their fingertips. It's just one of their things. But I didn't know that included talon-style toes. Yet that's exactly what Saita has—long curvy toenails that are painted black. Here's the trouble. She's using those claw-toes to scratch at the skinny, overly-pale and way too hairy shin of Lazare.

So much more than I needed to know.

Reaching forward, I try to grab the scepter. But Saita keeps changing the direction of her claw-toe scratch. Every time I try to grab the object of my desire, her nasty foot gets in the way. And now, I can see Lazare's leg shiver with some kind of emotion that I'd just rather not think about right now. Whatever it is, it's making the hairs on his furry leg stand on end.

Even more that I didn't need to know.

My idea had been to gently wrest the scepter away and carefully test out what kind of power is inside. Who knows what that thing really packs? Just touching it with my pinky might be enough.

It was a good scheme.

I blame his sticky-up leg fur for what happens next.

My temper snaps. Lunging forward, I grab the scepter with both hands. Power beyond imagining careens through my limbs. Every corner of my soul blazes with energy. Blasts of crimson lighting erupt from the rounded top of the scepter and slam into the table above me. The long piece of furniture hurtles into the air, where it then explodes into a cascade of kindling and dust.

The room falls silent.

Every eye locks on me.

I rise to stand. This wasn't how I pictured my entrance working, but I can adapt. I wave at Lazare. "Hey, guess what I found?"

The Protector pulls a wand from the folds of this robe. A new truth hits me. Lazare is actually a really skinny guy who packs a lot of accessories into his supernatural muumuu. Who knows what else is under there?

Whatever Lazare is hiding there's no way I can give him time for a counter spell. Pressing my arms forward, I point the scepter right at Lazare's face. Fresh arcs of red power beam straight into his eyes.

Somewhere in my peripheral vision, I notice how Lotti remains seated on a nearby chair, a bite of jellied cake held half-way to her mouth. I'm not proud of this, but the sight makes me realize something.

That's some good looking cake.

In my defense, if I'd had time to play around with the scepter first, I might have planned things a little more carefully. After all, spells take the shape of what you ask them to become.

In this case, the scepter just thinks I just asked Lazare to become a jelly cake.

Oops.

One second, there is a furious Lazare, whipping out his wand and looking incredibly ticked off at yours truly. The next moment, he's a lovely yet wobbly confection of yellow jelly cake.

In all honesty, this is my favorite incarnation of Lazare.

Then he explodes.

Just like the table before, Lazare bursts. Countless chunks of yummy cake fly across the room. A lot of it falls on Lotti, who takes the situation very poorly.

"You ruined my dress."

It's on the tip of my tongue to point out that I also exploded her father, but that would be rude.

"You ugly little troll, did you hear what I said?" Lotti whines. "You destroyed this gown!"

Now, all's fair once you call me an ugly little troll. "I also blew up your father, in case you hadn't noticed that part."

"I hate you!" cries Lotti.

"Hold that thought."

Turning about, I point the scepter toward where I'm pretty sure Dare is hiding out. This time, I picture the glamoured-up version of Dare turning into his healthy and very winter elfy old self. A new blast of crimson lighting slams into the back wall, bursting it apart.

I wince. I hope that got him.

The crowd loses their minds. Everyone races for the exits while slipping on bits of feast and jelly Lazare. It's a fitting end for the evil protector, in my humble opinion.

There's no sign of Dare, though. Best to send out one more healing blast, just to be sure.

The cold touch of metal presses against my throat. Halcyon's voice sounds behind me. "I told you Lotti was one my true love." Fake Dare presses his dagger more firmly against my throat. A single drop of blood oozes down my neck. "How could you destroy our wedding?"

I roll my eyes. "There's so much wrong with that statement, I don't even know where to begin."

Although I'm an aggressive little sass-mouth, I'm not suicidal. While talking back to Fake Dare, I take care to stand very still. This scepter is new to me. I don't want to blast off my own face while trying to destroy Halcyon.

A fresh voice echoes through the feasting hall. "I challenge you to a duel!"

I follow the sound and—*yay!*—Dare stands by the opposite wall, looking totally healthy and even more enraged.

"Who is this glamoured-up wizard?" asks Fake Dare.

Saita, who'd been quiet this entire time, now shifts on her golden chair. "That is my son, Halcyon. If he asks you for a duel, you are honor-bound to submit. Do not forget your place as a member of the summer court. And drop that ridiculous disguise."

The dagger leaves my throat. Saita pats the seat beside her. "Come sit here, Calla. You know the rules for a duel."

Which I do. No one can interfere, even super powerful friends with new scepter toys. I take my seat beside Saita and try not to worry.

After all, I just healed Dare. He should be fine for a battle. Only, I've never done anything like this before and the last two things I blasted with my magic exploded less than a minute later.

I cover my eyes a little. Maybe a lot. Through my fingers, I see Fake

Dare return to Halcyon form. The summer elf whips out an especially thin and pointy sword.

"En guarde," says Halcyon. "My rapier shall taste your blood."

Dare stride up to Halcyon and pauses before him. "Take the first strike."

Halcyon chuckles. "You can't be serious."

Dare grunts, which as I've said before, is his default when super furious.

"Oh, try to strike my son already," huffs Saita.

"As you command, your Highness." Halcyon swoops his rapier toward Dare. The prince grabs the golden blade in his first and squeezes. Crackling noises sound as the sword bends at an odd angle.

Dare can mush up swords in his bare hands? Who knew?

"My turn," grumbles Dare. Heaving up his arm, Dare punches Halcyon right in the chest. His golden armor turns concave. That's got to hurt. Dare grips Halcyon's head. "I grant you a quick death, which is more than you deserve."

Dare twists Halcyon's skull with such force, the head pops right off. I didn't even know that was a thing, and I really contemplated this topic, what with the Headless Horsewoman and all.

Headless Halcyon topples over. You really can't get more dead than being without having a skull anymore. Dare stalks off in my direction. "Are you all right, Calla?"

I wave my scepter in reply. "All good."

Now Lotti loses her mind. She races over to kneel by Halcyon's body. Setting her palm against his bloody chest, she turns to glare at me. "This is all your fault."

I purse my lips and think things through. "Yeah, you're probably right."

Lotti rises. "I hereby take my father's place as Protector of the Summer Realm." She steps closer. "And as my first act, I declare that Calla the Pixie shall be killed slowly."

"About that." I waggle the scepter. "You're not the heir of anything. I am."

Lotti pales. "What?"

Even Saita frowns. "That can't be. You're a faeling."

I scan the room, wondering if a *certain someone* had returned to join the fun.

Nope, no Mom.

Oh, well. I can do this solo.

Turning, I address my future subjects. "This would be easier if the Ley

Queen were still around, but she always has her reasons. It's like this. Tristan's my father and the Ley Queen is my mother. Surprise!"

No one cheers.

Dare steps over to my side. The solidarity is very much appreciated. "Calla speaks the truth. How else could she wield the Scepter of Summer?"

"My father wielded it," counters Lotti. "Once you hand it over, I'll wield it too." She makes grabby hands at my scepter, which I do not appreciate.

"He maybe used it a little bit," I state. "I can do a ton more. For instance, I can heal the blight right now." And in that moment, I know it's the truth. I also realize something else.

"That's how my parents met in the first place," I continue. "The blight is an illness of ley lines. By combining summer magic with ley power, they were able to end the disease. Now both powers exist within me. I can kick this blight's butt."

Lotti narrows her eyes. "Then do so or hand over the scepter."

"What a coincidence, that's next on my list."

Which it totally is.

~

Dear Diary,

I shall now draw how Lotti looked while making grabby hands at my scepter.

- Calla

Lotti

DAY FIFTY-ONE WITH LEY LINES

$\mathcal{D}$ear Diary,

No one touches my stuff.

Time to show Lotti *who's who* when it comes to the Scepter of Summer. Raising my right hand, I summon my ley power. Bits of golden tile go flying as a cord bursts through the floor. The ley line lands against my palm. Sadly, only a handful of blue threads cut through the gray cord.

Not a lot of time left to fix this.

With my left hand, I set the rounded end of the scepter directly against the ley line.

I picture what I want the power to do.

The scepter responds.

Red energy explodes from the scepter's end, surrounding the entire ley line in a web of crimson lighting. More power surrounds me as well.

Suddenly, it's as if every cell in my body burns with white-hot flame. I wish I could write that I stand all stoic and regal while this goes down. Nope. I scream myself hoarse and cry like a baby.

Yet I don't let go.

Bit by bit, the red energy of summer burns through the gray blight in the ley cord. In my mind, I can see the lines below the palace turn bright blue. My thoughts fly to the Ley Queen's palace, where I witness each workroom and its nest of cords. One by one, every ley line returns to a healthy shade of azure.

Next I see the people of Faerie. Elves, dwarves, naiads, pixies... disease vanishes from all the afflicted. Blight clears. Eyes open. Pain fades. The enchantments from the outer gardens get torn apart. All the topiaries are freed, just as I'd promised.

It is done.

Yanking my arm up, I separate the scepter from the ley line below. Instantly, my body cools. Agony seeps away. I have the distinct sensation of falling to the floor.

I stop.

Strong arms hold me upright. Somewhere along the line, Dare stepped to my side. Now he keeps me vertical in front of my future subjects. I pull in slow breaths as strength pours back into my limbs. While I do this, folks wander in through the blasted out walls. Some of the faces are familiar.

These are the topiaries from the gardens, now freed from their enchantments. Scanning the group, I notice the Griff's real parents in the crowd. Both appear healthy and well. It's nice when life works out that way.

The newcomers hang by the periphery of the room. Not that I blame them. Interacting with summer elves hasn't exactly worked out well for these folks. That said, I do get some cries of *thank you* and *you freed us!*

Which is certainly a nice touch. I wave in their direction. "You're welcome. I figured I'd take care of you guys while I was at it." I round on Lotti. "Convinced?"

Although Lotti hasn't exactly been the nicest person in my life, she also just got her wedding reception blown up, father turned into jelly before getting exploded, and her fake fiancee's head popped off. I'm willing to be reasonable here.

"As a matter of fact, I am convinced." Lotti pulls a wand from under her wedding gown and points it right at me. A bolt of yellow power careens in my direction.

With that, *reasonable time* is officially over.

With a swoop of my arm, I point my scepter right at Lotti. I didn't really picture what I wanted here—there wasn't a lot of time to plan—so my only thought is to destroy.

That's exactly what happens.

Blasts of crimson power fly off the scepter, smashing through windows and walls. The palace roof blasts up into the air, landing somewhere in the Buttercup Forest nearby to a chorus of snapped branches and snarling cats.

Not to brag, but my wand is way better than Lotti's. She's barely got a few inches of power out of the tip while I basically destroyed the whole building.

In fact, a bunch of debris knocks Lotti onto her back while she's still casting her spell. In the process, her wand breaks free from her hands to fly up in the air, pinwheel-style. In the process, the spell that was meant for me strikes Lotti full in the chest. A moment later, she's turned into stone.

The humans seem especially freaked out about this, so I gesture between them and the frozen Lotti. "Not to worry, guys. That was her spell for me. I have to say, that she could have been a lot meaner."

The Lotti statue explodes.

I duck down as little bits of rock fly over my head. Once the debris is done a-flying, I rise once more. Dare is giving me one of his sly grins.

I shrug. "Then again, maybe she was a total bloodthirsty freak who just got what she deserved."

"Could be," deadpans Dare.

I round on the audience of ex-topiaries. It's still mostly humans with a few summer elves mixed in.

"Hey everyone." I waggle my scepter high. "I'm Calla and I'm the rightful ruler of the summer realm."

I pause, waiting for the cheer. Nothing happens. *Oh, well. They'll get used to me.*

"Here's the deal," I continue. "If you're a summer elf who was frozen into a tree, welcome back! Lazare is gone and it's all good now. If you're a human, enjoy the moment! I'll soon cast a memory wipe spell and send you back to Earth, so none of this is permanent anyway. You're welcome. Again."

The elves seem totally fine with all this. The humans lose their minds. So I do what any reasonable ruler would in my situation. I zap them with my scepter so they all fall asleep. Sure, they're snoozing atop bits of Lazare jelly cake and stone Lotti, but it's not like any of that will hurt them.

And I have bigger things to do.

Namely, find Poppa and Muti.

- Calla

DAY FIFTY-ONE, POPPA AND MUTI

$\mathcal{D}$ear Diary,

I pull open the ley door in what's left of the feasting hall of Lazare's palace. Through the threshold, I spy the basement of the Pixieland Citadel. The cots all lie empty. Poppa and Muti's pillow sits, crumpled, lonely and abandoned. there's no sign of Bilge and Oinky.

Back in the summer place, steps up beside me. "You're going home now?"

I nod. That helps me avoid the actual question of where home really is these days.

"Do you wish for me to accompany you?"

"I'll do this alone, thanks." For some reason, I keep staring through the opened doorway and not moving.

Dare rests his hand on my shoulder. His thumb moves in soothing arcs against my skin. "You healed them, Calla."

And I know that's true. Still, the last time I spoke to Poppa and Muti, I was heading off to prison. They had big plans to build a party room in our acorn. I visited them when they were sick and everything, but it's not like we had extensive chats. I need to face the reality from the last time we spoke.

Poppa and Muti were basically glad to see me go.

They may not be thrilled that I've returned.

"If you need me, summon me," adds Dare.

"Thank you."

Standing on the threshold isn't helping things. I won't be at peace until I see for myself that Poppa and Muti are healed and healthy. So I step into the Pixieland Citadel. The door slams shut behind me.

Bilge waddles into the room. "It did so well!" In an uncharacteristic move, Bilge hugs me. Since he hasn't grown—and I most certainly have—this involves Bilge gipping my waistline. Oinky shuffles by my feet.

"Thank you, Bilge. I got some help." I wave the Scepter of Summer around for emphasis. "Are things okay here?"

"The pixies are helping." Bilge steps away, breaking the hug. "It must go home."

I nibble my thumbnail. "Not sure where that is these days."

"It goes to the acorn," says Bilge. And with that, my hobgoblin buddy waddles away.

Whether the acorn is my home or not, Bilge is right about one thing. That's where I'm most likely to find Poppa and Muti. Taking to the skies, I fly back to the oak tree where I grew up. As I approach, Jolly's face appears in the bark.

"I should spit sap in your face," says Jolly.

"I missed you, too," I retort.

Jolly then does something I've never seen before. He grins. An actual smile. Whoa.

And I thought finding King Tristan was a once in a lifetime thing. An actual happy Jolly is something else.

Shrinking down, I fly inside the acorn. As always, Poppa and Muti sit at their regular spots at the kitchen table. They look up as I enter.

I give them a decidedly awkward wave. "I'm back."

"Yes," says Poppa.

"We heard you talking to Jolly," adds Muti.

"Guess what? The Ley Queen is my mother and Tristan in my father. I grabbed the Scepter of Summer and healed the ley lines." As evidence, I raise said scepter. This is like show and tell, except with life changing magical items.

Poppa and Muti share a sad look. "We heard."

"Huh." I shift my weight from foot to foot. Talk about your uncomfortable conversations. "News travels fast around Faerie, I guess."

"We must be honest," says Poppa at last. "Turning your bedroom into a party pit was a silly idea."

"It didn't replace the sense of excitement that follows you everywhere," injects Muti. "We've put everything back the way it was. It's now a little shrine in your honor."

"Wow, thanks." Not sure what else to say. This should be a nice moment, right? Why do I feel like bad things are happening?

"We understand if you wish to sleep in the summer palace from now on," says Muti. "We aren't your real parents."

And there it is.

The true problem.

Now that I've discovered my birth parents, Poppa and Muti think they've lost me again.

I fly across the room and take a seat smack between the two of them. "You are my parents." I wrap my arms around their slim shoulders. "Nothing will ever change that. If my old room is ready, that's where I'm going."

"Good." Muti sighs. "I'll make you some galla root and then you can get some rest."

I'm not too sleepy, but it doesn't feel right to correct Muti when she's being maternal again. "That sounds great."

Muti also casts some grub for her and Poppa. She share a nice meal and talk about the latest gossip in Faerie. The big news is that Finster's widow has a new boyfriend. We discuss the perils of dating she trolls.

It's like I never left, and that's just fine with me.

After my meal, I flit back to my old room. Sure enough, it's back to the way it was the morning I left for prison... only without the heavy sense of doom hanging in the air.

Then I record everything in you, dear Diary.

It really is like nothing has changed.

And yet, everything is very different indeed.

- Calla

DAY FIFTY-THREE

Dear Diary,
    The topiaries are healed, even the ones at the school greenhouse. The blight is gone. Lazare and Lotti have literally self-imploded. Poppa and Muti are back to sleeping on the kitchen table on piddles of their own spit. Bilge and the sprites have cleaned up the citadel.

There's only one big thing left to do.

Visit Father.

And do I lose my badass chuck card if I drag Dare along for emotional support? I don't think so.

It's midnight on the nose when Dare and I step into the pocket realm where my father rests. My little llama buddy prances over to say hello. She's decidedly icy toward Dare, lifting her pink chin in his direction as if to say, *no winter elves here.*

I don't blame her, especially after what Reiver pulled.

We walk over to King Tristan. He lies still and quiet on his bed of apple blossoms. Stepping closer, I'm glad to see that my father's nose is healed up. All signs of colored mist or other spell debris are also gone. That's a positive.

I pause beside him. "Hello, Father. I'm here to wake you up." Pointing the scepter, I picture my father waking up.

Nothing happens.

I try again.

Still zero.

I lean in closer. "No offense, but you're really my normal parent. I'm pulling for you here."

Beside me, Dare clears his throat.

I look up. "What is—" The next words die on my lips. Why? A newcomer has entered the pocket realm.

The Ley Queen has arrived.

"Hey, there, you." I'm still not comfortable with the whole Mother thing. "How long have been standing there?"

"Long enough to know that I'm not your normal parent."

"About that…" I bite my lips together and try to think fast. "There's a really good explanation."

The Ley Queen is a master of the unreadable expression. She works that right now. "Do tell."

Still pressing my lips together, I tilt my head. *Come on, creative mind. Think of something good.*

I get nothing.

"It's like this," I say at length. "You're the Ley queen. You pull time around and see the future. That doesn't exactly make you normal, but that's not a bad thing, either. I'd just pictured my father as being more of a regular elf while you're my cooler, less predictable parent."

The Ley Queen stares at me for a long minute. In fact, her look goes on for such a while, I start to wonder if perhaps Dare and I should high tail it for the exit. At last, a slow smile rounds her lips.

"As images go, I think that's an excellent picture," she says smoothly. "I have some ideas on how you can awaken your father."

I exhale. "Good."

Notice how I say *good*, not *great*. That's because I can't help but notice how the Ley Queen says she has *ideas* on how I could awaken Tristan. As in, this is another quest situation from my mother. Those haven't turned out to be barrels of fun.

Still, if *whatever it is* ends up with Tristan awake, then I'm all for it.

Dare clears his throat again. I realize someone's been standing around and being ignored. "Oh, I forgot. This is Dare. He's my… Dare."

The Ley Queen nods. "I'm well aware of Prince Darius. I married a poorly glamoured up version of him recently. He may accompany you on the quest to revive Tristan."

Ha. Knew there was a quest.

"Glad to hear it." Perhaps this new adventure may not suck too much, after all. "Thanks, uh, you."

"About that." The Ley Queen's eyes soften with a look that I choose to define as genuine affection. "Why don't you call me Blue? That's what your father called me. It's my favorite name on Earth as well."

"Wait, you're the Blue Fairy?" I ask.

"That I am. Headless Horsewoman, Mother of Unicorns, and the Blue Fairy… those are but some of my Earthly titles. As I said, the Blue Fairy is my favorite."

This is a serious revelation. "Is there a Pinocchio running around?"

She winks. "Maybe."

"So that's a *yes*."

"I have other news for you as well," adds Blue. "I have reconstructed the summer palace as your father Tristan had it back in the day. If you'd like, we can return to Faerie and I'll give you the grand tour. I saved all his papers and such. You can get right down to the business of ruling."

"Yippee." In my head, that word came out with more enthusiasm. As it is, it sounds decidedly deflated.

"What about you, Dare?" asks Blue. "You perform much of the ruling for the winter realm. Care to join us and add your thoughts as well?"

"Happily." Dare says that word in such a nice and rumbly voice, I decide that learning paperwork won't be that horrible. Dare could read me the alphabet over and over and I'd probably enjoy it.

Who am I kidding? I'd totally enjoy it.

With that, I kiss my sleeping father on the forehead and head back to Faerie along with Blue and Dare. When we arrive, the summer palace looks a million times better after Blue's renovation. Everything is red flowers and natural wood. And we pend lots of hours reading stack after stack of incredibly important scrolls. I took tons of notes.

What, I, Calla Learned About Ruling

One. I have a team of elves to help me design and create outfits.

Two. There's a scrollorium somewhere around here with archivist elves who do stuff. I shall avoid this spot like it's the new blight.

Three. When people ask me to sign things, tell them no.

Four. I really need to awaken my father because this ruling stuff is the pits.

That said, there are some regal things that I really want to get done. For instance, I plan to retake the areas that Lazare shuffled off to Pixieland. Now that the blight is gone, we can get some trees and elf dancing action going there. I also need to tour my realm and introduce everyone to the awesomeness that is me.

Everything else can all wait until my father is awake because honestly? Ruling is really and truly a pain in the neck. The sooner my father is awake, the faster I can return to being sixteen and a smart-ass.

So after many hours of nodding and looking interested, I fly back to my home tree. Jolly is happy to see me and actually smiles once more before telling me to get off his bark. Poppa and Muti have a fresh dinner of galla root ready for me.

I write in my journal and fall right asleep.

All in all, a good day.

- Calla

DAY SEVENTY

$\mathcal{D}$ear Diary,

    First day on the new throne.

I wear my favorite pink dress under an ermine cloak. Comfort fashion.

Straightening upon my chair of red flowers, I look out over my domain. Right now, that amounts to a fairly large and empty chamber. Most of the summer elf nobles are still hanging back from court. In my opinion, they aren't certain if Lazare really got blown up.

That guy is gone, all right. Took my mice and birds a few days to clean up the mess.

Of course, Lazare still has two other daughters running around, so it's possible those two off causing trouble with the court. Not that I can focus on any of that right now.

I'm dealing with some serious adjustment anxiety.

Seventy days ago, I was a prankster pixie. Now I sit atop of the throne as ruler of all the summer lands. It looks pretty and all, but this rose-throne has prickles that stick into my butt. The scrollorium elves keep trying to corner me and make me read stuff with exciting titles such as Best Practices in Sludge Management. I'm running out of new ways to say, *I won't sign that right now.*

Being an adult is awful.

I can't wait for Blue to send me on that quest to wake up Tristan, but she says the right future thread has not yet appeared.

A handful of summer elves wait by the back wall. I wave them closer.

"My very first court is hereby in session," I state. "Come forward and be heard."

Dare leans by a nearby stretch of flowery wall. I told him he didn't need to sit through my first court, but he just grunted. Now he's glaring at the few attendees like one of them will leap forward with a dagger at any second. Dare is pretty convinced my own people are trying to kill me.

They can try. But they must get past Sammy the Scepter first.

Yes, I gave him a name.

Don't judge.

A pair summer elves march toward me throne. I recognize them immediately. "Blond and Blonder!" I cry. "You're here."

Blond frowns. "We're palace guards, not Blond and Blonder."

"I'm aware. You locked me up a few days ago. Don't you remember?"

Blonder winces. "Maybe? Was that the night we received the delicious wine?"

"We've been drinking it ever since," adds Blond.

"Okay, that explains a lot. Please do… whatever it is you *do*-do in court."

Blond pulls a scroll from under his breastplate. "We have a list of questions for you, Calla."

"Queen Calla," I correct.

Blond reads from his sheet. "First question. The nobles of the summer court wish to know why the blight began."

No idea.

"I'll get back to you on that." Although that answer is the equivalent of saying *I don't know*, I declare the words in a very regal manner.

Well done, me.

"Second question."

"Will the blight return?" asks Blond.

"That's in process with the other thingy thing." Not as convincing of an answer, but I'm still working my regal vibe. "Anything else?"

"There are rumors," states Blonder. "The court has heard that Queen Saita was romantically involved with Protector Lazare. Is there a chance for an heir?"

I shoot a glance at Dare, who rolls his eyes. The words are there, but no spoken: *fat chance.* Saita chooses her baby daddies carefully. They are all winter elf royalty and totally dead right after the baby is born. It's how winter queens have always worked things. Not my cup of tea, but then again, I'm not Saita.

"The winter queen's personal life is none of your business." *There, that sounded official.* "And you already have an heir. Me."

Blond checks his sheet again. "That's all I have."

"Cool." I stand and lift my scepter. "In that case, I hereby call my first court session to a close. You can all leave." I glance to Dare. "Except you, obviously."

The small group of summer elves dutifully file out the back of the chamber. When we're alone again, Dare approaches my throne.

"That went well," he says.

I scratch my back with Sammy. "My court sessions are different than at the Pinnacle."

"Which is a good thing, I assume."

"Remember what happened after my Hairless Elf Council Adventure? Everyone wanted a New Me. Mission accomplished, I guess."

"Not exactly." Three short steps lead up to the dais that holds my flower throne. Dare takes them in one leap. He towers before me, the embodiment of power and determination. Leaning forward, Dare rests his hands on either of my armrests, blocking me in. The prince carries a aura of confidence about him; now that sphere of strength envelops me as well. I suck in a shaky breath.

Dare moves in closer, stopping when our mouths are only a breath apart. "I have a secret for you, Calla."

Time was, a statement like that would have me waiting for a proposal. Not any more. Neither am I terrified, either. Instead, a warm sense of joy pulses through me. Something in my soul takes flight.

I've no idea what this is, but I'm going with it.

"Tell me," I say, my voice low.

"There was never a need for a New You," whispers Dare. "Your heart has always been perfect." Little by little, he raises his mouth upward, passing by my lips and eyes in order to set a gentle kiss atop my forehead. He leans back, straightens his stance, and smiles.

Oh, the dimples.

I remember what Future Me said about Dare breaking my heart. She can take a hike.

"So I'm the New-Old Me." I waggle Sammy a bit. "How does this look?"

"It's missing something." Dare moves to stand beside my throne. "Now, it's complete."

And so it is.

- Calla

The story continues in Calla, Book 2 in the Pixieland Diaries. Read on for an excerpt from Calla!

The adventure continues in Pixieland Diaries Book 2, *Calla*! Read on for an excerpt…

FAERIE DRAWINGS

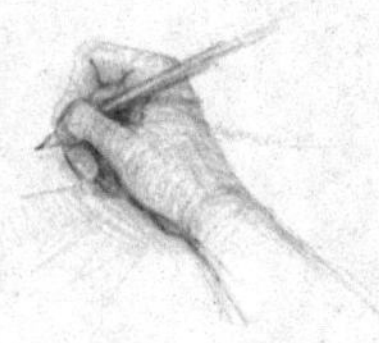

Check out these images from my homeland! All are drawn by yours truly...

   PS. These pictures are only available in this special enhanced edition because sometimes, we all need extra cool stuff.

Oinky

Summer Throne

Pixieland Citadel

Jolly

Summer Palace

ALSO BY CHRISTINA BAUER

ANGELBOUND

Order ANGELBOUND, the kick-ass paranormal romance! Read on for a sample chapter…

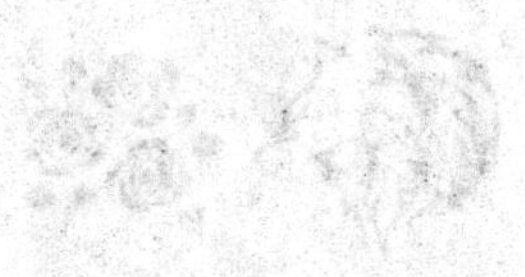

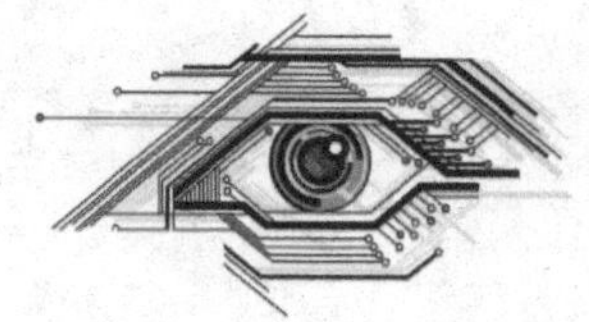

A kick-ass heroine + a swoon-worthy prince + an all-girl heist = the DIMENSION DRIFT series!

CALLA - EXCERPT

A SAMPLER FROM THE NEXT BOOK IN THE
SERIES. CHEETOS ARE INVOLVED.

DAY SEVENTY-ONE

*D*ear Diary,

Today I drop some ~~diabolic retaliation~~ harmless prankster fun on my new royal subjects, the summer elves.

Trust me, they totally have it coming.

Why the revenge? Yesterday I held my first formal court as Queen of the Summer Realm. It should've been some long chats with my elf nobles.

Only no one showed up.

We are not amused.

Time to get tricksy.

Today marks my second formal court… as well as my mega ~~payback~~ prank. While I write this, I sit upon a throne of red flowers. The shade goes perfectly with my pink hair, matching wings and violet eyes. And let's not forget my ermine cloak; it adds a splash of white to the look. *Clutch.*

Yet appearances come second to my dazzling plan for the morning. Although my subjects been avoiding me for weeks, that will end once the court doors reopen in just a few minutes.

I've so got this.

Sighing, I soak in the beauty of this moment. A huge atrium towers around me. Sunlight pours in through the open ceiling. The walls and tiles are all painted gold. A pile of tiny purple bags sit in the middle of the floor.

Bonjour, le elf bait.

Those packets hold fairy dust, which is powerful magic that any fae wants. My prank is how these bags also contain... *wait for it...* a freezing spell. Grab one and you can't leave the room until I say so.

My scheme is so brilliant, I can't stand it.

There will also be plenty of witnesses for my glorious success. My parents, Poppa and Muti, wait nearby. So does my best friend and major crush, Prince Dare of the Winter Elves. Let's not forget my buddy Bilge, the hobgoblin, and his piggy familiar, Oinky. Two summer elf guards—I call them Blond and Blonder—hang out by the back wall.

Speaking of the guards, they look expectantly in my direction. The moment has come to set aside my journal—it magically shrinks into a locket that hangs about my neck—and get ready for the fun.

Prank on.

- Calla

DAY SEVENTY-ONE AND A HALF

*D*ear Diary,

When we last left my life, I was about to ~~launch my tricky revenge on the snotty elves who've been avoiding me~~ begin a light-hearted prank in order to chat with my standoffish subjects.

My guards wait by the golden doors to my court chamber.

This is happening.

"Let's begin," I command.

Moving in unison, the guards heave the doors wide open. "Hear ye! Hear ye! Queen Calla now holds her second formal court. All noble elves may enter and be heard."

I cup my hand by my mouth. "Guys, you're forgetting the best part." I gesture toward the mountain of tiny silk bags that sit in the center of the floor.

"Right," say the guards in unison. "Free bags of fairy dust!"

Staring at the opened doors, I brace myself for the onslaught. Any second now, a horde of elves will rush into this room, only to get caught like so many little spiders in my massive royal web.

Yet no one walks in.

I wait some more.

Still nothing.

Minutes go by.

Nada in the visitor category.

Hours slowly tick past.

And wouldn't you know it? Not one summer elf shows up.

In my fist, I hold the Scepter of Summer, a golden stick that packs all my queenly magic. I named it Sammy because that's how I roll. I lift the scepter, a movement that should inspire awe in my subjects and friends.

That doesn't exactly happen.

Instead of gasping in amazement, Blond and Blonder screech in terror as they run away. The main doors close behind them with a deafening slam. I'd be surprised, but my guards do this every time I crack out Sammy. Who cares that whenever I wield my scepter, I blow a few things up? Sammy and I will fall into a magical groove eventually. Maybe.

From here, things get worse.

My parents—along with Bilge and Oinky—rush to hide behind my throne. This isn't the first time they've done a *duck and cover* move from my spellwork, either.

Dare saunters closer. Now I can enjoy one of my favorite views: the Prince of the Winter Elves. Dare is muscly and tall with strong bone structure and longish brown hair. Like always, he wears black body armor and a fur cloak.

"What magic will you cast with your scepter?" asks Dare.

"Another summoning spell." I don't need to explain why I'm casting it, either. You can't rule subjects that you never meet.

Dare pulls his brows together. "You've tried that before."

"Only four hundred times. Something keeps blocking my powers. Maybe attempt number *four-oh-one* will be my lucky number."

"Just point Sammy upward."

"Good idea."

This room wasn't always an atrium; it used to have a ceiling. During my tenth attempt to summon my elves, I somehow blew off the roof. It's an improvement, in my opinion. More air flow.

In any case, my next summoning spell will be the ticket. I tighten my grip on Sammy.

"Here goes," I announce. My cheering section from behind the throne goes into action.

"We've always loved you," says Muti.

"Don't kill yourself," adds Poppa. "Or us."

"I brewed extra healing potion, just in case," offers Bilge. Oinky snuffles his agreement.

"Thanks, guys." *What else can I say? They mean well.*

I raise my arm. Tendrils of golden light whirl about the top of the scepter. "I do hereby command thee, Sammy the Scepter—"

Suddenly, Sammy melts into liquid gold on my palm. From there, he drips to the floor, reforms as a ball and proceeds to bounce around the room.

Not again.

Little click-clack noises sound as Oinky runs out from behind my throne to chase Sammy around the chamber.

I slump back onto my seat. Which isn't a good idea, considering how the thing's made from prickly roses. "I don't get it," I moan. "Sammy worked great the first day I wielded him. Remember how I blew up all the bad people at Lotti the Snotty Potty's Big Fat Fake Wedding? That was awesome."

"It was." *And Dare should know.* It was his body double that almost wed the Snotty Potty in question.

"And there's more," I go on. "I even rebuilt the Summer Palace after the wedding, easy peasy. But now Sammy's being a DISOBEDIENT LITTLE CREEP!"

I have to yell that last bit because Sammy and Oinky are now dancing around the far side of the room. For his part, Sammy pauses in mid-air, spins around, and then keeps right on bouncing.

Smart ass.

Blond and Blonder burst back into the chamber, see Sammy and Oinky, scream in terror, and then sprint in my direction. The guards slide across the floor on their knees, stopping just before my throne. I'd be shocked, but Blond and Blonder do stuff like this whenever Sammy's hopping around.

"A message, your Majesty." Blond holds up a large envelope.

"Thanks." I hold up my hands. "Toss it here."

At this point, the guards are supposed to be some formal falderal where they step up to my throne, say a little speech, and then hand over any official message. *So annoying.* Earlier today, I issued the Royal Decree Of High Velocity Mail Delivery. Now they can just toss things at me.

Blond chucks the envelope at my face. Catching it, I tear open the message. *Boo.* A repeat. This exact same note has been sent to yours truly at least a dozen times.

Oh Queen Calla,

You are hereby invited to visit me at my palace in the Winter Realm. I have information to assist your reign.

- The Gargoyle King

I offer the letter to Dare, who scans the contents. "I can't believe he's still at it," says the prince.

Dare knows everyone in the Winter Realm. According to the the prince, gargoyles do live in the Eidolon Mountains. They never had a king, though.

"With your permission," states Dare, "I'll take this back to my court. Perhaps my mages will find some way to detect the author."

"Sure. Have fun."

Dare slips the envelope into the folds of his cloak. The Mages of the Winter Court have been casting spells to detect the Gargoyle King for days. Nothing has worked yet.

All of which is really beside the point. Writing a diary means being totally honest.

So here goes.

Today's Fairy Dust Prank is a total failure.

My subjects are still avoiding me. As in, the palace hallways are forever empty. People leave food at my door and run. It's unacceptable.

"Sammy!" I call. "Get back here! It's time to cast another summoning spell on my court."

My only reply is more boinging around the room.

I slump even lower in my seat, a movement which makes the rose prickles dig deeper into my butt cheeks. Maybe it's because Sammy always drains my energy, but I can't find it in me to care about a perforated butt right now.

Bilge tiptoes out from behind the throne. He's a squat green hobgoblin with a bald head, tiny eyes and pointy ears. Normally, tusks jut out from his lower lip. Not now, though. Bilge's tusks just molted. As a result, my hobgoblin friend thinks he's a sexy creature. In fact, when Bilge talks these days, he sounds like a human DJ on a racy radio program. I constantly imagine saxophone solos playing behind him.

"I know why the summer elves avoid it," says Bilge.

"Tell me," I declare. "Can't wait."

Which is a total fib. We've already had this *why everyone avoids Calla* conversation multiple times today. I could live without another repeat. But this is family and they're trying to help. And honestly? They might come up with something good.

"Perhaps the summer elves avoid *any* faeling," offers Bilge.

"That could explain things," I say.

See? Helpful.

For years, everyone thought I was a faeling, and that includes yours truly. Faelings are human babies who soak in enough magic to become a pixie or whatever. It's not exactly the height of cool in Faerie.

Poppa and Muti fly out from behind my throne. They're tree sprites with crinkly faces, long gray hair and short white robes. Their little wings flap in a steady rhythm. Is it weird to address ankle-high people as your parents? Nah. I got used to it ages ago.

"Bilge is wrong," says Muti.

I lean forward. "How so?"

"The problem are your pranks," adds Poppa. "You're not evil enough. Offering packets of faerie dust is just too nice."

This is an ongoing theme with my parents. *Calla is overly kind.* According to them, my soul will soon get chewed up by the other residents of Faerie. Hasn't happened yet.

"I'll work on being mean," I offer. My parents exhale with relief. I turn to Dare. "What do you think?"

Dare gives me the side-eye. So far, he only participated once in the *why everyone avoids Calla* conversations. The prince's theory is simple: Sammy scares people. And the Dare doesn't have to repeat that concept; I already know what he's thinking.

I shoot him the side-eye right back. "You're wrong."

Dare winks. "I didn't say a word."

"The problem is not Sammy. My scepter is awesome."

"Yet when you use it, the scepter tires you."

"Just a little."

Actually, a lot. As a matter of fact, just lifting Sammy earlier today was a total energy suck. Not that I'll admit this to Dare.

"Here's what's important," I announce. "Someone's magically protecting my court from being summoned to my wonderful presence. Who? Why?"

Dare keeps working his side-eye. I can imagine his voice in my head. *There's one answer to your many questions: It's all Sammy's fault.*

Sadly, in this case, Dare may be right. *Partially.*

"I suppose it could be Sammy... a little." An idea hits me. "I've got it! I'll practice wielding Sammy and show everyone what a great team we are."

Blond and Blonder race for the doors. "Run for your lives! The incompetent queen is about to kill us all!"

I really wish I could fire them, but they're the only two who enter my presence.

The guards aren't alone in getting spooked, either. Poppa and Muti flit away at double speed. "See you later, honey." They make a beeline out the missing ceiling.

"Oinky and I must also leave," announces Bilge. "It will draw my portrait while I'm gone."

Bilge pulls a small vial from his pocket and drops it onto the floor. Matching puffs of red smoke appear around him and his pig. When the mist clears, the pair have also vanished. Bilge is a potions master, so the *puff and go* is his version of an emergency exit.

I roll my eyes. "There was no need for everyone to run off. I didn't say I'd test things out *right now*."

"True." Dare tilts his head. "What was that about Bilge and a portrait?"

"Oh, Bilge wants to get a girlfriend before his tusks regrow. I said I'd draw him in a *less toothy state.* He needs it for some kind of dating exchange thing. I try not to ask too many questions."

"Indeed. When do you plan to practice your spell work?"

"First thing tomorrow. The Buttercup Forest."

"See you then."

Notice how Dare doesn't ask if he can join me? It's because I'd tell him *no*. He's a pushy prince when he wants to be.

Dare removes a wand from under his fur cloak. It's a gift from my mother, the Ley Queen, and it helps the prince transport back and forth between the Summer and Winter Realms. He waves his wand. Blue magic surrounds him.

One second, there's Dare. The next, I'm alone. Unless you count Sammy, who still bounces up a storm.

Honestly, who could find him scary?

I decide to spend the evening in the royal library. Sure, I've checked the place a kabillion times, but there must be a book in there somewhere about wielding my scepter. Maybe it got stored on the wrong shelf.

And if that doesn't work? I'll try something else. I simply won't give up until I figure this thing out.

After all, that's what it means to be queen.

- Calla

Bilge

DAY SEVENTY-TWO

*D*ear Diary,
Today was my first official test with Sammy the Scepter. I might have melted the Buttercup Forest.
Oops.
- Calla

DAY SEVENTY-THREE

$\mathcal{D}$ear Diary,

Second day of scepter testing. I got the Buttercup Forest back. All the trees can now talk. They keep saying how I suck at being queen.

Stupid trees.

- Calla

DAY SEVENTY-FOUR

$\mathcal{D}$ear Diary,
Day three of testing. Sammy was a total pain today. I spent all morning chasing his little bouncing butt all over the palace. Didn't cast one spell.

There must another way to find out what's wrong with my subjects. And it needs to include a good prank.

\- Calla

~

End of excerpt
Be sure to order Calla, Book 2 in the Pixieland Diaries!

APPENDIX

IF YOU ENJOYED THIS BOOK...

...Please consider leaving a review, even if it's just a line or two. Every bit truly helps, especially for those of us who don't *write by the numbers,* if you know what I mean.

Plus I have it on good authority that every time you review an indie author, somewhere an angel gets a mocha latte. For reals.

And angels need their caffeine, too.

ACKNOWLEDGMENTS

If you're reading my freaking acknowledgements, chances are, I should thank you for something. So, for the record: you are awesome, dear reader.

That said, huge and heartfelt thanks must go out to my husband and son for their rock-solid support. Being an author means a lot of early mornings, late nights, long weekends, and never-ending patience. You two are the best guys in the universe, period.

After that, I must thank the extensive network of reviewers, friends and colleagues who helped me build my writing chops in general. Gracias.

Finally, deep affection goes out to my late, much loved, and dearly missed Aunt Sandy and Uncle Henry. You saw the writer in me, always. Thank you, first and last.

ABOUT CHRISTINA BAUER

Christina Bauer thinks that fantasy books are like bacon: they just make life better. All of which is why she writes romance novels that feature demons, dragons, wizards, witches, elves, elementals, and a bunch of random stuff that she brainstorms while riding the Boston T. Oh, and she includes lots of humor and kick-ass chicks, too. Christina lives in Newton, MA with her husband, son, and semi-insane golden retriever, Ruby.

Stalk Christina on Social Media

Blog:
http://monsterhousebooks.com/blog/category/christina

Facebook:
https://www.facebook.com/authorBauer/

Instagram:
https://www.instagram.com/christina_cb_bauer/

Twitter:
@CB_Bauer

VLOG:
https://tinyurl.com/Vlogbauer

Web site:
www.bauersbooks.com

BEVERLY
HILLS
VAMPIRE
A NOVELLA BY
CHRISTINA BAUER

AN AFTERWORD BY CALLA

Dear Reader,

Sheesh.

You wouldn't believe what I go through to get Christina Bauer to write my story! CB is all about writing strong chicks, so that was forever a fit. But then, she wouldn't actually spit out my tale into paper, electronic or otherwise. Years went way. Ages, I tell you!

Between us, I suspect CB got nervous because I wasn't Little Miss Battle Babe. You know, in the traditional sense of chopping off heads and all. Plus, I dress really well, which is necessarily a match for the traditional warrior vibe.

There's more, though.

Not sure if you've read the other folks CB covers, but there are some ladies who go through a total suffer fiestas. (I'm thinking about you, Elea from the Beholder Series!) Now don't get me wrong. I have bad stuff happen to me. That said, I have a certain female Ferris Bueller thing going on. It isn't exactly sweeping the literary world. I force risks.

Long story short, it took me a while to wear old CB down. Yet I eventually busted her resistance like so many elf wafers under a very large hammer. Go me.

I hope you enjoyed my story.

- Calla